The Answer to Your Question

Also by Paulette Alden

Feeding the Eagles

Crossing the Moon

The Answer to Your Question

Paulette Alden

4900 Washburn Ave. S.
Minneapolis, MN 55410

Published in the United States of America

ISBN 978-0-9885189-8-8
First Radiator Press Edition 2013
Library of Congress Control Number: 2012919935

Cover by David Janik

Radiator Press Logo by Rebecca Swift

For Jeff

Part I

Chapter One

Inga

I remember the day Ben was born, how they laid him on my chest all mottled pink and squirming. When I rubbed my cheek against his tender head, he clutched my finger with his tiny ones as if to claim me. At that moment I thought I understood everything I needed to know about life, as if everything that had been dark became bright, everything that had been ponderous was lifted up on wings of air. There he was in my arms, my baby boy, flesh of my flesh, a miracle beyond comprehension. A miracle because he existed!

And being, he made me. I became myself, Ben's mother. I understood my role, my meaning. I would love him and protect him and raise him up to be a fine and gentle man. I would let no harm befall him. Now it seems to me that that was the last simple thing: how the love I felt for him suffused me until it became embedded in my very cells. Of all the things I'll never really understand, that love is the biggest mystery of them all. It's just an animal thing, I know, a way nature has of insuring the survival of the young. But we like to think we're more than animals; we like to think we have free will, spirits, souls, even. In that way we imagine that we're in control. That we have choices and reasons for why we do the things we do.

Of course that was before everything else. Before Tony Nichols, before I left Charles, before the four girls and Jean. Before the police came knocking on my door. I don't know how many of us there are whose lives are cleaved in two so abruptly. For me it happened on September

10, 1968. At some point the book I was reading, *Slouching Toward Bethlehem*, dropped from my hands and woke me up, or maybe it was the sharp rapping at the front door. In all the years I'd lived in the north end of Tacoma, I'd never known of such a thing. I considered not answering, but the rapping intensified, so insistent that I pulled on my robe, switched on the porch light and looked through the peephole. That peephole was Ben's idea—that, and the chain lock so I could open the door a crack but no one could force his way in. I had scoffed that I didn't need such protections, it was a quiet, safe neighborhood after all. The only "crime" I could remember in the eighteen years I'd lived there was when the Gleasons' son threw rocks through the sun porch windows of a duplex down the block.

Outside were two men, their faces ballooned into monstrous size by the lens. One was wearing a police uniform and the other street clothes, though I could see a miniature gun in a shoulder holster, black against his white shirt. I slid the chain off and opened the door. Beyond were three squad cars, their red and blue lights flashing, and several police were running toward the back of the house, the strangest thing.

The one with the shoulder holster asked if they could come in, and he called me by name. Something in my chest lurched then. The uniformed one swept right past me with his gun drawn, and I turned in bewilderment to the older man. "Is Ben all right? Is he hurt?"

From the day Ben was born I feared something would happen to him. I worried that the small lump in his groin when he was a toddler was cancer, though the doctor said it was cat fever from a scratch, a swollen lymph node that would resolve itself in time. I gave the cat away then, though I loved her. Whenever I read stories in the paper of accidents—the child found at the bottom of a swimming pool with the mother a few feet away—that was Ben face down in my mind, or those car accidents with teenagers out for a joyride, until the car flips and rolls. I spent many an anxious night when Ben was in high school pretending to read, trying to familiarize myself with new books we were getting in at the library, but unable to concentrate until I heard the back door open. It had only been in the past few years, since he left home for college in Seattle and took an apartment there after graduation, that I'd been able to relax my vigil.

"I'm Detective O'Loughlin." Just then I heard the lock on the kitchen door turn and voices in the kitchen. "They have to search," he said, as if I'd understand. Several policemen were running through the house, opening doors with drawn guns. They left a smell of fear and sweat in their wake, masculine and alien, as if their presence had changed the molecules in the air. I pulled my robe tighter. The house is just a little bungalow, two bedrooms, it didn't take long, and all the time the detective and I just stood there in the foyer, waiting, for what I didn't know. I wanted to ask about Ben again, but found I couldn't speak.

"All clear, Ron," the first policeman came back, and in a moment I heard the squad cars start up out front, then pull away into the night. I knew the neighbors would be astir, and I was already forming a story to entertain them: "It was the wildest thing ... police all over the place ... false alarm. Can you imagine!" But even as I was spinning it, somehow I knew I'd never tell it.

"Why don't we sit down," Detective O'Loughlin said, and he steered me into the living room with a hand on my elbow, as if I might stumble. I sat down stiffly on my mother's green velvet Victorian sofa. Why she had wanted such an uncomfortable, formal thing in northern Minnesota I'd never know, and why I then wanted it when I moved to Tacoma I'd also never know. For some reason I felt like apologizing for it, the awkward ugliness of it. The detective sat at the edge of the wing chair, perching there really, then pulling it close to where I sat. He introduced the younger, uniformed one as Sergeant Reinhart. He had those intense blue eyes that some Germans have, and high stern cheekbones, with no fat to soften his bony face. He couldn't have been more than twenty-four, twenty-five years old, around Ben's age. I tried a smile on him but he turned away.

The older one, O'Loughlin, looked to be in his late fifties, a sexy kind of man with a cleft in his chin, a little overweight now in middle age, a man who liked to flirt with women I could tell, though now he was dead serious. I felt clairvoyant, as if I could see it all: the wife, the grown kids, the grandkids whom he indulged outrageously. A family man, a man who believed in the law, who was looking forward to retirement in a few years and didn't want to get killed in the meantime by some thug.

"We need to ask you some questions about Ben." He looked at me so intensely I had to look away. I wondered if sweat had broken out on my forehead or upper lip.

"He's never been in any trouble," I said. "What could you possibly want with Ben?"

"Do you know where he is right now?"

"Why do you want to know?"

There was a long, uncomfortable silence. I didn't know what to do with my eyes, where to rest them. I looked at the framed photograph of Ben on the end table, his high school graduation picture. He had always been a good-looking kid, with thick brown hair, only his was naturally curly, something I could have used. I used to pretend to snatch it off his head and put it on my own when he was little, making him laugh. He had been a happy, bright child. He lost some of his playfulness as he got older, though I thought that was natural. Life becomes more complicated for all of us as we grow up. The officer was waiting me out.

"His apartment in Seattle, I assume. I can call him …" What I didn't say was that I hadn't seen or heard from Ben in weeks. Though that wasn't unusual. I intended to get up, go to the phone, but I didn't move. My mouth was so dry my words smacked.

"Get Mrs. Daudelin a glass of water, would ya," O'Loughlin said, and Reinhart disappeared down the hall. When he returned I had to hold the glass with both hands, it shook so hard when I brought it to my lips. My throat felt parched, but I had trouble swallowing.

"Ben isn't at his apartment, Mrs. Daudelin. We have men there now. Do you have any idea where he might be?"

"Please tell me what this is about."

The way he looked at me made me go hot and cold at the same time.

"We have reason to believe your son is responsible for at least one and possibly up to four murders of young women. I'm sure you've read about them—the bodies found up in the Alpine Lakes Wilderness area."

My hands flew to my face as if it had caught fire. An idiotic grin distorted my mouth and I let out a weird guffaw. "You have got to be kidding!"

O'Loughlin looked down a moment and the sorrow on his face frightened me more than his words. "I'm sorry, Mrs. Daudelin. This is no joke."

"Excuse me just a moment," I said quickly, and I hurried to the bathroom. Almost before I could pull up my robe and gown I erupted with diarrhea. God, was I going to vomit too? Lightheaded, I had to sit there a long moment, my nightgown pulled up around my hips, my naked legs weirdly white in front of me, as if I'd never seen them before. My right leg started jumping like a fish out of water. I wondered if I'd be able to get up on my own, but the idea of the policemen having to come in, find me like that, boosted me to my feet. I stared at the strange person in the medicine cabinet mirror. I ran cold water on a washcloth, bathed my face. Patted down my cowlicks with the washcloth, ran a comb through my hair. Looked around, as if a secret panel might open and I could escape.

There was a soft knocking on the door. "Are you okay in there?"

"Just a moment," I said, and when I heard the footsteps recede I came out, shutting the door quickly behind me, worried about the smell. I walked back to the living room on legs that felt like a sea creature's, hoping I didn't look as bizarre as I felt. O'Loughlin rose like a gentleman as I took my seat again, but it angered me to see the look of pity and concern on his face.

"You're going to be back here one day apologizing to me for this!"

He leaned forward in the wing chair, resting his forearms on his legs, looking down for a few beats, as if gathering himself. I stared at the backs of his hands, how they were covered in dark hair. "I know this is hard, Mrs. Daudelin, but I need you to understand that Ben is in very serious trouble. Has he been here?"

"I can assure you Ben is no murderer!" I wanted to sound indignant, but my voice wheezed out like a balloon losing air, so that by the time I got to "murderer" I could barely say the word.

O'Loughlin sighed and took a sip from my glass of water on the coffee table. I wondered if I should offer him something. I was shivering, but his face was sweating, so maybe the room was hot. I couldn't tell. There was a *Time* magazine on the coffee table, the cover a photo of Nixon and Agnew clasping hands and holding them up above their heads, with the caption "The G.O.P. Ticket." I didn't even know who Agnew was. I wanted to pick up that magazine and read it more than anything in the world. I clasped my hands together to keep them from reaching for it.

"What evidence do you have?" I squeaked out.

"One of the girls at the erotic massage parlor where Angela Cruz worked knew Ben and identified him as the man Angela left with the night she went missing. We got a positive ID on him from Sissy

Bockman's roommate who was with her at the bar the night she disappeared. All the bodies were found in the same area and appear to have been killed by the same man. We think that man might be Ben."

I was about to explain that Ben would not be at an erotic massage parlor. But what did I know of what Ben did? My mind veered away from it, the idea of it, whatever it was that happened in such places. I had never been able to talk to Ben about sex. When he began growing body hair, when I realized he had wet dreams, I told him it was time he started washing his own bedclothes, and even that embarrassed us both. I had been an only child, no brothers, I didn't know much about boys. How I wished then that Ben had a father, but Charles had been out of our lives for years. I had heard he had remarried, that he was living on the East Coast. It was as if we had never known each other, let alone brought a child into the world. I was staring off into space.

"Maybe you should call someone. To come be with you."

"I don't ... What? You mean, like a lawyer?"

"Right now, Ben is a suspect. There'll be time for legal counsel. We need to find Ben, talk to him. Anything you can do to help us."

"I see," I said, not seeing at all. Instead I was thinking about Ben, trying to draw him into my mind, get a fix on him. I couldn't seem to think straight about him. Who was he? And didn't I know? Of course I did. He was ... Ben, he was ... It was like trying to describe myself.

"Could I call someone for you, Mrs. Daudelin?"

"No, no. It's not necessary. Just give me a moment. How were they killed? I mean, I must have read ... I can't ..."

"Bound and strangled," Reinhart said coldly.

"That's enough," O'Loughlin waved him off.

Something huge and hard was growing in my chest, pressing on my lungs, making it hard to breathe. "Then it couldn't have been Ben," I said.

"Do you mind if we have a look around?"

I got up on my crab legs, not knowing what else to do, and led the way.

I showed him Ben's room first. It was in perfect order, neat, clean, the way it never was when Ben lived at home. His posters of a '57 red Corvette and a '53 red Maserati on the wall, his stereo in the corner, the Fender

Stratocaster guitar he wanted so badly and then never learned to play, his books, science fiction and fantasy mainly, not my taste but at least he read something. I gazed at the black globe on his nightstand, which projected stars on the ceiling when the overhead light was off. When he was a boy, still mine, as I thought of it, before he got more complicated, more … distant, we'd lie across his bed and recite the names of the constellations, Sagittarius, Orion, Scorpio. Those were happy times, peaceful times, of that at least I was sure.

Detective O'Loughlin was looking in the closet. I'd spread out into Ben's closet, since he never spent the night anymore, hanging my summer and winter clothes there, depending on the season. So much of life was not what I had expected or would have chosen, but I'd gotten used to it. I would have wanted a child who kept in closer touch, came home more often, took more of an interest in my life, but since that was not the child I had, I'd adjusted. It was closet space going to waste, which I could use.

He looked in my room, the double bed where I slept alone, tousled now from when I leapt up to answer the door. An old maid's room, I felt him thinking, a dried-up aging woman, though I wanted to protest that I was only forty-six. But maybe he was right. I'd only had one lover in the twenty years since I divorced Charles—David Dunn, our family doctor, and given the way I was, it didn't work out. We were back to being friends. Well, regardless of what this policeman thought, I liked the room, with its white spread, opaque white curtains that let light in but kept eyes out, a feeling of sanctuary. A pretty room, feminine without being sweet, comfortable with its reading chair with cream cushions that blended nicely with the whites, a floor lamp and stack of books beside it.

"Nice," O'Loughlin said, giving a nod, somehow embarrassing me.

We peeked in the bathroom, nothing to see there, no lingering odor, thank god, and went down to the kitchen. I always did the dishes and put them away. I tried to view things through this detective's eyes, how he'd see I was a person who didn't let things go, a stable woman with a job, a few friends, a father and a grown child. Not the kind of woman who would have a murderer for a son!

O'Loughlin led the way back to the living room, again with that light touch on my elbow.

"Mrs. Daudelin," he said. "I should warn you. There will be reporters. It'll go national very soon now that we have a lead suspect. There's been a lot of interest … and fear … around the … girls."

I couldn't let my father find out on the news! I rushed to the phone stand in the hall and dialed his number back in Minnesota, up on the north shore of Lake Superior. It rang and rang, after one a.m. there, but I had to wake him. When I heard his voice, *hello, hello, who's there?* I couldn't say a word, my throat closed. All I could do was hand the receiver to the detective.

He cleared his throat. "Sir," he said slowly. "This is Detective O'Loughlin with the Pierce County Sheriff's office. I'm here in Tacoma with your daughter—"

"Inga," I said idiotically, "It's Inga."

He paused, then, "With your daughter Inga," and I could imagine Dad on the other end, frightened, still trying to wake up.

"No, she's okay, sir. Just upset. That's right. I'm sorry to have to tell you, sir—but Ben, your grandson, Ben Daudelin, is a suspect in—"

Another pause. "No sir. I'm afraid it's much worse … Murder … possibly more than one, actually."

I motioned for him to hand the phone to me. "Dad, Dad … just listen now for a moment. I know. Listen to me, Dad, it'll be all right. It's all a mistake. A big mistake!" and I looked O'Loughlin right in the eye. "No, don't come now. They're looking for Ben. No, I don't know where he is! When they talk to him, it will all be cleared up. It'll be okay, Dad." I wanted to say *I promise*, but couldn't. "Don't watch the news. Don't turn on the TV. I'll call you tomorrow, okay. Go back to bed, try to get some rest."

"He loves Ben so much," I started to say, but suddenly my legs crumbled beneath me, I sank to the floor, my hands coming up to cover my face. It wasn't true! How could this be happening? We had to fix it! How could they accuse him? Ben! Ben! Strange guttural sounds were coming from my mouth, tears were streaming down my face.

"Kleenex," O'Loughlin ordered Reinhart. I went cold and clammy, as if blood were gushing out of my body. Am I dying, I wondered. Is this what it's like?

O'Loughlin was helping me up, steering me over to the wing chair. "Put your head down between your knees," he was saying from far away.

He pressed on the back of my head until I leaned over. "Take slow, deep breaths," and I tried to do as he said. Still, everything was turning black around the edges.

The next thing I knew I was in an ambulance, with an oxygen mask over my face, which I wanted to rip off. I couldn't believe what was happening. I thought wildly of being at home, in bed, asleep. I struggled to wake up. "Just try to stay calm," someone was saying as he took my pulse.

At the hospital they hooked me up to an EKG. I tried to think what to do, who to have them call. David, he was a doctor, he'd know what to do. He knew Ben, he would tell them it couldn't be true. When he arrived I reached for him and he put his arms around me. David's eyes had been damaged in the war, he wore thick glasses under which his eyes seemed to swim. Except for the brief interlude when we tried to be lovers, he'd been our family doctor since Ben was ten.

"Did they tell you?" I asked him wildly.

Through his thick lens, I saw bewilderment, but he didn't say a word, just rubbed circles on my back.

When my heart settled down, they let David drive me home. We sat in the living room, he offered me a scotch, even though it was four a.m., or a Valium, but all I could think was that Ben was wanted on suspicion of murder. They didn't know where he was. The word *nightmare* was too mild. My imagination couldn't contain what had been shoved into it so brutally.

David stayed the rest of the night, sitting there in the living room, while I went and lay down on my bed. There beside me was the book I had been reading when I dozed off. I stared at it as if I had never seen it before. If only I could go back, back to the person I had been, the life I had known, before the police came knocking on the door. But the day outside my white curtain brightened, and a life I couldn't conceive of commenced.

Chapter Two

Jean

Mrs. D hasn't been at work for two whole weeks, what with all the commotion about Ben in the news. The police are looking everywhere for him, though they haven't a clue where to find him. All his teachers and friends, the folks who've known him his whole life, can't believe Ben Daudelin could kill those four girls. Just last week his high school principal went on TV to say how Ben had been an excellent student, well liked by all, with leadership potential. But I can believe it, even though I've never met Ben. Things are not always the way they appear. My Ganny has a gift for knowing stuff that other people can't know, and she says I have it too.

People are wondering about Mrs. D too, now. Like maybe she did something to make Ben do the things he did, like dropping him on his head when he was a baby, or withholding love. There's this girl at work I don't like, Margery, who's always going on about Mrs. D being a murderer's mother and how she'll be afraid of her when she comes back to work. It's just foolishness and makes me mad. No one could be afraid of Mrs. D. I can't wait for her to come back.

Mrs. D was the one who hired me in August when I came looking for a job after Jimmy got sent to Nam. I haven't looked it up on the map, though we have a lot of big maps at the library. It's like a made-up word in my mind, Nam.

First thing she asked me was how old I was. I told her sixteen. She asked where I was from. I told her Carolina, like that song they play on the radio all the time. When she looked blank, I sang a little of it: "*In my mind I'm going to Carolina. Can't you see the sunshine, can't you just feel the moonshine …*" She laughed a little then, like she liked me even though she had just met me. I liked her too, like I had known her a long time. She asked me why I wanted the job. I told her about Jimmy being in Nam, and that I didn't know much, but that I liked books. When she asked me what I liked about them, I said all the words. She looked at me then, reading me like one of her books. She has shiny brown hair that she tucks behind her ears when it gets in her way, like she doesn't know about perming or curling it. Her face is no-nonsense but delicate-like, pretty for someone her age. Her eyes are hazel, kind and bright, with eyelashes so thick it's like she's wearing mascara, but I don't think she is.

It was Mrs. D who taught me how it all makes sense. She wanted to train me right, she said, for the future. She showed me how to understand the numbers and letters on the spines of books. We were on the fourth floor, and she said to me, "Each book has its place and no other place will do." She took a book off the cart and studied it, then she ran her finger over the other books in front of us until she found the right place, the only place, and put the book exactly there.

We were getting along just fine until the police came looking for Ben. That first morning after it came out on the news, it was like a lightning bolt had hit the library. Some folks were crying, others were shaking their heads, some didn't say a word, and some took off during their lunch breaks to shore Mrs. D up, tell her it couldn't be true. I guess Mrs. Haskell was the one who took Ben's picture off Mrs. D's desk. It was Ben in knickers and a winter jacket, a thick scarf wrapped around his neck, a red wool cap on his head, holding up what looked like a big moose antler, snow-covered pine trees behind him. You could tell he was Mrs. D's son. Then suddenly his picture was gone, Ben was gone, and Mrs. D was gone, and what had made sense didn't make sense anymore.

Now sometimes I stand among the stacks, and time goes by without me doing a thing. I'll be afraid an hour has gone by, but usually it's only twenty minutes or so, and no one has missed me. I can't remember what I've been thinking or feeling while I was standing there, but it's different from being asleep.

At home in the evenings I'll sit down to read and the same thing will happen. I'll look down and see the open book in my lap, and it'll be time to go to bed, when I've just got up from supper. Before Mrs. D left, I would read all the time, actually following the words and making sense of them. When she was around, I'd find inter-esting things in the books I shelved, and the day would go fast. Now the days feel stuck, like a clock that's broke.

Lots of days Ben's high school graduation picture is in the paper. You can see why those girls went with him. He has a head of curly hair, a sweet smile, and a black mole by his right eye, a beauty mark like Marilyn has, only hers is by her mouth. It's funny but I feel I have Ben to thank. I already knew the easy things, like not going out at night, not opening the door unless you know who it is, looking in a car before you get in, always locking the doors and never ever walking anywhere alone. But Ben taught me that it doesn't always happen one of those ways—something you can understand and guard against.

Finally our big boss, Mr. Reynolds, told us Mrs. D was coming back to work the very next day. Everybody was so excited, and nervous, too. Mrs. Haskell, who has been telling us shelvers what to do while Mrs. D was gone, broke down and cried. When I heard the news my stomach did a somersault.

At the end of the day Mr. Reynolds had us all gather in the conference room, so he could tell us how to act when Mrs. D came back. While we were waiting, Margery leaned over and pinched my arm to make me look her way. "The apple doesn't fall far from the tree," she said, to get my goat. I felt like snatching that dyed yellow hair right off her head, but just then Mr. Reynolds came in and everyone got real quiet and still.

Mr. Reynolds is tall and bald and always wears these brown V-neck vests that match his brown pants. When he's nervous, he runs his pink tongue over his lips, like he's found something good to lick there. "As you all know," he said, lick lick, "Mrs. Daudelin will be returning to the library tomorrow. We will welcome her back, of course, but without too much … fanfare." Lick. "Of course. I just want to remind you all to mind your manners. Don't stare. And for Pete's sake don't ask her anything about Ben … But don't avoid her, of course. Just act normal." Lick.

"Normal like a murderer," Margery whispered in my ear, and I slammed my elbow into her side.

"She won't be wearing a name tag," Mr. Reynolds said, "to protect her from the public."

But everyone in town already knows who she is. She went on TV right after Ben became a suspect to ask him to come home, but he never did.

On the bus ride home I thought about what I could say to Mrs. D tomorrow. Mr. Reynolds said don't say anything to her about Ben. All I ever say to her is yes ma'am and no ma'am, and ask her which carts of books she wants me to shelve. But maybe this time I would get up my nerve. I would tell her Ben wasn't her fault, that she was a good person and never forget it.

I opened the icebox to see what I could eat for dinner. All that was in there was a half a package of hamburger turning brown. I couldn't remember when I had bought it, but I fried it up. When I smelt it I ate soda crackers instead. I stayed up late watching TV, though what was on I couldn't say. I thought about the four girls and the things that were coming out in the newspaper about them, how their hands had been bound behind their backs, how their throats had been squeezed until they could breathe no more. At some point I fell asleep on the couch, but then I woke up with a terrible start, my heart beating hard. I sat straight up and said, "Monstrous! Monstrous!" though I didn't even know it was a word I knew.

I overslept and didn't have time to fix any lunch. I was afraid I'd miss the bus. I flew down the stairs to the parking lot in front of the apartment complex, and there was Jimmy's truck, grinning at me with its wide metal grill. I hardly ever drove it, 'cause I was afraid of wrecking it. It was Jimmy's pride and joy, a 1960 Chevy pickup, two tone, with a white roof and body, a green hood and the top half of the back was green. White wall tires. It didn't have any rust, except in the truck bed. The last thing Jimmy told me before he left for Nam was to take good care of it. I wouldn't drive it even if I was late to work on this of all days, but I was in luck. The bus was just pulling up to the stop on Military Way when I got there, out of breath and wet, 'cause I had forgot my umbrella.

I was hoping it would be Mrs. D giving me the carts of books to shelve but she was nowhere to be seen. It was Mrs. Haskell again, who is nice, just not as nice as Mrs. D. Maybe Mrs. D hadn't come into work after all. She wasn't at her desk like I thought she'd be. It was a letdown for sure, but I carried on, putting each book in its exact and only place the way she taught me.

Since I hadn't had time to make lunch, come noon I had to walk three blocks to McDonald's and spend money. When I started across Eleventh Street, I glanced down the steep hill to the Port of Tacoma. White smoke was pouring from smokestacks and a couple of big ore boats were docked down there. Behind them the snow-covered mountains made me think of the mountains at home. There was that stinky smell in the air from the paper mill, Tacoma aroma. All at once I got the dizzy-head. I was afraid I might puke right there on the sidewalk.

I went on down to McDonald's, thinking maybe food would help. I got a fishwich and a coke and sat down near a girl with a kid. Now I figure that was an omen. She kept putting the baby down, but it pulled itself up by catching on the leg of her jeans. She wasn't but a young girl herself, and the kid had a big moon face with those pimples that babies get. The girl was real skinny, and I wondered if that baby had sucked all the fat out of her. Normally I wouldn't have put my mind to them, but for some reason I couldn't help staring at the kid, the way it pulled at her and looked around so serious, like it had something important on its mind.

Before he left for Nam, Jimmy said he wanted us to have kids. But I told him we needed to wait. It was nothing I could connect with me. Once you have kids, everything is laid out for you. A circle is drawn around you and everything that happens from then on is going to be inside that circle. Like the girl at McDonald's. Her circle was already drawn.

The sick feeling had almost passed, so I figured maybe I was just hungry. All the time I was eating my fishwich that baby was picking up dirty French fries from the floor and putting them in its mouth. Then it pointed straight at me and looked me in the eye, like it knew something.

"Why's your kid pointing at me like that?" I asked the girl.

The girl shrugged and pulled the kid up on her lap. It nearly yanked the neck of her T-shirt down to her titties. Then it squirmed to be let down. As soon as she put it down, it wanted to climb back up. It grabbed and pulled on her, and her just a scrawny worn-out looking thing.

"You wanna hold him?" she said to me. "You hold him awhile."

She jumped right up and delivered him into my arms. He was heavy as a sack of grain, and he made a kind of sucking sound that 'bout made me sick again. He started whimpering, and I knew he was winding up. His face turned red and a blue vein thumped in his temple.

"Here," I said to the skinny girl, shoving him back to her. He clutched onto my sweater and wouldn't let go, but I pried his greasy fingers loose. "He doesn't like me."

I was feeling kinda funny again. Maybe that baby had put a spell on me. I ate the whole fishwich 'cause I'd paid for it, even though I'd lost my appetite. When I was walking back up the hill I thought I was going to throw up right there on the sidewalk. I couldn't help picturing that fishwich, how they keep them sitting around too long, how the gob of tartar sauce oozing around the brown square of fish was hard and yellow.

I made it up the library steps, but saliva was flooding my mouth, the strangest thing, just like used to happen when I'd get carsick on windy mountain roads on the way to Ganny's. I ran past the checkout desk up the three stairs at the back to the girls' room, and spilled out everything I'd eaten into the toilet. I sat back on my heels, right there in front of the commode, a dirty place to be but not as bad as the men's. I figured if I could just rest a moment I'd be fine.

That's when Mrs. D came into the bathroom.

She froze like she didn't want to see me, like she wished she could hightail it out of there. But then she sighed big and swooped down beside me. She took me to the sink and patted my face with a paper towel. She smelled clean, like a cucumber, not sweet like perfume. I wanted to put my head on her shoulder, rest there a bit.

My legs felt shaky, like they might fold up beneath me. Mrs. D took me by the arm and led me into the back room where everyone gets their coffee. There were little pink packages of opened sugar scattered on the yellow table, and a bunch of mugs: Mrs. Reynold's black-and-white one that says "Boss," Mrs. D's dark blue one, Mrs. Haskell's red one oversized like her that says "When Your Wrong, Your Wrong." Eight or ten other ones, all with brown stains inside. It smelled like stale coffee and there was an open box of donuts on the counter.

"Jean—?" she said, like she might have forgot my name she'd been gone so long and so much had happened. There was something different about her face now that she was back, like she'd been slapped. "Are you okay? Maybe you're getting the flu... ."

I told her how I'd gone to McDonald's for lunch, how I'd eaten the fishwich and felt sick walking back up the hill. "But I'm okay now, Mrs. D." In truth I still felt queer.

"Have you been sick at your stomach prior to this?"

It was true that I'd thrown up a couple of times lately. I thought it must be what seasickness felt like, though I'd never been on a ship. But until that moment, I had made myself forget about it, like it never happened. That was a trick I learned early in life.

"Jean—you should probably see a doctor."

"Okay," I said, though I didn't mean it. I didn't want to hurt her feelings. But I was not going to go, not to some strange man who'd look at me with hard eyes and poke me with hard things.

"Jean—could you be pregnant?"

Every thought drained from my head.

Then this one thought rose like a mountain in the middle of the road: Jimmy hadn't used a rubber the last time before he shipped out to Nam. I had figured it didn't matter. But now I knew that it did matter.

Time passed, as it is bound to do. Then Mrs. D was giving me something, placing it cold in my hands: a mug of ginger ale. To settle my stomach she said. My mind had sat down in the middle of the road like a mule that refuses to budge.

She tore open the saltines package with her teeth, and handed me one. I put it in my mouth because it was there, and I chewed a little piece of it, salt and cracker. It felt like my whole life was rising up inside me like floodwaters, but I couldn't speak a word. Two big tears spilled over and ran down my face but I didn't even know what I was crying for, 'cause it was nothing that had a name.

Chapter Three

Inga

I knew that girl was pregnant the moment I saw her kneeling there in front of the toilet. She looked so stunned when I said the word, as if such a thing had never crossed her mind! But then I didn't realize I was pregnant either at first, even when I missed my third period, even when I was sick myself. Charles was just home from the war, we married within the month, and I got pregnant with Ben right away. I was twenty years old, a virgin, I didn't know much about sex, my body, or getting pregnant.

She was a little peculiar from the start. When I interviewed her for the shelving job, I could tell she was not like the girls we usually get, not coarse and shallow like Margery or a female doormat like Babe. I remember how she sang to me that day, charming but strange. Her face was solemn and innocent, and there was something about her I couldn't put my finger on. Was she simpleminded or wise beyond her years?

I had my doubts about hiring her, but I thought I'd give her a chance. Those first weeks I had to help her learn her job, at least enough to keep it. She was so shy she hardly spoke, and then in a Southern accent that Margery mocked, until I told her to cut it out. I wondered how long she'd last but she … Jean … wasn't my problem. I hardly knew her, she was just one of many shelvers that came and went.

I had just returned to work that day, after being away for two agonizing weeks. I wanted nothing more than to get back to the library, to regain some sense of normalcy. I had been shocked that first morning back at how everything was just the same: the bright, open, calm space;

the blond wood tables, the sturdy chairs; the usual mix of patrons, some regulars who knew me from Before, who eyed me now with sympathy, fascination, or disgust maybe; the street people we tolerated napping as long as they didn't snore; the white buzz of the overhead lights; the canyons of the stacks; the silence of concentration and focus—these were normally a comfort. But how could it all be the same when the world had tilted on its axis? Still, even if the world had tilted, the bills kept coming in, the mortgage was about due. I came into work. So what if I were sleep walking?

But there she was, throwing up into the toilet. She didn't speak when I led her to the sink and pressed a wet paper towel to her forehead. In the mirror I saw how young she was, how pale. I could hardly recognize myself, as if the events of the past two weeks had rearranged my features into a permanent grimace.

I took her to the break room and sat her down. "I'm okay now, Mrs. D," she said, using the nickname the shelvers use, short for Daudelin, Charles's French Canadian name. Of course everyone knows my last name … Ben's name … now.

I asked her if she had been sick prior to this. I couldn't resist brushing her bangs back from her forehead, where they hung limp and damp. There was something waiflike yet dignified about her. Her hair was light brown, straight and fine, pulled back in a ponytail, her face a pixie oval. She wore a navy skirt and a pink pullover sweater that had been washed too many times.

She raised her eyes to mine, looking directly at me, and yet she didn't answer. Her eyes were hazel, serious and calm. We stared at each other for a long moment, as if something hung in the balance. Was that the moment I might have turned away? Could I have? Or maybe there was already a connection between us, something beyond our control. I certainly don't believe in past lives, but why do certain people come together, as if they're just picking up where they left off?

I asked if she could be pregnant, even though I already knew she was. Her face went so white it frightened me. I recognized the feeling: her life had been cleaved in two. I told her to take the rest of the day off if she needed to, but she stayed on at the library, as if she didn't know what else to do with herself.

Maybe the same could be said about me.

• • •

I was hoping that returning to my job would help order my existence again. My simplest thoughts and actions felt fragmented and confused, as if I'd received a blow to the head. I was still reeling from that late night visit two weeks earlier.

I wouldn't have thought I could eat that first morning. David cooked breakfast, I remember that, he set the plate in front of me, and when I first looked at the two sunny-side up eggs, my stomach heaved. But my hand picked up a piece of toast, tore it in two, dipped it into the runny yoke. I ate ravenously, like a hungry dog.

We didn't need to turn on the TV to find out Ben was all over the morning news. By seven a.m. there was a buzz outside, the drone of reporters. But inside we were in a sealed hive, the bees couldn't get in. We took the phone off the hook, and David opened the front door just long enough to put up a sign: "No visitors at this time." As if my house were a hospital room with a terminal patient. Maybe it was. From the kitchen, where I had started washing the breakfast dishes, as if it were just any day, I heard shouts, loud and then muffled when David slammed the door. The plate I was holding slipped from my hands and shattered on the linoleum floor.

I was picking up the pieces when we heard a ferocious knocking on the kitchen door. David and I looked at each other in alarm, but I told him he better open it. It was Detective O'Loughlin, carrying a bag of donuts. Seven-twenty-five a.m., I remember looking at the clock over the stove. David finished sweeping up the broken plate, and I made another pot of coffee. None of us spoke. O'Loughlin ate a donut while the coffee was brewing, and then I poured three cups and we went into the living room. O'Loughlin sat in the floral wing chair, his chair, I suddenly saw. I sat on the edge of the sofa, my hands pressed between my knees. David pulled up a dining room chair. I realized I was still in my nightgown and robe, and I thought about going to get dressed, but I just sat there. When I balanced my coffee on my knee, the cup rattled in the saucer and we all stared at it.

"When was the last time you saw Ben, Mrs. Daudelin?" O'Loughlin began.

"Call me Inga," I said, and my mind went blank. I couldn't remember when I had last seen Ben. How was that possible?

"Just take your time," David said. He was staring at me kindly through his thick glasses. "It's okay. Just tell him what you can."

My mind turned like a wheel trying to gain traction. I remembered that it was a holiday. It had to have been the Fourth of July. I told the detective how Ben had come down from Seattle, how we had cooked steaks in the backyard. Then I fell silent. I looked away from O'Loughlin. I was remembering that I had been irritated at Ben because he seemed so preoccupied that day. I had accused him of being self-absorbed, putting him through a veritable deposition, so hungry was I to catch up with his life. But he hadn't told me much about himself and he hadn't asked me a thing about myself. He had mocked me that day, asked what exciting thing had happened at the library lately. Had someone thrown up in the biography section, or maybe someone forgot to flush a big doo-doo down the toilet. I reminded him that that job had put him through school, put food on the table, paid the bills. I sent him home early, tired of his company. It was the last time I had seen him.

O'Loughlin wanted to know how Ben had seemed that day, if anything unusual had happened. I told him nothing in particular. I didn't know what to say. I didn't expect perfection or for Ben to be on his best behavior around me. I was hardly perfect myself. He could be distant, moody, sarcastic, but that was just Ben. It didn't make him a murderer.

"What's Ben like? What does he like to do? Anything you can think of."

"He always wears black sneakers," I said. "It's kind of a trademark … He's always been restless … full of nervous energy, always shaking his foot when he sits down. He grew a shoe size every year in high school, until the twelfth grade when he hit size 12. I can't remember the last time he wore a suit and dress shoes. Always the jeans and blue or white oxford cloth shirts with the sleeves rolled up … I'm not sure what you want to know."

"Has he ever been in any trouble, Mrs. Daudelin?"

"He started smoking in ninth grade. I told him it was a nasty habit, I ordered him to give it up, but of course by then I couldn't make him do anything he didn't want to do. He didn't smoke in the house at least, but he'd come in reeking of it, his clothes, his hair, his skin …" I saw O'Loughlin and David exchange a look. I had lost my mind.

"Would you excuse me a moment?" I asked in a faint voice. I stood up stiffly, as if I might crack in two, and made my way to my bedroom like a drunk. I sat down on the bed and for a few moments I panted. When my breathing had slowed, I picked up the framed photograph on my nightstand. The two of us, Ben about ten years old, standing in front of me, my arms around him, my hands clasped in front to hold him tight. We balanced in our tennis shoes on the big boulders on the North Shore of Lake Superior. At Dad's. He's mine, that's what the picture said. He'll always be mine. Behind us the waves of the lake splashed ice cold against the rocks, even though it was August.

Dad taught him to fish the summer he was seven. We'd visit Dad every summer for two weeks, and up until he was about ten, Ben would cry when we had to leave to come back home. Something else … How Ben wanted to step on the little fish when he landed them on the dock. He'd mash them down with his tennis shoe, so that their mouths and eyes bulged. Why would he do such a thing? Of course Dad put a stop to that right away, and I figured it was just Ben being a boy, a kid. Experimenting, seeing what it was like to have that kind of power.

Were there things I missed? Things I didn't understand?

No. No! It wasn't possible that it was Ben!

David knocked on the door, opened it slightly. "Are you okay?"

"Yes, I just … maybe I should get dressed …"

"The detective left. He left his card on the phone stand with his home number on it. You're to call him day or night if Ben shows up. He said he'll be back but if you think of anything in the meantime …"

"Thank you, David," I said. "For everything."

He just looked at me solemnly and nodded. What could he say?

When he shut the door, instead of getting dressed I lay back on the bed.

I was still lying there when Lorraine Haskell came bursting through my bedroom door. "I knocked and shouted at the back until David let me in," she said. Ten years we'd worked together at the library, big, red-haired Lorraine, dramatic where I was reserved, sure of herself where I was unsure. She took me in her arms, crushed me to her big breasts, I smelled her familiar scent, Midnight in Paris.

"Why is this happening," I gasped into her neck. "It can't be Ben! It can't be! It isn't!"

"No, no, it can't be," she said. "It'll be all right. They'll find the right guy. It's a big awful mistake."

"You know Ben," I said, pulling back and looking into her brown eyes. I saw she had been crying. "He wouldn't do such things!"

"I know, darling," she said. "It's … they'll straighten it out. Now let's get some clothes on you. People will be coming."

"People—"

She was right. Friends began to arrive, bringing comfort, support, food. Lorraine got me dressed, and I went out to hugs and reassurances from people who had known us over the years, from Ben's schools, the library, the neighborhood, even the pastor from the church I had stopped going to when Ben was twelve. I myself was totally calm, totally unreal. As if I were actually there, though where I was I had no idea. My stand-in greeted people warmly, reassured them, and they commented on my "strength." Everyone expressed shock, disbelief, outrage. There were tears, though none were mine. The woman who passed for me felt energized, determined, defiant, assuring others it was all a mistake, it would all work out. When I heard myself speak, I believed those words. I felt confident and certain, while another part of me stood apart, appalled, without a clear thought in her head.

It felt like a party. Or maybe a wake. It was like Ben had died, or maybe I had died, I didn't know. The press was camped outside the door, trying to interview anyone who had known Ben, from the janitor at the high school to the Marvins next door, who had only lived there a year and didn't even know him. Did he have a girlfriend in high school? Was his hair long or short now? Did he smoke marijuana?

At some point I went on TV, begged Ben to come home, talk to the police, clear his name. It would all be over in a few days! When he didn't come forward, I was furious at him. When had he stopped doing what I told him? Twelve, thirteen? When had he veered away, become separate? But what if something terrible had happened to him, what if that's why he didn't turn himself in! He could be dead for all I knew. But wouldn't I sense that? Wouldn't I feel it somehow? *Ben not in the world*. I would know.

Sometime during those first few days Christopher and Amy came to see me. Christopher had been Ben's best friend since kindergarten, and Amy Ben's girlfriend in high school. I hadn't seen Christopher in maybe three years. He and Ben had grown apart once they graduated from high school, Ben off to the University of Washington, while Christopher had stayed in town, becoming a mechanic at Good Karma, after several false starts at various jobs and trades. It was always Christopher who was in trouble when they were growing up, some shoplifting incidents, a couple of drunk driving arrests. Next to him Ben had always been the golden boy. I had read in the paper that Amy had gotten married this past year, but when I mentioned it to Ben, he just turned away, and said something to the effect of "lucky guy" sarcastically.

Christopher was over six feet, and he engulfed me in a bear hug. I realized when he began shaking against me that he was sobbing. I patted his back, he buried his face in my hair. I could feel the wet tears, annoying, really. *Why waste tears when Ben was innocent.* "It's okay, Christopher," I said, and pushed him away. "Ben'll be okay. It'll all get straightened out."

He wiped his face with his handkerchief. Amy just stood to the side, looking embarrassed and uncomfortable. She was slim, pretty, long blond hair, with short square teeth in a wide mouth. Ben had considered her a prize, and I understood it had really hurt when she dropped him, though he kept it to himself. I never knew what happened between them, only that she ended it. I expected Ben would have many girlfriends before "the one." But he had never brought another girl around again. After awhile I stopped asking him about his love life.

Christopher was agitated, veering from nostalgic stories of the past to outrage and disbelief about the accusations. He wanted to "do" something, what I didn't know, and it was coming to me that all any of us could do was wait.

I congratulated Amy on her marriage, as if we were having a social chat. When she told me how sorry she was about Ben, tears shone in her blue eyes.

"Tell her," Christopher said. "Tell her no way could it be Ben."

I looked at Amy, curious to see what she would say, but it didn't matter. Something in me didn't care what anyone said. She explained that a detective had asked if she saw anything in Ben when they dated, but there was nothing, really, just that he was immature, and she didn't want to get so serious in high school.

"Being immature hardly means he would kill someone," Christopher said sharply.

I stopped listening. I rested in a place inside, a haven, a round sphere of peace.

Lorraine or David stayed at the house with me that first week. O'Loughlin came several times to ask questions. He looked at me with compassion, so much so that I had to look away for fear I'd break down. I was afraid if I started crying, I wouldn't be able to stop. He exuded a masculinity I was not comfortable around. It brought back memories from a long time ago. Despite his weight and his going bald, there was still a trace of the boy in his face.

He wanted to know about Charles, Ben's father. I told him I hardly knew his family, but that his father had been institutionalized, for what I didn't know, because Charles wouldn't talk about it. He was dead before I even met Charles. Charles had been on the front when the Allied troops invaded Sicily, and was sent home with shell shock. I assumed he'd get over it once he was home and safe. We married that November and he entered graduate school on the G.I. bill. I had just graduated. I would have liked to go to graduate school myself, in philosophy of all things, but it wasn't like these days, with the women's movement telling women they could be anything. I got an office job in an insurance company to support us. Charles was irritable and distant, as if he were someplace else, and maybe he was. After I missed my third period, I went to the doctor. They still used rabbits to confirm pregnancies back then, injecting the human urine into the rabbit and then examining its ovaries. I remember feeling sorry that the rabbit had to die. When I told Charles about the results, I told him *Have children young, grow up with them.* I was excited, happy, thinking this new development would change things for us, but Charles still brooded and had headaches that put him in bed for days in a dark room.

Toward the end of that first week, I told Lorraine and David that they didn't need to stay over anymore, that I would be fine on my own. I wanted to be alone. I was used to being alone, and I needed to be alone—alone with my thoughts of Ben. O'Loughlin said he would have a policeman stationed outside the house. I started to object, but then didn't have the energy.

I began to go into Ben's room at night and lie down on his bed. I couldn't remember the last time he had spent the night at home. The red corduroy spread smelled like an absence, no lingering scent of him. My whole body ached with longing. Where was he? Why didn't he come home? When the pain would be too much, I'd roll onto my stomach, bury my face in his soft pillow. Questions pummeled me. I thought of the notebook I had found under his mattress when he was fourteen. The drawings had burned a hole in my brain. But I had accepted David's opinion that Ben was just being a teenage boy, with violent fantasies that didn't mean much. I had put it out of my mind, since Ben was basically a good boy, a good son, conscientious when he wanted to be. He always did his homework and got good grades, especially in English and history. He wasn't perfect, I knew that. He was often restless and got bored quickly. I considered that a sign of his intelligence. He was cranky at times, sometimes depressed. These were things to worry a mother, but nothing to raise a real red flag. People were attracted to him, that was the thing. It made me proud the way folks were always asking about him. His teachers and coaches … no one ever said a bad word to me about him. He was so bright, so personable, so good-looking. Wouldn't someone have detected something? Wouldn't I?

But by the time he was in high school it seemed we lived separate lives, even in the same house. I usually had my nose buried in a book. We were always polite and civil—though maybe we were just avoiding each other in some essential way.

For some reason during those first few days I thought a lot about my mother. She died when I was twelve, a painful death from breast cancer. I went from being a child to a woman with no in-between. We were stoic people, not given to shows of emotion. Repressed, people would say these days. I always wondered if she had lived, would she have told me about all the womanly things I felt I missed out on. Probably not. Now I felt robbed all over again. I wanted my mother in exactly the same, hopeless way I had wanted her after she died.

I called Dad every day. He sounded bewildered, trying to find words that would convince people the police had the wrong fellow. It wasn't in his constitution to even imagine something like this. We weren't "those kind of people," whoever such people are.

What if I hadn't had that transgression? What if I had stayed with Charles? Ben would have had a father, a man in the house. Maybe there would have been siblings. I tried to fill in the empty spaces as best I could. Coaches, Boy Scouts, the church until he was twelve, so he'd have role models. It was my fault there was no man at home.

What had happened to those girls was outside anything I had ever had to imagine. O'Loughlin had told me that there had been a bite on Angela Cruz's breast, two inches deep. They would get a dental imprint from suspects to look for a match. I couldn't bear to think about what the girls' families were having to live through. But I kept coming back to one thing: it couldn't possibly be Ben! It just couldn't be. *Not Ben … not Ben.* I repeated it like a mantra until my heart settled down.

I'd lie on his bed, seeing the room brighten as he must have done all the mornings growing up. I had made his curtains, beige linen with a light-blocking material behind them. He had wanted something red but I thought it would make the room too garish. Why had I thought that? What did it matter?

There was something else … I could feel it. It had nothing to do with thoughts, words. Something so much deeper than that, so beyond words. He lived in me. Ben. I couldn't put it into words. The way he was so embedded in me, like my own bones, my blood.

Chapter Four

Jean

What I need to think on is my Problem. The thing that's growing inside me. What Mrs. D told me about. I can't hardly believe it's true. But since Mrs. D said so, it *is* true. Before she told me, I didn't even have a problem. Now I've got a big one.

Even though I know it's wrong, I can't help but think of it as cancer. Tumorlike, that'll get bigger and bigger, until one day it has to come out. That gives me the creeps. When I put my hand right below my belly button to see if I'm swelling up, I'm flat as a fritter. But that won't last long. I keep wishing it'll just go away on its own. I can't even remember the last time I got the curse. If it showed up now, it wouldn't be a curse, it'd be a blessing.

Mrs. D is the only one who knows and she hasn't said anything else to me about it. She has other things on her mind. At least she's still coming to work again every day. I know I ought to write Jimmy to tell him about it, but I don't want to. He's the one who gave me the Problem in the first place. I'm hoping that any day now the Problem will be gone. But what if it hangs on? Then what will I do?

When Jimmy wore his uniform, it was hard to tell him from the other soldiers. It was camouflage green and brown, and he wore high black boots. He might have been anybody, a stranger, though I've known him my whole life. He was two years ahead of me in school, and I don't know why he wanted me so bad after forgetting about me for so many years.

His family lived on County Road C, and we went to the same schools and church, Lima Baptist, where I sang in the choir. I used to be real religious around the time I was twelve, thirteen. I'd look people in the congregation right in the eye when I sang those hymns ... *I walk in the garden alone, Amazing grace* ... I'd try to convert them with my singing, make them believe what I, a young girl, believed. But then I began to wonder if it was true, Jesus being the son of god and rising from the dead. The side of me that didn't believe, couldn't believe such a tale, got bigger and stronger while the side that did believe shriveled up and died.

My first real memory of Jimmy was in the back of a pickup truck going down County Road C. It was summer, 'cause the corn in the bottomland was high, and it must have been Sunday, 'cause I had on a dress. Our mamas were up front in the cab, and they were smoking. I had never seen Mama smoke until that day, so that's mixed up with the first memory of Jimmy too.

I was only five or six, the road was rough, we were bouncing around and had to hold on to the sides to keep from flying out. One time Jimmy slid right over almost on top of me, and that's when he got it in his head to try to pull down my undies. We both had to let go when he started in on me. I remember thinking that I'd let him pull up my dress—I couldn't hold it down and keep a tight two-handed grip on my panties. That was the first time I can recall having a thought. We struggled in complete silence. I wasn't mad or afraid, it was just something that I wasn't going to let happen. We went on for a long time that way, both silent and determined.

The truck slammed to a stop, throwing us against the hard metal cab. I was afraid some animal might have run across the road and got hit by the truck. There were always dead animals along the side of the road out there in the country. Driving at night meant a slaughter of frogs hopping toward the light. Frogs and turtles, their shells broke open, and coons, possums, and sometimes deer, their necks stretched out on the shoulder.

Then I saw my mama's face through the cab window, knotted up like a fist. She jumped out and jerked me over the side of the truck, like to wrench my arm out of my body, the way a doll's arm gets broke off. She kept holt of me, me squirming to get away but caught like a critter in a trap while she hit me again and again on my bottom. I heard my own voice whinin', "Don't, Mama, no no! I didn't mean to!" though I didn't even know what I had done. But inside another voice was saying like it always did, *I won't let her hurt me. She can't hurt me.*

Jimmy and his Cherokee mama stood on the side of the road and watched the whole thing. I couldn't stop the sobs when it was all over and we were back in the truck, going down the road again. Jimmy didn't look at me then, he just stayed on his side of the truck, and it seemed like he didn't look at me again until his senior year.

My daddy was a soldier like Jimmy. When I was little I didn't know what was wrong with him. He was always having operations, like his insides had teeth that was biting him. It wasn't until I was old enough to leave home that I heard the story, and then Mama acted like I had known all along. It happened in a bar in Germany. Daddy went to open the bottle by hitting it on the counter, to bust the cap off. Mama said it was dark, so he couldn't see that the top was all shattered. He drank some shards of glass down inside him, and it was then he started to die, though it took years and years to finish. It was just one of those fool things people do and have to pay for. We had to pay too.

I once thought I'd make a nurse. But that was before I got enough of nursing taking care of Daddy. Toward the end he was so little and shriveled up and miserable that it about dried up all the human kindness in my heart. Mama worked second shift at the textile mill, and I'd take care of Daddy, changing his diaper, pureeing his food in the blender, and spooning it into his mouth like he was a baby bird. He stayed in a big old recliner in the corner of the kitchen, and he prayed every day to die. He'd cry, scream, hit, and spit. I learned how to gauge his moods, stay out of range if I had to. I couldn't even feel sad when he passed. Mama didn't shed a tear neither, as if all the tears had been wrung out of us so long ago we were dry as sand in the sun.

Now I want to be a librarian like Mrs. D.

Today when I get off work, I don't go home right away, feeling troubled like I do. I walk down Tacoma Avenue past the county jail and McDonald's to Wright Park. It's getting dark, the street a little spooky and deserted, what with Ben running around loose somewhere. Margery is always trying to scare me, telling me that Ben is gonna get me, stuff his big cock in my mouth and choke me. That's the way she talks, plain nasty. Still, I wouldn't want to run into Ben Daudelin.

My favorite place in the park is a glass building they call the conservatory, full of living green plants, some so tall you can see them pressing against the glass of the dome, like they want to break through. It's like a crystal castle where a princess might live, or maybe a plain old lizard. I sit down at a picnic table just down the hill from it, and it kind of glows in the waning light.

I study on my Problem, on what I'm going to do. I try to remember what we learned in school, about those tubes that connect to the uterus, and how the egg and sperm travel through them, or is it just the egg? Eggs make me think of the round, smooth, warm ones that I took from the chickens' nests in the coop out back at home. But human eggs are more like gum drops, or maybe like frog eggs you see in a pond, watery and clear. I don't really know, having never seen one.

All I know for sure is I don't intend to let any egg inside me grow. I can't get my mind around the idea that another person will be living inside me, even if it's only a baby. I mean, I know it's the way of nature, a fact of life, but you have to admit it's too weird for words. The idea of it getting really big, seven pounds I believe, heavier than a sack of sugar, and then trying to come out my hole seems like a stupid joke, if it didn't scare me so bad. It isn't anything I intend to go too far with.

But how does one get rid of an egg growing inside? I know I'd better do something quick, but what? I can't recall anyone ever talking about what to do, though everyone knew Ella Mae Cantrell back home went away and came back without her Problem. I figure a doctor who could take care of it would cost a lot of money, and how would I find one? I could try looking in the phone book under *A*. I could ask Margery or Babe, or some of the other girls, but I don't want them to know my business. The natural person to ask is Mrs. D, but I wonder if she'd think less of me. I wonder if she ever wishes she had gotten rid of Ben when he was still an egg.

Then I think about writing Ganny, because if anyone would know what to do it's her. She lives way up in the North Carolina mountains near Cullowhee and doesn't have a phone, but she can read. She's the only one of her generation to get a high school education. Ganny is the one who told me not to marry Jimmy, to finish high school, but Jimmy was just a train moving down the track, and I hopped on board. I can trust Ganny to tell me what to do.

When it begins to get really dark, I know I had better catch the bus before it gets any later. There are two Colored boys waiting at the stop too, only Coloreds want to be called Blacks now. They can't be more than thirteen or fourteen, looking me over and trying to jive me. "What ya doing, white girl? Wanna come home wid me?" I ignore them, turning my back, pretending I'm deaf. After awhile they get bored with me and start jostling each other, talking all kinds of trash. A few other people arrive, an old Indian man and a couple of soldiers going back to Fort Lewis. We all stand in our little spaces and don't look at each other, while the two boys show their asses, as we say back home, acting too big for their britches.

I sit up near the front, near the driver, like I always do. He knows me from picking me up in front of the library, and while he isn't what you'd call friendly, he does nod and raise his bushy eyebrows at me as if to say, *Why are you getting on here instead of at the library?* I just shrug. That's the kind of conversations we have. The two kids sit in the back and turn on a portable radio real loud. They want attention, why I don't know. It must be their way of trying to be somebody, even if that somebody is nobody anyone would like. I can't study on my Problem because their boogie music is filling up my ears. Maybe it's just as well, 'cause my own thoughts seem stuck in my head, not able to go forward or back.

We bump along down South Tacoma on the way out to Lakewood. In the dark now the fir trees are huge and black, pointing up to the sky like big hands raised in prayer. I get off at Military Road S.W. and walk around the corner past St. John Bosco Church. Up ahead is our apartment complex, the one Jimmy and I lived in before he went to Nam. Now it's just me.

The first thing I do every day when I get home from work is check the mailbox. It isn't really a box, not like our big black mailbox on the side of County Road C, tilting on its post because a car sideswiped it, probably a drunk some dark night. It's really just a little slit in a wall of other slits, and I have to open it with a tiny key. If I ever lost that key, I'd die. Usually there is nothing but an advertisement for something or other, but ever once in a while there's an actual letter.

So far I've never gotten a letter from Ganny, but sometimes I get letters from Jimmy and Mama. Jimmy's letters come from so far away that they take a long time to get here, plus he never bothers to put a date on them, like we learned in school. How to write a business letter. How to write a thank-you note. How to write a letter to a friend, where you put the date in the upper right corner. Miss Furman was our teacher in that class in junior high, and you could tell she was somebody, that she came from somewhere—not like us country people. She had been to college in Columbia, the capital of South Carolina, and she wanted to teach us the proper ways, like Mrs. D wants to teach me. She only lasted a year. Word had it she moved to Greenville, and began teaching at a private school there. Jimmy must not have ever had her class, or more likely he didn't pay attention.

Jimmy's letters are never enough. What is missing? He signs them love, *Love, Jimmy*, but they don't tell me much. He must write them in the jungle, because that's what Vietnam is. I know that men are dying there all the time, but Jimmy doesn't talk about that. He writes like he's having fun, smoking dope, jumping out of helicopters, playing "I Fell into a Burning Ring of Fire" on his tape player full blast all night long to spook the commies. A couple of his buddies are Colored, or Black I should say. He wrote me about Denny from Tuscaloosa, Alabama, who grew up picking cotton and now he's into Black Power. Maybe being Southern Jimmy and Denny have something in common. Jimmy doesn't like Yankees. They make fun of his accent, but a lot of the soldiers are from the South, he says, so he's not lonesome, except for me. A lot of the soldiers are Colored. Black. Jimmy said over there it doesn't matter, because a bullet is color-blind.

Mama is working at the mill, sometimes doing double shifts, and she's not much for letter writing. It's a textile mill out there in the country between Pickens and Pumpkintown, set way back from the road with pastureland all around it. Cows with dark red hides graze on that land, and an empty road runs through the pasture, except when there's a shift change. Then the cars pour out and in, and you might be in New York City is how it feels, not that I've been there. Only there aren't any buildings except the plant. When Mama does write she tells me news from home, how Gloria my older sister is doing and how my little nieces Beth Ellen and Ginny Lou are coming along. Five and three. They'll be half-grown before I get to see them again. But I got married, and moved out here to be with my husband, and Mama says you got to sleep in the bed you make.

I climb the two sets of stairs up to our apartment, K-11. I look behind me to make sure no one is there, but it's as deserted around here as ever. It's only when I have the door shut and locked behind me that I feel safe. Even if Ben isn't around, there are bound to be others like him. You can't be too sure.

Before I do another thing, I get out my box of stationery that came with its own envelopes. Pink with what looks like pansies all around the border. Got it at the drugstore in Cashiers before I left home, figuring I'd be writing a lot of letters out here. I sit down on a high stool at the kitchen counter and write Ganny: *Dear Ganny, guess what, I'm way out here somewhere at the edge of the world on my own and Jimmy's somewhere all the way on the other side of the world and I'm in the family way and I'm scared and don't want it. Please advise. Hope you're doing okay. Miss and love you, Jeannie.*

I don't even know how Ganny's doing. I hope she's not sick. Mama never mentions her, but Ganny is Daddy's mama, and truth be told, Mama doesn't care for her much. They don't keep in close touch, and Ganny would never turn to Mama for help.

I love Ganny. I remember all the times we'd drive up to her place, a rambling, low-slung farmhouse in a hollow surrounded by steep ridges, painted white in its better days, an open porch on three sides, wood piled to the porch ceiling near the front door. She has outbuildings of gray weathered wood that has never been painted, smooth as satin to the touch, and lots of wild cats going in and out of the barn that has fallen in on one end. Ganny puts out corn bread crumbled in milk from her cow in tin plates for those cats. They won't let no one come near 'em. There's usually smoke coming out a stovepipe on the roof 'cause she cooks on a wood-burning stove. She always has plenty enough wood to last a hard winter up there in the hills.

I decide I had better tell Jimmy. *Boy, are you going to be surprised*, I write. But why should he be surprised, when he was the one who didn't use a rubber. Still, knowing Jimmy, I'm not sure he'd make the connection. What is in his mind I don't really know—his plans, his dreams. He isn't the kind to talk about all that. He's part Cherokee, hair black as crow feathers and cheekbones like craggy cliffs. I figure it happened that last time before he left for Nam. So it wasn't an immaculate conception. How weird it must have been for Mary, to be with child and not even have done it. And then to have to be the mother of Jesus, well, who would want that, even though it's supposed to be an honor and all. Who would want to see their boy nailed up on a cross, son of God aside.

I cross out the part about being surprised. *I'm expecting and it's all your fault*, I try again, then I cross that out. But it *is* his fault and now I'm stuck with it inside me. I tear up that letter and start another one. I won't tell him about the baby because I don't intend to have it. I'll find some way to get rid of it. I write him that it's still raining and that when I had the oil changed on the truck, the guy said I was eighty thousand miles overdue. Jimmy must never have changed the oil! I seal the envelope and put his APO address on it.

Then Ben comes into my mind. I wonder where he is, what he is up to at this very minute. I decide to write him a letter too while I'm at it, even though he has no address, correct-like with the date and salutation, like I learned. What should I say to him?*Dear Ben*. But that's not the way to start, because Ben is not dear, not at all, not after the harm he done those girls. I can't help wondering what they must of thought, what they must of felt, when they realized that he was like a hawk that swoops down and grabs a mouse in its claws. They must of felt caught, about to be torn apart alive by the hawk's beak. Here's what I write to Ben in my letter: *I hate you. You broke your mother's heart and that's not right. Why did you do it, Ben Daudelin? Why why why? What were you thinking? Maybe you don't even know yourself. Maybe you just wanted to, the way people do sometimes. You wanted to do something mean, no matter what harm it brings to other people. I hope you fry in Hell. Sincerely, Jean Parker.*

But I don't put my return address, even though you're supposed to.

Chapter Five

Inga

I was using Larry's office where I could shut the door. I've known Larry Reynolds forever, since he hired me eighteen years ago. He's dull but as good as they come, and I love him for it. He's been so great during this awful time, letting me take time off when I needed to, protecting me from the press and public, understanding when I had to stay home and brood, or when I couldn't stand to do that either. His tall, skinny frame, balding head and familiar bland, worried face are a comfort to me whenever I come into work.

There was a soft knock on the door, and when I said *come in*, it was Jean. My mind was in such turmoil all the time I'd almost forgotten about her. I'd see her at the library when I came in, but Lorraine was still supervising the shelvers, so I hadn't had much to do with her. I was surprised to see her, since the shelvers never came to Larry's office. I wondered how she knew where to find me. When I raised my eyebrows at her in surprise, she just stood there looking awkward and shy. I felt my face contract into a frown.

"What should I do?"

Sometimes I could hardly hear what she said, it was such a whisper. And then there was that Southern accent of hers. She pronounced "hi" as if there was a *y* in it somewhere, though I wasn't sure where.

"Mrs. Haskell is supervising you now, Jean. She'll tell you what to do."

"I mean about the other thing. You know." She pointed to her belly.

Honestly, she reminded me of the Little Match Girl, a story I hated as a child because it made me cry. I couldn't take her on, Match Girl or not.

"Jean, don't you have any family you can go to?" I couldn't keep the irritation out of my voice. "What about friends, a girlfriend maybe? Maybe you should go back to the South, back to your mother."

She just looked at me with those calm, clear eyes and shook her head, no.

Sometimes I'd see her reading in the stacks, running her finger over the page to follow the lines. What was she looking for? If I'd check to see what book she'd been reading, I'd find it was way over her head. I'd wonder what she got from what she read, if she could even make sense of it.

"Don't they have any military services for dependents? A doctor you can see at Fort Lewis? Honestly, Jean, I can't help you with this."

The look on her face made me feel ashamed. She just nodded, but she didn't make a move to leave.

"I have problems of my own, you know," I said. She cast her eyes down, blushing, and then looked right back at me. Her hazel eyes were serious and deep, old eyes in that childlike face. I wondered what her story was, who her people were, how she had gotten herself into such a predicament so far from home.

"Okay then," she said, and backed out, leaving the door open. I got up and shut it, and then leaned my back against it. I didn't know if I wanted to cry or beat my head on something. A big wad of dry cement was stuck in my throat. *Where was he, why didn't he turn himself in?* It had been twenty-six agonizing days since the police had come knocking on my door.

A few days later I was looking for some resource material for a patron when Larry came to get me in the stacks. "That detective is here," he said. "He's waiting for you in the conference room."

O'Loughlin came to the library occasionally. But he'd always call ahead, not just show up. I followed Larry back to the main floor, though my feet didn't seem to hit the floor right. In the conference room O'Loughlin was seated at the table, in his usual street clothes, a white shirt, no tie, a worn tweed sport coat, khaki pants, with a mug of coffee Larry must have given him. He met my eyes and immediately said, "He's okay. They have him in jail in Portland. No gunfire. No violence."

I sat down quickly. "You're sure it's him?" My mouth went dry, and one leg started shaking violently.

"He was driving a stolen car."

I shook my head in disbelief. How would Ben even know how to steal a car? How many more things were there I didn't know about him?

"There were handcuffs in the trunk."

"No!" I said. "No! It's got to be a mistake."

"We'll be testing them for fingerprints and DNA. We've got a court order for the teeth imprint." He was watching me closely.

"What has he said?"

"He's not cooperating with the authorities there. Maybe he'll talk to you. We're getting an extradition order to bring him back."

I tried to speak but my mouth felt numb.

O'Loughlin looked at me in that way he had, a mixture of compassion and gravity. "He'll be returned here shortly. There's no physical evidence yet linking him to the crimes. Just the eyewitnesses. But I expect that will change at some point—when we get the bite print results. If they match we'll be charging him with the murder of Angela Cruz. Probably the others." He let this sink in. "He'll be assigned a public defender."

"I don't see why you believe he's guilty," I said. "Based on … before you know all the facts."

He just looked at me.

"I see," I said, though I didn't. I stared at him in bewilderment, trying to understand.

"Mrs. Daudelin …"

"Inga," I said. "Call me Inga."

"Okay. Ron then. I know this is awful for you. I'll do what I can to help. If you want to see him in Portland, I'll make the arrangements."

"Tell me about the girls," I said. I hadn't wanted to ask before.

He looked at me for a long moment. Then he nodded. "Michele Rodele. Nineteen, studying biology and history at the community college. Something of a party girl, from what we know. Liked to drink, dated lots of boys."

I nodded, looking away.

"Cecilia Bockman—Sissy. Short, perky, a ski racer and tennis player. The only girl in a family of four boys. Twenty. The one whose roommate ID'd Ben as the guy they met at the bar the night she disappeared." Now he was the one who looked away, then back at me, to see how I was handling it.

"Go on," I said.

"Monica Morgan. About to graduate from the University of Washington. Had a fiancé. They were going to get married this June after her graduation. Disappeared walking back to her sorority house."

"And Angela," I said. "Tell me about Angela."

He sighed. "Older. All of twenty-seven. Latina. Worked in one of the erotic massage parlors on South Tacoma Way." He paused. "We figure they went willingly. Trusted their killer. Sensed no danger, at first. He was smart, nonthreatening, probably good-looking. A good talker, no doubt."

"Someone like Ben, you mean."

"Yes."

In a daze I made my way to Larry's office. I told him I had to go home, that they were holding Ben on suspicion of murder. I ran into Lorraine as I was leaving by the back door. She took one look at me and said, "What?"

"He's in jail in Portland. They found handcuffs."

"Oh, Inga," she said. She was staring at me in amazement, as if she didn't know me or herself even. Then her face crumbled and tears filled her eyes. "I'll come home with you," she said. "You shouldn't be alone. We'll go to Portland. An attorney … We'll figure out what to do."

I shook my head. It was coming to me that I wouldn't be going to Portland. I wasn't ready to see him. "I have to go," I told Lorraine. "I need to get home."

When I got to the house, a couple of reporters were already there. I parked in the garage and ran to the back door, holding a newspaper over my face while a flashbulb went off and a microphone was shoved at me. Once inside the house, I locked the back door and leaned against it, as if they might break it down. I was breathing hard and still I felt short of breath. I tried to think what to do next. But nothing came to me. The phone started ringing. I took it off the hook. I sat down at the kitchen table. When I next looked up, it was dark outside.

I was searching my memory constantly, trying to find anything I might have missed about Ben. I thought about how Charles had believed in spare the rod. He would get upset over the smallest things you have to expect out of a child—tears, laughter, excitement, tantrums sometimes. Little things upset Charles. He had those headaches, and believed noise triggered them, though I thought anything could cause them, it really had little to do with Ben. I hadn't been able to stop Charles from turning Ben over his knee and spanking him hard. I saw the fury and shame on Ben's face when he got spanked, but I knew to try to stop Charles would have made it worse. I tried to comfort Ben afterwards, but he'd just want to be left alone. This at three, four years of age.

I forced myself to think about those nights the year Ben was four, when I'd be late or go out, pretending I had a meeting, when in truth I was seeing my transgression. I don't know what went on at home then, except that Ben grew more fearful and resentful when I'd say I had to be away in the evenings, so much so that I quit going out at night. That was when I decided to divorce Charles. It wasn't because of Tony Nichols. I had no illusions that I would ever be with him. It was just that I didn't want to be with Charles anymore. I had never known my father to raise his voice or hand in anger. I didn't want Ben to grow up around a man who did both.

After we divorced, Charles stopped coming around, and then we didn't see or hear from him again. Not Christmas, not Ben's birthdays. No card, money, nothing. I hadn't even heard from him since Ben became a suspect, though it had been all over the national news. I know it pained Ben that his father abandoned him like that. He had loved his daddy, in spite of the spankings. Maybe he blamed me for him losing his father. Maybe he sensed the secret I was keeping from him. Maybe Ben knew there was something more important than him in my life.

I met him, my transgression, in the coffee room of the office building where I worked as a receptionist for Pacific Life Insurance. Charles and I had been married not even five years. He was a lawyer in the same building, and we'd find ourselves on the same coffee break. At first I was intimidated by him, he close to fifty and I a young twenty-five. Distinguished looking, with his silver gray hair, and a face that suggested experience of a sort I was not acquainted with. Something knowing about his look, the way his eyes appraised me. For the longest time—though it must have only been weeks—I couldn't meet his eyes. I was afraid to for some reason, it would be too—revealing. I knew he was looking at me in a way I wasn't familiar with, a way that excited and disturbed me, worming its way into my thoughts. I tried to be nice, polite. That was all I knew to be, do. I figured if he saw something in me, it was only that I was young, pretty in the way most young women are pretty. We made conversation, nothing much, but I began to look forward to my coffee breaks, I began to pay extra attention to my hair, my clothes. I felt happier during those fifteen minutes when I was around him than I felt at any other time in my life, even with Ben. I had never felt that kind of happiness before, certainly not with Charles. I didn't know what it was at the time, but something was building in me, something that had to find release.

I remember the first time Tony Nichols touched me. I was holding the coffeepot, offering to top off his cup. He just touched my hand lightly, purposefully. He stopped time with that touch. He might as well have touched my whole body, such was the sensation that shot through me. Charged, changed. No turning back.

He introduced me to my body. I had never had an orgasm. It wasn't something girls like me knew about, and Charles didn't have much experience with women. It's something Tony Nichols showed me about myself. We would go to a motel out near the office, and he would do things to me with his mouth, his hands, his penis, that Charles had never done. I would go home to my husband and son, and I was one thing to them, and another to my transgression entirely. Entirely other. It got where that was all I could think about … how he would bend me over the bed, how I would do anything for this … and this … and this … I hardly knew myself, I was double, two things at once. But I didn't feel guilty at the time, that was the thing. I had no guilt at all. The other was too important.

It ended because I confused love and sex. Years later I could see that, though I couldn't see it then. I just wanted more of him, and I couldn't have more. We never even spent the night together, we never talked for hours at a time. I wanted to *know* him, that was it. I thought that was love, and maybe it was. I didn't understand that sex was his form of love. I only understood that much later. He was so keen on my body, he loved making love to me. He was busy, married, with teenage children, and sex was what he wanted, and what he had to give me. I never knew what his thoughts and feelings were. It was nothing we could talk about. I had no wish to be married to him, to take him on in that way. I didn't even know what I wanted. Just him. Then I saw how much Ben hated for me to be away, and I knew that I was neglecting my son. Not in any obvious way, but he was not foremost in my mind. I could hardly concentrate on him. I was always thinking about other things, private things. Sensations, feelings, images.

I told Tony I had to stop, and he didn't question me or ask me to explain. Didn't ask me to stay. I imagine he thought it was because of Charles or guilt, but that wasn't it. I knew it was better for me not to keep wanting more and constantly being disappointed. His desire was straightforward, fair enough, but mine had tendrils that wound around and through my whole being. I knew I had to end it, even though I wanted to keep on with it. To never end.

I didn't go into the coffee room after that, I stayed at my desk or went out to the corner drugstore for coffee. It was very painful for a long time. But eventually when we'd see each other, in the elevator or on the street, it was as if we didn't know one another. We pretended until it was so. I had loved him more than I could understand.

What I had found out about myself scared me. The way I could do wrong. I did know it was wrong, the way I cheated on Charles. I cheated Ben too, as it turned out, because my actions led to the divorce, led to him not having a father. I decided after that that I would be good. Be an adult, is how I thought of it. Trying to reduce things, make them simple, manageable. Now I wonder if Ben learned it from me—to have a secret, hidden, transgressive self? A side kept secret from everyone. To be two things at once. If he did what the police were saying he did. If he possibly could have.

I decided after the divorce I wouldn't date. I would put my mind on raising Ben and supporting us. But was I really what I should have been for Ben? I can see him in my mind's eye now, how he came running up to me when he was six or seven. He'd dug a huge hole down at the creek, "mining" for silver. Excited that he would make us rich. His curly brown mop of hair. Showing me the shiny pieces of mica in his open palm. Eyes wide with amazement at our good fortune. I was in graduate school then in library science, working at the library, and always tired. Always. Money was tight, Ben knew that, he envied the things other kids had. I was preoccupied, fretting over mistakes I had made—Charles, Tony Nichols. I was often irritable, nowhere near the perfect mother, not the kind who was home after school, who baked cookies. I told him it was just dirt, to throw it away and go wash his hands before dinner. I turned away but not before I saw the look on his face.

We had a life, no better or worse than most.

But nothing that would create a murderer.

I forced myself to reexamine that time when he was fourteen and I found the notebook.

Things had gone more smoothly for us once I got my degree and began working. I had regular hours and was home in the evenings. Time passed and things seemed fine. Ben did well in school, had friends, sports, Boy Scouts. If he was quiet and even withdrawn some of the time, I knew from my own experience that things weren't simple, that people had private, even secret selves that they kept from others. I figured that was his right, and maybe part of growing pains.

Mostly I stayed out of Ben's room, respecting his privacy, but this one time I decided I had to clean up in there. I was going to dust behind the bed where the dust bunnies had proliferated, even wash the mattress pad while I was at it. When I pulled the bed out from the wall to strip off the sheets, I felt something between the mattress and box spring, far back against the wall where no one was likely to reach it.

It was a dark blue spiral notebook, the kind kids use in school. I sat down on the bed and began to page through. My breath caught in my throat. He had drawn a vagina with a knife stuck in it, red ink like blood flowing from it. A huge penis inserted into a woman's behind, her face contorted in pain. Another woman down on all fours with a collar around her neck, a stick figure man with a huge penis standing over her, her breasts severed from her body, the two mounds lying beneath her torso. There were intricate drawings of butcher knives, hunting knives, swords. I shut the notebook quickly and sat there stunned, my mind scrambled.

Then I jumped up, agitated to get rid of that notebook as quickly as possible. Even holding it felt dangerous, as if it were toxic or might explode. I couldn't just throw it in the trash under the kitchen sink or in the can out back! I felt half-crazy, crazy to kill it. I lit some newspaper and kindling in the fireplace, and set it atop the flames, watching it burn and curl to a black crisp.

Ben was at a Boy Scout meeting of all things. When he stepped in the door, he said it smelled like smoke in the house, and I said, "That's right, that's your … art … going up the chimney." His eyes opened wide in surprise but in an instant he shut down, his face impassive. I took him by the shoulders—he was nearly as tall as I by then—and shook him hard. I wanted to hurt him, I feared for him, I was disgusted by him. I had never hit him, but we both felt it in the air, that I might slap his face, which had turned white. He jerked away and said in a low, mean voice, "What I do is none of your business, you dirty bitch." He might as well have hit me. I stared at him in amazement. At that moment he was a complete stranger to me. Hatred flared in my chest.

He ran to his room and slammed the door. I was so stunned I didn't know what to do. On automatic I went in the kitchen and began frying pork chops for dinner, my mind racing in every direction, the smell of cooking meat turning my stomach. After maybe a half hour he came in and sat down, resting his elbows on the table and burying his head in his hands. I wondered if he was going to cry. I hadn't seen him cry since he was ten. His whole demeanor was one of abject misery. He had changed out of his Boy Scout uniform into his pajama bottoms and a white T-shirt. He needed a haircut, his hair curling in spirals all over his head like Medusa's. I was still hurt and angry, still flabbergasted by the drawings, but the sight of him wrung my heart. I sat down at the table, told him we had to talk. He rubbed his eyes hard, as if preparing to face the music, and then without looking at me, he mumbled that he was sorry for the way he had talked to me. He didn't know why he had been so mean. Would I forgive him? All in a strained, low alto that squeaked a little now that his voice was changing. He was passing over from boy to man. It occurred to me that it was his hormones kicking in. Maybe that was what was driving him. Maybe the drawings were … I didn't know. Normal for a boy that age? Fantasies that had nothing to do with his real self?

I studied his face, trying to see into him. He had fine features, a beautiful face really, with that mole a perfect accent by his eye and his crown of curls. *You dirty bitch*. Was that how he felt about me? And those drawings. Where did such images come from?

"Ben, what's going on?"

He slid his chair roughly away from the table. I held my breath to see if he'd leave. I tried to push on. "Ben," I said, "… I mean … why …"

He didn't look at me. "I said I was sorry. Can't we just forget it?"

"Don't … do it again," was all I could come up with. I wanted to touch him, as if that might ease things somehow. I brushed his hair back from his eyes, told him to get a haircut tomorrow. He was stiff under my touch, as if barely enduring it.

After that he was more secretive. I kept searching his room, looking for … I'm not sure what. I never found drawings again or anything else that would give me pause. Over the next few weeks I tried to make sense of the incident. He was a young male, he had hormones, he might be exploring sexual feelings in ways I couldn't understand. I didn't expect him to draw hearts and roses. Everything—except the drawings—appeared to be okay, that was the thing. There would be times, moments, days, when I would relax, think, *You fool. Everything is fine! Ben is fine!*

I hadn't wanted to talk to anyone about all of this, I had wanted to protect Ben, not let anyone know about what I didn't understand myself. To talk about it would have made it into a problem that I didn't want to have. I didn't know who I'd talk to about him. I couldn't imagine telling anyone about the drawings.

Still, it weighed on me, keeping me awake at night. About a month later I did try to talk about Ben to David. I figured a doctor would know whether what had happened was normal or not.

I felt so foolish I had trouble getting the story out. I told him about the drawings, and how Ben had become secretive in a way I had trouble describing. Cipher was the word that came to mind. Sometimes he would fall into black moods, be sullen or flare up over nothing. If I asked him to clean his room, or take out the trash, he'd sometimes slam a door or leave the house and be gone for hours. But when he'd return, he'd be himself, or at least one of his selves. The one who could charm me with his smile and words.

David had me make an appointment for him to see Ben, and Ben easily passed. David told me he thought Ben was just sensitive and self-conscious, needing to separate from me now that he had reached puberty. Mood swings were pretty normal at that age. Striking out with ugly words showed a lack of impulse control, nothing too unusual for a teenager. It all made sense. As for the drawings, well, boys were hormonal firecrackers who have fantasies, even violent ones. David thought Ben was very bright and maybe bored with school. Just watch him and if nothing else showed up, don't worry so much. Ben was a fine boy. I should be proud. I was reassured, trusting David's opinion, feeling not so alone about the incident.

Shortly after that, David asked me out, and though it meant he could no longer be our doctor, we started seeing each other. I had been lonely for years but I had tried to ignore it, at least until Ben was older. For the first few weeks it was exciting and romantic, but as the months passed we were missing some spark. I remembered Tony and how it had been with him. We went back to being just friends, though I know it hurt David. I think he'd even thought of marriage. David became our family doctor again and, to his great credit, remained my friend.

Time passed, and the notebook faded in importance as life continued with no indication that Ben was troubled. But was that the truth? Or had I been sleepwalking through our lives? Was Ben just very clever at hiding his dark side? Or was he who I thought he was?

Chapter Six

Jean

I'm still toting around my Problem. The days just keep passing, and it just keeps getting bigger, though in truth it's just a li'l swell, or maybe that's the chicken potpie I ate last night. Mrs. D told me she can't help me with it. I keep waiting and waiting to hear from Ganny. I can hardly think sometimes for a roaring in my head, like it's under a big faucet, the way Mama used to wash our hair in the bathtub.

I get to where I talk to the Problem, begging it to just go away. *I know you're in there,* I tell it, *and you're going to get big. Neither of us wants that, right? It'll hurt to come out, I'm just telling you. It will squeeze your head into a little pointy point, and you won't like that one bit, you hear? Better bail now, while you're just a mite. Okay? Okay?*

Nary a word back. But I just keep talking, even though I don't have to say a thing out loud. I know it can hear me, my inner thoughts. Sometimes I fuss at it: *Why you want to do me this way? What have I ever done to you? You're gonna take over in there. There's not room for the two of us. I was here first, you! Go away, now, just drop into the pot like a big, messy period. I don't need you. I don't want you! You hear!* But it's stubborn to a fault.

Today is Mrs. D's first day back since Ben got arrested. Margery was carrying on about Ben in the break room, like it was a big joke. "They'll fry him up for good now that they've got him," she said. "Stick a fork in him when he's done," and she laughed her nasty laugh.

"Now don't go talking so mean," Babe shushed. "Mrs. D might hear you." Babe's a lot older than us, at least thirty-five if she's a day, wears her black hair in a beehive that looks like something live could be nesting in there. She's sweet as sugar candy and not the brightest bulb. Men watch her in the library, and it's not hard to see what they have on their minds. She has a mean husband, which is probably why she recognizes mean when she hears it. One time she came in with a black eye, said she had walked into a door knob. Margery asked her what she was doing walking around on her knees.

"Ben's innocent until proven guilty," I said, just to stick up for Mrs. D. But I didn't believe it for a minute.

Margery just flounced her blousy hair back. She dyes it that stupid yellow color not found in nature. "Are you nuts! Ben Daudelin killed those four girls and everybody knows it. He killed those poor girls, and he'll kill you if he gets the chance. You are some kind of fool, Jean, you know that?"

"Now girls," Babe soothed. "Oh look, our break is over! Back to work!"

"Am not," I said to Margery across the table.

"Are too."

That's when I leapt up and snatched her bleached hair and pulled it hard. She screamed like I was scalping her, and here come our big boss Mr. Reynolds skidding into the room on his soft-soled shoes. He won't tolerate a commotion in the library. I feared for my job.

"Girls, girls," he said excitedly. "We're all under a strain, given the—circumstances. Now if you can't get along ... Well, you know what that means."

"She started it," Margery said. We were back on the playground in third grade.

"What does it mean, Mr. Reynolds?" I said. "If we can't get along."

"Well," Mr. Reynolds looked surprised. Lick. He paused for a moment, like he didn't know himself. "It means one of you will have to go, Jean."

"It won't be me," Margery hissed. "I have seniority."

"That's enough, from both of you." He shooed us away. I went back to my cart and pushed it mightily into the elevator and rode up in a huff to the second floor. I hated that damn Margery! And what was I going to do about my Problem?

• • •

The next day I waited outside the library's back door for Babe to get off work. I figured if anyone would know what to do it was Babe. She had been around, you could tell. Maybe she had found herself with a Problem she needed to get rid of. She was the kind who would know about such things. That's the way it came to me. Besides, time was running out and I had no one else to ask.

I walked with her in the drizzle up the steep hill behind the library. Shelvers weren't allowed to park in the parking lot, so she had to find a place on the street way up the hill every single day, and it wasn't easy. Another good reason for not driving Jimmy's truck. Babe had a kind of twang to her voice, like she was raised in Texas. She called everyone honey. I had forgot my umbrella again, so she shared, tucking her arm into mine and pulling me close. She smelled like roses past their prime. Something about Babe reminded me of a dog that's always rolling on its back to show its soft belly in the hope it won't get hit again.

"Babe," I began. "I have this Problem. You know, in here," and I pointed to my belly.

She stopped in her tracks but I kept going. A cold rain had commenced and streamed off the umbrella down my jacket collar onto my neck. Babe pulled me back under the umbrella and snugged me close to her. "Oh honey," she said. "That's no problem! You're a married lady. Your husband'll be home soon and yall will have this precious baby."

"No," I said. "I don't want it. I'm afraid for it to come out." I was shivering. Maybe she wouldn't help me.

"Oh honey," she said, "it'll be okay. Women have been having babies since … well, forever. It does hurt some, I'll grant you that, but then you'll forget about it when you see its precious face."

"No," I said again. "I don't want it. I'm not ready for my circle to be drawn. I've got to get rid of it."

We started walking again. The rain had picked up and was seeping through the umbrella. We were both getting wet. I was panting a little from the hike up the hill. What if she wouldn't help. What would I do then?

I looked into her face, which just missed beautiful. It made me think of valentine hearts. Rain or tears were spilling out of her eyes, making her eye makeup run, black mascara smears down her cheeks. She looked away for a long minute, like I had lost her.

"I have a number," she said. "A doctor who can take care of it. It'll cost you. He's taking a big chance with the law. It's jail time if he gets caught. Oh honey, you're just a baby yourself. Are you sure?"

"Yes, ma'am."

She gave me an extra good hug. We had come to her car. The door on the driver's side had a big dent, like someone had kicked it. She had to pull hard to get it open.

"I'll bring you the number."

I walked back down the hill to the bus stop. I was soaked from head to toe, cold and shaking, but a stone had been lifted from on top of me.

She brought me the number the next day, scribbled on a piece of paper. I called as soon as I got home that evening. A man answered, but he didn't say anything except hello. I had expected him to say he was Dr. So and So or something … but no. Suspicious like. I told him I had a Problem and that I heard he could help.

"Where did you get this number?" He didn't sound very nice. I stuttered out *Babe*. I didn't even know her last name.

"Write down this address," he said. "Come on Monday at two o'clock. Don't discuss this with anyone. Bring someone with you. You'll need someone to drive you home. Don't eat anything the night before." He talked so fast my head was spinning.

"I don't have anyone," I said.

"That's not my problem," he said. "Bring five hundred dollars in cash."

"Five hundred dollars!"

He hung up.

I barely had enough to pay the bills, what with Jimmy's pay and what I made at the library. I turned the sewing basket where I kept my rainy-day savings over on the rug. A mess of needles, thread, thimbles, and money came tumbling out. I counted forty-two dollars in bills and some loose change.

I went outside to the parking lot and stared at Jimmy's truck. I sucked in my lower lip and bit down enough to hurt but not to bleed.

The next morning I got up extra early, cranked up the truck, and drove the short distance to that filling station in Lakewood where the mechanic had changed the oil. One thing my daddy taught me was to always change the oil. Why Jimmy hadn't seen to that I didn't know.

"How much?" I said to the guy when he came out of the office. His overalls were clean, and he didn't have oil smeared on his hands and face the way he did last time. But it was early in the day. I flipped my thumb toward Jimmy's truck.

He reared back on his heels, like he was shocked. "You trying to sell that piece of junk?" He went over and leaned his head in the open window to see the odometer although he already knew the mileage from when he changed the oil. "Oh boy," he said. "You oughta pay me to take it off your hands." He winked at me. His two front teeth were missing, and his face was a fascinating web of deep wrinkles.

"Five hundred dollars," I said. "It runs real good."

He whistled through the hole in his mouth where his teeth used to be. "I'll give you three hundred fifty. I'm doing you a favor at that."

"Five hundred," I said. "And I mean it."

He jumped back in mock fear. "Whadda ya gonna do," he said. "Pull a gun on me?"

"Please," I said. "I have a Problem."

"We all got problems, kid. Four hundred."

I thought about it. I had the forty dollars at home. I needed four hundred sixty. I knew from his voice that the doctor wouldn't take less.

I bit my lip again. "This is my last offer," I said. He snorted at that. "Four hundred sixty."

He walked around Jimmy's truck, kicked the white walls. I put my hand on my tummy. *You are going to get me in a lot of trouble*, I said to it inside. *Jimmy's gonna kill me if I sell his truck.*

"Four hundred fifty, Little Lady. And that is *my* last offer."

"Sold," I said. "Cash."

"You drive a hard bargain for such a little bit," he said, but he went in the office and brought me out the money. He counted it into my hands and it was right: two twenties, a ten, six fifties, and a one hundred. "Don't spend it all in one place," he smirked. I handed him over the two keys.

"I need ten more," I said. "Would you take this watch here? Ten dollars. It's worth a lot more."

Ganny had given me the watch when Jimmy and I got married. It was an Elgin made right in South Carolina. I handed it over and without looking at it he slipped it into his overall pocket.

He pulled a ten-dollar bill out of his wallet. "Now get on out of here," he said. "You got all my money."

"Where's the bus stop," I asked, and he pointed down 140th Street. I tucked the bills into my bra. My breasts were tender and swollen from the Problem.

If only I could have gone right then, that day, to the doctor's, but I had to wait all weekend. This was my Saturday off, so I couldn't even go to the library. I turned on the TV to the cartoons, *George of the Jungle, Spiderman, Birdman*. Then it was football, and the Saturday movies that night. Sunday was the best, *Walt Disney, Ed Sullivan, Bonanza* with Hoss and Little Joe. I had stopped talking to the Problem. I felt right lonely, but I didn't want to encourage it, give it any ideas. The weekend seemed to last forever, but I knew from experience that time would pass. And eventually it was Monday morning.

I called into work as soon as the library opened. I should have asked for Mrs. Haskell but I asked for Mrs. D. I told her I might be coming down with something and I wouldn't be in today, and maybe tomorrow.

There was silence at the other end. Then she said, "Well, I'm sorry you're sick, Jean. Is there anything you need?" I felt a pang inside and thought about telling her about the doctor. But she might try to talk me out of it. I told her no ma'am, that I was just going back to bed. I felt lonesome as a stray dog when I hung up the phone.

I got out my bus schedules and map. The doctor's office was on the other side of town, an area I had never been to. It took me two hours and three transfers to get there, but I was way early. I was surprised that the address was a house, not an office. I wondered if I had it right. But I had been extra careful when I wrote it down: 610 East Twenty-Sixth Street. It wasn't a good neighborhood. The frame houses had paint peeling, screens hanging out of some of the windows, overgrown yards, and dog poop on the sidewalks.

It was almost noon, and I was starving. I hadn't eaten anything for dinner last night, just like the doctor said. Now my stomach was fussing at me. I didn't know what to do with myself for two hours. I walked down the street from the doctor's office. At least no one was around, and for once it wasn't raining, though it was gloomy with mist. There was a sorry little park with a swing set nearby. I sat on the swing and felt sorry for myself. I wondered what everyone else was doing. Where was Jimmy and what had he been thinking to give me such a Problem? What was Mrs. D doing right now? Was she eating lunch in Mr. Reynold's office by herself, the way she did. I wondered what she was eating. My stomach fussed louder at me. And Ben? They had caught up with him in Portland the papers said, and were shipping him back to Tacoma any day now. At least he was off the streets.

I felt kinda sorry for the Problem. It was hungry too. Well, that couldn't be helped. It was a Problem, that was all there was to it, and soon it would be a Problem no more. I wondered if it would hurt to get rid of it. I felt weak-kneed just thinking about it.

At a little before two o'clock I walked back to the house. It sure wasn't what I had expected. A two-story pink house with the window shades pulled, and a chain-link fence around the yard. I opened the gate and walked up the concrete steps to the screen door of a three-season porch. The doorbell was hanging loose. I wondered if anyone in the house could even hear me knock from out here. I tried opening the screen door. It was unlocked, so I trod across the porch, which was full of moldy-looking upholstered furniture, and knocked on the door. I felt like I was going to throw up. But there was nothing to throw up.

A short, middle-aged man slowly opened the door, not friendly like or like he was even expecting me. He had on a blue shirt that wasn't tucked in, and black pants that looked shiny, like car upholstery. His gray hair was in a pony tail, but strands of it were licking out all around his head, making him look crazy. He didn't speak to me, just peered behind me. "Didn't you bring someone to drive you home? Come in, come in," he said and put his hand on my back and shoved me into the house.

"I'm Dr. Oates," he said. "I'll be performing the procedure. Did you bring the money?"

I nodded and got it out of my pocketbook. I had put it in one of the envelopes from my stationery box. I handed the envelope over and he tucked it in his shirt pocket without even counting.

"Are you really a doctor?" I asked.

"Of course," he said. "Let's get on with it. Come with me and I'll explain everything." He pointed to a closed door on one side of the living room. "I'll tell you what to expect after you get your pants off."

I was feeling funny, like there were brakes inside me I hadn't even known about. I didn't move.

He looked at me as I stood there, my eyes cast down. "Do you want to do this or not?" he said. "I thought you wanted to do this thing."

"Will it hurt?"

"Of course it will hurt. But nothing you can't stand. I've done a lot of these. How far along are you?"

"Jimmy … that's my husband, he's in Nam … left in August." It was November now. Halloween had come and gone.

He had started toward that closed door, like he was in a big hurry, but now he stopped and turned slowly.

"So you could have gotten pregnant anytime before he left. When was your last period?"

I looked around, like I might find the answer written on the wall or somewhere. With the shades pulled it was dark in the living room. It didn't look homey, like someone actually used the room. There were no knickknacks or pictures on the wall, nothing but a sofa and two straight chairs. Maybe it was the waiting room.

"I can't remember," I said. "But I think it happened right before he left. 'Cause he didn't use …" I couldn't say the word rubber to this strange man.

"You may be too far along," he said. "We'll have to see."

My legs felt like they might give up on me, and my chin was quivering the way it did before I was about to cry.

I followed him into the room. There was a single bed hiked up high on cement blocks, and a sideboard with glass jars of instruments, towels, and a metal bowl. A gooseneck light at the foot of the bed looked like a strange metal animal peering at the mattress.

"Take off everything below the waist," he instructed me. "Lie down here, feet this way. I'll have a feel inside to see how far along the fetus is." He went out and closed the door behind him.

I was shaking so much I had trouble taking off my slacks and panties. How could I let him see my privates? But that's where the baby was, that's where it had to come out, through my hole and privates. I climbed up on the bed, and just then he came back in, pulling on rubber gloves. "Okay," he said, all business, "let's get on with this. Bend your knees up so I can get in there." All of a sudden I felt something plunge into me, his finger or maybe his whole hand. The other hand was kneading my stomach like it was bread dough.

"Ouch!" I shrieked.

"Hold on," he said. "I'm just at your cervix here."

"It hurts," I cried. "Stop it!" I felt dizzy and sick at my stomach. What if I passed out?

"Did you think it wouldn't hurt?" he said. "It's gonna hurt, girl. I'll give you a little shot now that will help."

But I was leaping up off the high bed, scrambling for my pants. I pulled them on fast as I hobbled into the living room, leaving behind my undies. I grabbed my jacket and pocketbook and headed out the front door.

I was almost down the steps when I remembered. *My money. Jimmy's truck.* How could I get it back without the money? I ran back into the house. "My money," I said when the doctor came out of the bedroom. "Give it back."

He ran his hand over his crazy hair. "What money?" he said.

I stared at him. "My money … the five hundred dollars."

"You better go now," he said. "I think you should go." He took me by the arm and shoved me out the door and onto the porch. He shut the door behind me, and I heard the double bolt click.

I still had the Problem. And I had sold Jimmy's truck. Now I had two Problems.

My head had such a roaring, I couldn't even think.

Chapter Seven

Inga

By Wednesday, Ben was in the Pierce County jail in Tacoma. It had taken them two weeks to extradite him from Portland, fourteen sleepless nights and long, exhausting days for me. He had been assigned two public defenders, and one, Alan Margoles, had offered to come to the library from his office nearby to walk with me to the jail at ten o'clock this morning. I hadn't met him but we had spoken on the phone. Did I want to see Ben? I did and I didn't.

For the first week after Ben was arrested, I stayed away from work. There was just too much "excitement" in the news, which I knew would extend to the library. But at home I had too much empty time on my hands. I began to feel angry that my life was on hold. I realized it was up to me to hold my head high and carry on. Or at least carry on. It would just look worse for Ben if I hid at home, as if he were guilty. As if I were ashamed of him. There had to be some explanation for all this.

Since I especially didn't want any extra time on my hands on the day I was to see Ben, I went in to work as usual, hoping it would distract me from the terrible case of nerves I had. My stomach was in a knot, and my breathing felt unreliable. I noticed that Jean hadn't come in again today, after calling in sick yesterday. Normally she never missed work, so I wondered what was going on with her. Maybe something had gone wrong with the pregnancy. I toyed with the idea of calling her, but I didn't want to give the impression that I was more involved than I was. Then I looked up her number on her application and dialed it. It rang and rang, but she didn't pick up. Now I had another thing to worry about, when I was already consumed.

I forced myself to fill out an order form for some new children's books. I tried to focus totally on the task at hand, not letting any other thoughts in. But I kept glancing at Larry's wall clock in spite of myself. I wondered if it was running slow, maybe winding down. When I checked my watch, it had the same time. I wrote down *Where the Wild Things Are.* What would Alan Margoles be like? Our future depended so much on him. Would he be competent, aggressive, committed to Ben's case? So much felt out of my control. I turned back to the order form. *Always Room for One More. Sam, Bangs, and Moonshine.* But every now and then I caught myself staring into the middle distance, wondering what it would be like to see Ben and what he would say.

Finally it was nine-forty, almost time. There was a soft knock on Larry's office door. Before I could get up from the desk, the man I assumed was Alan Margoles came in, shaking rain off like a dog. He paused for a moment to straighten his baggy raincoat and flip back his hair. Then he came over to me and gave me a long, damp handshake. I was shocked by how young he was, maybe twenty-six or twenty-seven, not much older than Ben. I felt like saying, *No, this won't do, you won't do, we need someone older, experienced!* But I didn't want to offend him in case he was all we could get.

"Are you ready for this, Mrs. Daudelin?" he asked.

"Inga," I said. "Please call me Inga."

We went out the back door of the library into a light rain. Under Alan's big golf umbrella we walked down Tacoma Avenue, past McDonald's to the Pierce County Jail. I'd never paid any attention to the jail before. Now it was the most important place in the world to me. Though it was just down the street from the library, and though I saw them all the time, I'd never given a thought to all the bail bond places around there. But now Ben's bail was set at $300,000. Our friends, led by Christopher, were trying to raise the 10 percent cash, but we needed a pledge of property worth the balance, and my house wasn't worth that much. Bail was not going to be within our reach.

Alan and I walked in silence. At one time I had thought Ben might go to law school and become a lawyer. He seemed to have the right talents for it, excellent writing and speaking abilities. He had won the state Latin award in high school, beating out private school kids from Seattle. He went through a period where he loved quoting Latin legal phrases, *caveat emptor*, *res judicata*, and bragged his senior year of high school about becoming a lawyer. He started out as a poli-sci major at the University of Washington and seemed on track for law school. But then his grades dropped, I never knew why, and he switched to a sociology major his junior year. Gradually all talk of law school faded.

"I know you have a lot of questions," Alan said. "I'm just getting on board on your son's case myself. I've had a contact visit with Ben, and I've been over to the county attorney's office to make copies of the police reports. It gave me a chance to have an informal talk with the prosecutor. There'll be time …"

"There's one thing I have to know now," I said as we walked along briskly. "The death penalty."

Alan didn't break stride. "It's very rare these days," he said. Then he put his hand on my arm, stopping me on the sidewalk. He looked me right in the eye. His eyes were bloodshot, as if he'd been up all night. He was someone's beloved son. "We'll do everything we can to get him life if he's convicted," he said carefully. "Now let's just concentrate on proving him innocent."

But a cold wind roared through me. If they convicted him, they'd execute him.

The jail was an imposing building, stern and inhospitable looking, gray as the day. Inside we took the elevator straight to the fourth floor, where visitors checked in. A man behind a wire cage checked our driver's licenses, and Alan showed his attorney license. Then another officer came and took us through a series of locked doors and down a long, empty hall to a waiting room. From there we were escorted into the family visit room where we'd see Ben. It had a long table running lengthwise, with a thick Plexiglas divider on it. The room was putrid with stale cigarette smoke, but at least we were the only ones there. My heart was beating so hard I wondered if Alan could hear it. I sat down nervously to wait for

Ben, while Alan leaned against the wall behind me. I looked at my watch. Nine-fifty-five.

The door on Ben's side of the room opened and there he was across the Plexiglas shield from me. For a moment I thought it wasn't Ben, that there had been a mistake! He looked so skinny and haggard, as if he'd aged years! He was wearing blue cotton pants with a drawstring and a blue short-sleeved cotton pullover shirt, like he was in pajamas. His thick curly hair was gone, replaced by a buzz cut that made him look skinned. But it was Ben, all right, and he gave me the crooked, ironic smile I knew so well, as if to say, *Fancy meeting you here*, like we were in a play and he would play his part. He put his hand up to the glass. I met it with mine from the other side.

He sat down opposite me. My eyes filled with tears, I was too choked up to speak. Ben's eyes brimmed too, and his ironic bravado crumbled. He looked vulnerable and shaken, his face suddenly ashen. Alan handed me a Kleenex, and I tried to hand it to Ben but hit my hand against the Plexiglas. "Thanks anyway, Mother," he said and I saw how he was struggling for control.

I wanted to put my head down on the table and cry my heart out. Instead I concentrated on taking some deep breaths. I wanted to get through this meeting, and crying was not going to help.

"Are they treating you okay?" I finally managed. "Are you eating? You look gaunt!"

He glanced around, maybe composing himself, maybe to see how much he could say. There was a guard standing behind him against the door he came through. "Well, I wouldn't say it has all the comforts of home. But they're not beating me or anything. Food's okay, institutional I guess you'd say." He crinkled his eyes, giving me an expression I'd seen many times, as if grimacing at a bad joke.

"I ... I'll have to fatten you up ..." I said. "When you come home. Alan here—" I gestured toward Alan behind me but then didn't know what I wanted to say. Something reassuring, comforting. But what could that possibly be?

"Hi, Al," Ben said. "I'd shake your hand but under the circumstances ... Thanks for bringing Mother. But shouldn't you be working on my case?"

The attempt at humor fell flat. Ben snorted a little, acknowledging that there was no way to lighten things up.

"Oh Ben," I murmured, and it was strange, really, how the love surged in my chest. Such love must be a biological thing, beyond one's control, the way you can love a newborn, the way I loved him the moment they laid him on my chest.

"This is a horrible mess," Ben said, shaking his head. "I'm sorry … for the embarrassment and everything."

We sat there in silence. I had had so many conversations with him in my mind, but now I felt blank. I couldn't find a place to start.

The silence stretched out. "So how are you holding up?" he asked at last.

What could I say? The more I felt, the less I could speak. "Okay," I finally managed.

"How's Grandpa?" he asked.

"Ben," I said sharply. "Help me. I don't understand. I want to help. But you have to tell me the truth."

"Of course." He cast his eyes down. He had always had such long eyelashes. They gave him almost a feminine, sweet look at times. But now his face had hollowed out, sharpening his cheekbones and nose. He was clenching and unclenching his jaw.

"Why didn't you turn yourself in, Ben? Why did you run?"

He shook his head. "I'm an idiot," he said. "It was a big mistake. I should have turned myself in right away. But I panicked. I mean that anyone could think … I mean, me—! I couldn't think straight. I just took off, and then I didn't … I don't know. I just … I'm sorry," he said sheepishly, as if he hadn't taken out the trash when I had asked him to.

"What about the handcuffs, Ben?" A shiver went through me. I knotted my fists and dug my fingernails into my palms.

"Mother," he said in a pleading voice. "I don't know anything about them. I stole that car, but I had to get away. I couldn't let them catch me. Because they wouldn't believe me. The police must have planted those things. What would I be doing with them? It doesn't make any sense." He hadn't been looking at me, but now he quickly glanced up and then away.

"Ben," I said, "whatever the truth is, just tell me. I'll help you, I promise, but you have to tell me the truth! Did you kill those girls?"

We hung there. Then he leaned forward, bringing his face close to the Plexiglas. "Look at me, Mother! You *raised* me. I'm innocent! Totally innocent! It must be a case of mistaken identity or something, but it's *not me*. You of all people have got to believe me!"

Innocent … innocent. The word rang in my ears.

But it was not what I expected. Not relief … it was … I couldn't name it.

I pushed back my chair, almost knocking it over as I got up.

"You believe me, don't you, Mother? Mother!"

I felt Alan's arm around my shoulders as I pushed through the door.

Alan took me home and offered to stay with me awhile, but I said no. I couldn't stay in the house, I couldn't go to the library, I didn't know what to do with myself. With shaking hands I laced on my tennis shoes and drove to Point Defiance Park, where Ben and I had spent so much time. I parked near the rhododendron garden and took off down the outer loop trail, moving as fast as I could. There was no one much around on a weekday morning. I was running as if my life depended on it on the well-maintained trail, oblivious to everything around me, my shoes rubbing blisters on the back of my heels. I had forgotten to wear socks. I was surprised to see I was running in the clothes I had worn to work, a khaki skirt and oxford cloth blouse, no jacket. The words *Innocent, I'm innocent, You've got to believe me!* pounded in my head.

Finally I was breathing so hard I had to slow down. I stood for a long time looking out at Puget Sound and the Narrows Bridge in the distance, trying to regain my breath, trying to calm my racing thoughts. *Ben couldn't have killed those girls. But what if he had? Innocent. But the handcuffs.*

It took about an hour to complete the loop, and then I walked it in the opposite direction, killing another two hours. I couldn't stand to go home, I was afraid of being overwhelmed by my thoughts. I went to the mall, and wandered around the stores until they closed. Then I went home, hoping I'd exhausted myself enough so I could sleep, but it was not to be. I stared into the dark, unable to get the picture of Ben leaning close to the glass out of my mind. *Innocent! You've got to believe me!*

But how could I?

At midnight I was still wide awake. I couldn't stay in my own skin another minute. I got up, still in the same skirt and blouse I had started the day in a million years ago, grabbed my purse and my peacoat hanging by the back door and went out to the garage. I didn't know where I was going, just that I had to go. I had the strangest sensation, that worms were crawling through my body and that I'd do anything to get rid of them. I drove my Nova through the quiet North End without a clue where I was headed. It just felt necessary to be out in the dark, doing something, going somewhere, in the middle of the night. I felt a little calmer driving. I had to pay attention to what I was doing, stopping at stoplights, concentrating on making turns. From what I could tell, the whole world was asleep. I went down Division and turned onto Pacific Avenue, which was a different kind of dark and at the same time desperately bright. I had seen this stretch of downtown many times during the day, when its clubs and bars were closed, when it just looked seedy and sad, the pavement stained with vomit and sticky with spilled beer. But now it shouted excitement, booze, girls, fun! Men, mostly soldiers from the base, were milling outside the bars, a whole world I wasn't familiar with. I had never been out like this on my own in the middle of the night. I would have thought I'd be frightened, but I felt the way men must feel when they're looking for a fight. *Just try starting something with me.* I realized I was seriously, deeply angry.

I parked in a diagonal space and went in the first bar I came to, a place I had never expected to enter in my life. Loud rock music was blasting, assaulting my hearing, as if determined to blot out all thought and talk. Good. The room was so dark and smoky it took a few minutes for my eyes to be able to see anything. It felt like everyone in there had turned to stare at me as I stood near the door. I didn't see any women. I realized I was shivering, suddenly unsure of what I was doing. But I wanted a drink. Isn't that what people did when they felt like worms were crawling under their skin? If I had a drink, maybe that would relax me and then I could go home and sleep. I wanted more than anything in the world to sleep.

I didn't know what to do or where to go, whether to sit at a table or take a bar stool. I knew there was some protocol but I had no idea what it was. I hoisted myself up on a bar stool, away from a couple of men seated there who looked me over. It seemed to take the bartender forever to notice me, I wasn't sure whether to try to get his attention or just wait. My face felt burning red, but something in me was determined to see this through. Finally he came over, a beefy, bald guy with intricate tattoos all over his arms, blues and reds, eagles and snakes, hearts and eyes. He must have been a boxer at one time, his face looked as if the bone structure had been shattered and then healed in odd angles. "Hey, apologies," he said jovially. "Didn't see you down here. What can I get you, young lady?" and he slapped a napkin down in front of me. "A margarita?" I said hesitantly. I really didn't know anything about drinks. I had had a margarita at Kay's Mexican restaurant, and I had liked the sweet limey taste with the salt.

"Sorry," the bartender said. "We don't do those green things."

"Oh. Well, what do you recommend?"

"I've got just the thing. I think you'll like it," and in a few moments he set a short glass of what looked like a milkshake in front of me. "White Russian," he said. I raised my eyebrows at it skeptically, and he laughed. "Go on. Try it."

I took a sip. "Delicious!"

It was exactly what I had in mind. I realized the words in my head had stopped since I'd walked in the bar. I lifted the White Russian toward the bartender in a toast, then tilted it back and took a big gulp, almost choking. The bartender laughed and told me to slow down. My ears had adjusted to the loud music, and now I liked the way it filled me up, blanked my mind. I was surprised that my glass was empty. I was staring at it in disappointment, wondering if I should have another, when I realized someone had taken the stool next to me. "Another round," he motioned to the bartender, indicating my glass and his. He leaned close to my ear to be heard over the din, and introduced himself as Jack.

"Oh. Well, thank you," I said. "I don't mean to be rude but I was just planning on having this one drink and then …"

He put his hand on mine where it was resting on the sticky bar.

"Shhhh, shhhh, you don't have to explain," he said. "I can tell you're not a lush. Not even much of a drinker, are you? Just keep me company for a little bit. No expectations. But of course I'm open and flexible … What's your name?"

The bartender sat another White Russian in front of me, and another drink in front of Jack.

"What is that?" I asked. He explained it was a Seven and Seven—Seagram's 7 and 7-Up.

I was feeling light-headed, more relaxed, as if things weren't so bad. I sipped the new White Russian and it was even better than the first one. For some reason this made me laugh.

"That's better, isn't it," Jack said. "It's okay to have a little fun. You look like you could use some."

I turned to look at Jack. He was a little loaded but not so bad. In his early forties, I'd say. He had a wedding band on his finger, which seemed reassuring. I pointed to it and asked him if he had kids, which he did, a fifteen-year-old boy and a ten-year-old girl. I asked their names. I had hit a vein. Jack told how his boy, Stan, played quarterback for Yakima High, and how the girl, Evelyn, wanted to be a fashion designer. He described in detail how she was always dressing her Barbies in elaborate scarf outfits, which I found fascinating. We're having a good conversation, I thought. He motioned to the bartender for another round, and I thought why not.

He talked on about his job, selling wood by-products, whatever those were, in a four-state area. He was just in Tacoma for one day. At some point he asked me if I had kids. I hesitated. "No," I said, "No kids."

"Not married?"

"No," I shook my head, and suddenly I felt sad, where a moment ago I had felt gay. I was about to cry. A big lump blocked my throat. I suddenly felt as tired as I'd ever felt in my life, and sort of dizzy.

"Excuse me," I said to Jack. I gathered my purse and almost fell off the bar stool getting down. My legs seemed stupid, and I lurched with embarrassment to the ladies' room. My head was spinning, or maybe it was the room. I felt sick. I peed, sitting in the stall to try to stop the spinning. I wanted to lie down. When I went back out, Jack was still there. How would I get rid of him? I wondered how long I had been in the bathroom. I felt strangely altered, and all I wanted to do was to go home.

"It's been nice talking to you," I tried to say, but my words came out slurred. "Oh boy," I said. "Time for me to go!" But then I realized I didn't have my purse. I must have left it in the ladies' room. In a panic I rushed back to the restroom, but my purse wasn't there. Did I even take it to the ladies' room? The room was pulsing and I was getting a throbbing headache in my right temple. How would I get home? My car keys were in my purse.

I climbed back up on the bar stool, which was an effort, and said to Jack, "I think I've misplaced my purse. You haven't seen it, have you? Did I take it with me to the restroom?" I couldn't seem to make the words crisp.

"Honey, you're smashed," he said. "You're in no shape to drive."

"No," I said, "I'm fine, really. My purse. My keys …"

"Tell you what," Jack said and squeezed my hand. "Let me give you a lift. It's the least I can do. I feel responsible."

I looked at him and he was grinning at me. *We figure they went willingly. Trusted their killer … sensed no danger, at first. A good talker, no doubt.*

"No," I said. "I'll call a friend."

I could barely think. David … Larry … Lorraine … any of them would come. But how would I explain myself. I had been drinking in the middle of the night in a bar downtown. Not only was I too drunk to drive home, I had lost my purse and my car keys.

"Would you dial this number," I asked the bartender. I recited Ron O'Loughlin's home number. He had given it to me in case Ben ever showed up. I'd taped the card next to the hall phone, where I saw it all the time without even thinking of it. Now it came right back to me.

The bartender dialed and handed me the receiver across the bar. Ron picked up almost immediately, as if he were wide awake, though it was getting on toward two a.m. "O'Loughlin."

I almost hung up. I tilted on the bar stool. "It's Inga Daudelin," I said. "I'm … I'm …"

"Where are you," he said. "Do you need help?"

"I'm … can you come get me?"

"What's going on? Where are you?"

I asked the bartender the name of the bar, and told Ron the name, and that I had lost my purse. He said he'd be there in a few minutes.

I covered my mouth with my hand. I was so ashamed. Jack had disappeared, thank god. I thanked the bartender, who told me to take care. I felt as if I might fall down when I got down from the bar stool. I made my way to the door by hanging onto the backs of chairs, but once outside I had to sit down. I didn't know how long it took Ron to arrive, because

I shut my eyes. I must have slept right there on the sidewalk on my haunches. The next thing I knew Ron was taking my arm.

"It's okay," he said. "I'm taking you home."

"My purse," I said. "The ladies room …"

He was helping me into his car. I slumped down in the passenger seat, and then I was asleep again.

Ron was helping me to my back door. "I'm so … so … I'm so," I said, slurring my words. I hated that! "I'm so drunk! I'm so … what's the word I'm looking for. Starts with an *m* … Em … em …"

"I think the word you're looking for is 'human.'"

"That's my purse!"

"It was hanging on a hook in the ladies' room."

"Oh! God! The Nova. I've left it somewhere."

"You can get it tomorrow."

He unlocked the back door with my keys and was helping me down the hall into the living room. "No, I'm fine, really," I said, and sat down heavily on the hard Victorian sofa. The room was whirling.

I was about to thank him, to thank him sincerely, but a powerful undertow pulled me down into a depthless sleep.

Chapter Eight

Jean

I didn't feel like going to work today, which isn't like me, 'cause I always feel like going to work. But I was expecting to be rid of my Problem, and I still have it. I thought maybe going for a walk would help. Ganny used to say sometimes it's better to think with your feet than your brain. I went down the open cement stairs and stood for a moment in the parking lot out front. The place where Jimmy's truck used to be had been taken over by someone's giant red Cutlass. I hadn't gotten rid of the thing I wanted to get rid of and I had gotten rid of something I shouldn't have got rid of.

I began walking out the street that led into our complex. When I came to the corner, it was like I was seeing it for the first time, even though I saw it every day. St. John Bosco Church. I don't know much about Catholics, except that they have nuns and priests and are more religious than anyone else. I'm not much for the religion. I got enough of that when I was growing up. Sunday school and church every Sunday, Bible study on Wednesday nights, choir practice, Bible drills where Mr. Maggin—we called him Maggots behind his back—would call out a scripture verse. We'd be holding our Bibles down by our sides like pistols we were about to use in a duel. We'd whip up our Bibles to see who could find the verse the fastest. I used to know all the names of the books of the Bible in order. I can only get as far as Leviticus now.

St. John Bosco was some pretty church, like it was carved right out of the forest of Douglas fir that surrounded it. Dark wood, low to the ground, and not much of a steeple, like it was too shy or modest to announce itself. The yard around the church had big rocks placed here and there like nature had heaved them up, only men had put them there. There were odd, stubby blue-green evergreens branching out to the side instead of up. I followed a path of pebbles and sat down on a wooden bench, amidst the peppery smell of pine. It was so different from where I went to church, Lima Baptist, which sits on the very top of a steep hill with a range of blue mountains in the distance. There are mountains here too, but they don't look the same. For one thing they're snaggle-toothed and covered in snow. But the most amazing thing is the big mountain, Mt. Rainier, and how suddenly you'll be going along somewhere and it'll pop up, ghostlike, hulking over you like it's watching you. Like it sees and knows. Maybe that's what God is like.

I felt drawn to go inside the church. I pushed on the dark wood door, expecting it to be locked. But it opened easily, like it was expecting me. I stepped inside, where it was hushed and cool, dim except for some low lights glowing along the walls. Little candles were burning in a long tray, and it smelled rich and sweet inside, like the incense Jimmy bought at head shops. I would have liked to light one of those candles, but I didn't know if I was supposed to. I'd light one for Ganny to answer me soon and tell me what to do. 'Cause I didn't know what to do about my Problem.

I stood for a moment taking in the colored window at the front of the church. It was a river of blue glass with a brown glass boat floating on it, the sun sending down yellow glass rays. In front of the window Jesus was hanging from a big gold cross in a diaper, his legs tucked up. I went down toward the front and slipped into a pew, stumbling over a low bench on the floor. That must be what they kneel on. We never had such in our church.

It was so peaceful and quiet in there, like the church was dozing. I just sat and tried to let my thoughts clear. What came into view inside my head was that big ghostly mountain watching over me. It felt like it was keeping me safe. At least I hoped so. I put both hands on my stomach. *What am I going to do about you?* I asked it. *It's just you and me.* I had sorta missed it when I stopped talking to it over the weekend. I was staring on that when I heard someone come into the sanctuary behind me. My heart beat double time.

Just as I jerked around to see who it could be, an elderly gentleman came strolling down the aisle right up to me. He was not in a robe like they wear, just a gray cardigan sweater and gray pants, the same color as his hair. Still, he must have been a priest, he must of belonged here. "I didn't mean to startle you," he said. He looked at me in the soft light, trying to figure me out. I was used to that.

"I hope it's okay," I said. "I'm not causing any trouble. Am I?"

He laughed gently. "Not at all, my child. You're welcome to stay … and pray … as long as you like."

"I'm not much for praying," I said. And then I couldn't help myself. "But I do have a Problem." Two big tears rolled down my cheek, just like when Mrs. D first told me.

"God will help you with all your problems," he said, and he slid into the pew behind me. I turned so I could search his face. It was a kindly face but stern too, the way I imagined God's to be.

"How?"

"How will He help you?" I seemed to have taken him by surprise. I was used to that, too.

"When you give your life to Christ, he bears all your sins."

"But how exactly does that help with a Problem?" I could see he didn't really get it. The kind of problem I had. "I need to get rid of it."

He stared at me in a way that made my face burn. I wanted to leave, but that might be rude.

"You mean, get rid of your … problem?"

Maybe he was a little deaf. "Yes," I said louder.

A different look came over his face. It was like a hand passed over it, and now it was not quite as kindly. It had tilted in the direction of stern.

"That would be a mortal sin, my child," he said. "No, that would definitely send you to hell for eternity."

We both sat in silence, studying on this.

"I wouldn't want that," I said finally. "No sir. But are you even sure there is a heaven and hell? I don't think so myself. It doesn't make sense."

"There are better ways," he said. "There's … you know … loving couples, married couples, who would welcome … your problem."

"I'm married," I told him. "But Jimmy's in Nam. I sold his truck. That's my other problem."

"Let me help you," he said. "Maybe that's why you're here today. Maybe that's why you came in. To get some help."

"Could be."

"Why don't we go down to my office. We can talk better there. Let me get some information."

He wanted my name and address. He wanted my phone number. He wanted to find a home for the Problem. I knew what he was talking about. But now I wasn't sure I wanted to get rid of the Problem anymore. At least not till I heard from Ganny what to do.

"Thank you very much," I said. "But I have to be going now. Someone is waiting for me."

I gathered my jacket and pocketbook quickly, and then I ran out before he could chase me, maybe tackle me to the ground. Take away my Problem. But he couldn't have it. It was mine. Of that I was sure. *You come with me*, I told it as we galloped out the door. *Let's get out of here. It's time for supper.* Suddenly I had my appetite back. *I'm hungry, aren't you?* It had stopped making me throw up anything it didn't like. Sometimes I got the feeling it was hungry for something weird, not pickles and ice cream like the old wives' tales, but licorice, which was the one food I myself hated, or malted milk balls, which I could live on. When I was not trying to reason with it to leave, I told it about what happened at work that day, what Mrs. D said to me, or about some book I'd poked into. I told it about home, how we had a club when we were kids, with a secret password and a club house in an old CCC boys' icehouse. It was right good company, come to think of it, and no loving couple was gonna take it away from me.

When I got home, there it was, a letter in my mailbox. I could tell by the printing that it was from Ganny. I tore it open and read what she had wrote: *Dear Jeannie, I have studied the situation. It is not easy to do. It might cause more harm than good. You will be okay. We do not always know what is best. That is what the man upstairs is for. I am not one of those to just believe blindly. But that has been my experience. I am an old woman now and I see things differently. It is better to give than to receive. So give life. That is my advice. I am okay, knees about give out but keeping on. Love Ganny.*

I folded the letter and put it back in the envelope. I kissed the envelope, smelling as it did of buttermilk, wood smoke, and bittersweet. It wasn't what I was hoping to hear, but it was what Ganny said. I trusted her judgment. I thought maybe she was right. Give life. I understood what that meant. Not because you expect it to turn out pretty or easy, but because that's what there is. It was the main thing, was what it was. I thought I knew that before, but now I knew for sure. I thought of those pictures on TV of those boys in Nam, how they'd give anything to keep theirs. Life. How they didn't want to spill it out on that foreign soil. Even the enemy, Charlie like they called him, he wanted to hold on to his life too. I knew that, just like I knew that underneath everything in Jimmy's letters was a silent prayer: *let me live*.

I went up the three flights of stairs and unlocked my apartment door. I turned on the lights inside. Jimmy took this apartment because it has a little balcony with a sliding glass door, and when you step out on that balcony, it's like you're in a tree house almost, the fingers of the Douglas fir close enough to touch. They want to touch their fingers to mine, so sometimes I do. When I pull my hand away the tips of my fingers smell green.

I opened the icebox and got out the bread and peanut butter. I ate a sandwich and drank a whole glass of milk. Then I rolled up three pieces of baloney and ate them. Then I ate some Fig Newtons.

I ran a bath because I had work to do. I had life to give. It was time to start drawing my circle. When the bath was full and warm, I took off my clothes and stepped in, feeling how the water made my muscles relax. I eased down inch by inch, taking my time. Soon enough I stretched all the way out, my head resting on the back of the tub, my scrawny body laid out in front of me, my feet up on either side of the faucet. I looked at my breasts, which didn't even look like my own little breasts anymore, and at my stomach, where I thought I detected a definite swell. What would it be like when it came out?

I won't hurt you if you don't hurt me, I said inside.

Nothing.

After awhile, I realized maybe I had to try harder. *I'll try not to hurt you if you try not to hurt me.*

And then, in the exhale of my breath, in the silence that rushed in when the roaring in my head stopped, came one word: *Okay*.

Chapter Nine

Inga

I was still asleep on the Victorian sofa the morning after my debacle at the bar when I heard a phone ringing a little after six o'clock. First it was just a distant annoyance, but then as I began to come to, I realized it was ringing right in the hall and wasn't going to stop until I got up and answered it. My mouth felt tacky, and I lurched to the right as I got to my feet. I was still in the same khaki skirt and oxford blouse from yesterday, the skirt sticky on the back, from what I didn't want to know. What had I been thinking last night! My head felt misshapen, my joints stiff, and then I remembered with a groan that I had actually called Ron O'Loughlin to come get me.

God, it was Ron on the phone. When I heard his voice, blood rushed to my face. Before I could apologize, he said he'd be at my house in ten minutes.

That only gave me a few moments to freshen up, brush my teeth, and get out of my awful clothes. I'd have given anything for a shower but there wasn't time. When I stripped, I saw myself in the dresser mirror. Like Ben, I had lost weight. I was as thin as I'd been when I married. I still felt like a girl inside, hard to explain. Or maybe I just felt like myself, outside of time. I cupped my breasts, feeling strangely lonely and alone. The alone part wasn't new, but the loneliness was. I thought I'd gotten over that years ago. I paused there, looking for a long moment at my body. It set off a longing in me, the way I had felt for a long time after Tony Nichols. I turned quickly away, pulled out some fresh clothes, a gray wool skirt, white blouse, and navy sweater, disappearing back into my practical, sensible, invisible self.

Ron didn't need to knock before I opened the door. I couldn't meet his eyes. I wondered what he thought of me. But maybe he had news. I felt nervous, but I'd already met the worst: Ben in jail about to be charged with murder. He'd looked like a stranger yesterday, something grim about him I'd never seen. The way he clinched his jaw so hard, the deep trouble he was in. And thin. That blue prison shirt just hung off him, the sleeves too long at the wrists. *Innocent. Totally innocent!*

"Why don't we just sit down," Ron said. I followed him into the living room, too tense to sit as he took his regular seat.

"About last night," I began awkwardly.

He cut me off. "People do crazy things when they're in pain. But that's not why I'm here." That's when he told me Ben had escaped during the night.

"What?" I asked dumbly.

"Ben escaped from the jail sometime overnight."

"He escaped?"

"That's what I'm trying to tell you."

"How could he escape! I don't understand. How could they let him escape?" I started pacing back and forth, pressing my fist against my mouth.

"They discovered he was gone at the five-thirty bed check. When they went to wake him it was just ... sheets wadded up, some crumbled newspaper, I don't know what the fuck all, two or three pillows, the spread pulled over it all."

"Where would he get extra pillows?"

"They're trying to figure that out." Ron tipped back in the wing chair and rubbed his hands over his face. He looked disgusted and exhausted. He had a dark five o'clock shadow, which must have itched. He's a good man, I thought. He doesn't want this any more than I do.

"I'll make some coffee. You look like you could use it."

He waved me off. "He removed the metal light fixture in the ceiling of his cell. Widened the opening to about a foot square, enough so he could squeeze into the crawl space with the heating ducts and electrical wire. He squirmed and crawled his way toward the north end of the building and broke through the roof of a hall closet in the sheriff's department annex."

"And?"

"From there he dropped to the floor, went down the fire escape stairs, and walked out the door."

"I can't believe it."

"It's true. He's gone. They're searching for him now."

"It's because of me," I said.

Ron looked at me. "What do you mean?"

"He thought I didn't believe him. I asked him to tell me the truth. He said he was innocent. I just got up and left. He must have thought I've given up on him."

"Did you? Believe him?" He gave me such a penetrating look I had to look away.

I hesitated. "I'll never give up on Ben."

"I doubt seriously that Ben escaped because of you. He has better reasons than that." Ron sighed heavily. "I'll assign someone to watch your house."

"No."

"It's for your own safety."

"You don't honestly believe Ben could hurt me."

"We don't know."

"You don't know him! I know him, Ron. You don't."

It was a standoff. We sat in silence.

"Nevertheless, I'm going to assign an officer here. Let's just say it'll help me sleep better. Now let's go pick up your car."

"But …"

"Let's go," he said. "I have to get back to the office. You can't leave your car there all day."

I grabbed my coat and we rode down to Pacific Avenue. I thought of something Scott Fitzgerald said: The test of a first-rate intelligence is the ability to hold two opposing ideas in mind at the same time and still be able to function. I didn't have a first-rate intelligence, but I was holding two opposing ideas at the same time: *He did. He didn't. He was. He wasn't.* As for functioning, at least I hadn't killed myself.

Chapter Ten

Jean

Mrs. D didn't come to work for a whole week after Ben broke out of jail, but I went every day on the chance she'd be there. When she finally came back, I was waiting for her by the back door. I told her I was going to give life. She just nodded, looking confused, like she didn't know what I meant.

"Do you know a doctor that sees girls in my condition?"

"Oh. Yes, you should definitely see a doctor," she mumbled and started to walk away. "Prenatal care is very important, you know."

"Can I go to your doctor, Mrs. D?"

She turned back to me, looking surprised.

"Jean, that's not really … I don't want …" But then she just sighed and said, "Well, I guess I could make an appointment for you. But just this once. Then you're on your own."

"I had to sell Jimmy's truck," I said. "It was a mistake but it's gone. Will you carry me?"

"Carry …" she started, but then she just nodded. "But just this once."

A few days later when she hadn't said anything, I asked her when we were going to go to the doctor. "Go …" she said, like she'd forgotten. But then she said she'd make a call, and that afternoon she told me she'd take me the next day at three o'clock, that she had cleared it with Mr. Reynolds so we wouldn't even have to come back to the library afterwards.

When we started out the next day, the afternoon sun made it feel like a holiday. It was the first clear day we'd had in I couldn't remember when. Mrs. D drove a blue Nova, and the inside was clean, no cigarette packages and McDonald's trash all over the floor like in Jimmy's truck. I dreaded telling Jimmy it was gone, but at least it could wait 'til he got home. I would write him about the baby as soon as I got home from the doctor today. Maybe that would make up for it.

When we started down the hill toward Division, Mrs. D didn't say a thing, concentrating on the traffic. She didn't have on any earrings, but there were holes in her lobes. She was wearing a navy blue pea jacket with big matching buttons down the front, and on the seat between us was her black pocketbook, the kind that would hold everything you'd ever need. I wanted to learn things from her, how to do and be. We rode in silence until we cleared downtown and headed south on I-5.

Then out the front window to the left, there it was, Mt. Rainier, rising huge and spooky in the distance. The top was covered in snow and clouds were swirling around the peak. It about took my breath away.

"Look at that!" I said to Mrs. D.

"What?" she said.

"The big mountain. Mt. Rainier."

"Rain*ier*," she corrected my pronunciation. "It is magnificent, isn't it? We usually don't get this clear a view of it."

"It watches over me," I said.

She glanced over at me but didn't say anything. I kept my eyes on it as long as I could, until it disappeared behind the forest alongside the highway.

We rode in silence for awhile, both thinking our own thoughts. Then she looked over at me with that worried look she always has now. "How's your husband getting along in Vietnam?" she asked. "What do you hear from him?"

I told her how Jimmy couldn't write too many letters because he was busy looking for Charlie. "He's an RTO on a track. Operating the radio is an important job. You're the one to let people know what's going on. Otherwise, the men are out there in the jungle all alone."

"I can't imagine," Mrs. D said. She was driving with two hands on the wheel. A ray of sun was coming in the front window. I leaned forward so it could warm my face.

"Jimmy says tracks are good, because they're like a big metal can all around you and they move fast. The guns on them are kick-ass. Oops."

Mrs. D smiled a little, the first I'd seen in a long time.

I told her how Jimmy said that the people are horrible poor, so poor you wouldn't believe their stick arms and legs and the way their bellies stick out. "The children run alongside the tracks, begging for food, and when they bang their fists against their open hands, it means they want you to buy their mother or sister. For sex. Two dollars."

"Goodness."

"I sold Jimmy's truck," I said. "He's going to be mad when he gets back."

She didn't say anything for a few minutes. "Well, you never know how people will react. Maybe he'll be so glad to see you and meet the baby that he won't mind. Maybe he'll get an even better truck."

"Maybe."

Ahead was a big green sign saying Puyallup, a funny name I couldn't pronounce. We went east and all too soon we turned onto a frontage road. I wished we could just keep talking and riding down the highway, all the way to California. I got an afraid feeling and I put my hands on my belly. As if she knew, Mrs. D said, "You'll like Dr. Dunn. There's nothing to be nervous about." Up ahead I saw a long, low cedar-shake building tucked into a forest setting. That had to be the doctor's office, not like that other doctor's office that was just a run-down house. The cat had got my tongue. "It'll be okay," she said. "He'll examine you and make sure the baby is okay."

"Okay then," I said. I followed Mrs. D in.

The doctor wore glasses thick as jelly jar bottoms, but once I got used to his buggy look, he was sweet. Mrs. D sat next to me in the examination room, like we was mother and daughter, and Dr. Dunn sat on a round stool he could roll around on. He asked me questions, like did I know when I'd had my last period, if I had ever had a pelvic exam before, if I had had any previous pregnancies. I said no sir to ever one. Mrs. D had to leave the room then so he could examine me, but a nurse came in and she talked about what a sunny day it was, taking my hand and holding it. The doctor had me put my feet up in metal stirrups, and he stuck something in me like pliers to hold open my hole. He pressed down on my tummy and it felt like he stuck his other hand up in me, though maybe it was only a finger. I about died of embarrassment, plus it hurt but not as bad as that other doctor. He acted like it was all normal. I was glad, though, because now that I was going to give life, I didn't want anything to go wrong. I didn't want my feet and legs to swell up with too much sugar in my blood, I didn't want to have a baby who had a water head or a hole in its heart. All the stories you hear.

On the way home from the doctor's Mrs. D stopped at the drive-in and bought us each a hamburger and a chocolate shake. I ate mine so fast, before she was even half-done, that she just looked at me and ordered me another one, just like that.

We sat in the car and ate and drank, listening to the radio. When the news about Nam came on, she turned it off.

"Jean, have you ever thought about going back to … is it North or South Carolina? To have the baby. Where you have family. I'm sure your mother would want to help out."

"North," I said. "But no ma'am. I want to stay here."

"I see," she said, as if she didn't see at all. But she hadn't met Mama.

We sat a piece more in silence. Then she said, "I'm sure your mother loves you, Jean. I bet she'd surprise you. Do you think?"

"No ma'am."

"What about other family? Someone you could turn to."

"There's Ganny," I said. "Some say we're just alike." I told her how Ganny's a real mountain woman, how she has common sense and knows how to keep her head in a crisis. I told about the time we were walking down the road behind Ganny's place and how we came upon a giant rattlesnake wrapped around the trunk of a pine tree. I was maybe five or six years old. I'd been warned of rattlesnakes all my life, how they rattle and strike and then you're dead, so seeing that snake bigger than a man's upper arm was like seeing all the bad things I'd ever feared come to life. I told how my legs just gave out and I fell down on the road in a crumpled heap. Ganny gathered me up in her arms—she's not very big, but strong from chopping wood and toting water and doing a million chores—and carried me home. "If she was afraid herself, Mrs. D, she didn't show it. A few minutes later I heard a gunshot. Ganny had gone back and shot that snake dead. She skinned it and nailed the skin to the house, to warn off other snakes she said."

"Your grandmother sounds like quite a woman," Mrs. D said. "Maybe you could stay with her until Jimmy comes home."

"Maybe," I said. "But I want to stay here with you."

"With me!" she said, and snorted a little. Then she looked over at me and shook her head. "Jean," she said. "I don't mean this unkindly but—how can I put this—you're not like other people."

"I know," I said. "I get that from Ganny."

Later I thought what a coincidence it was that I told Mrs. D that particular story—out of all the millions of stories in the world I could have told. Ganny believes there aren't coincidences, that everything fits together, things happen for a reason even if we don't know why. Maybe she was beaming herself to me across the miles, reminding me to keep my head like she did that day. Maybe she was telling me in some mysterious way what to do. I don't know.

What I do know is Mrs. D dropped me off at my apartment—that's how he figured out where I live. It's called a complex because there are many buildings that look just the same, and it's complex to find the one you live in. Mine is the letter *K*, but it is next to *C* and *A*, don't ask me why. The soldiers who live here—the ones waiting to be shipped out to Nam—spend a lot of time washing their cars and playing loud music on their car radios. The smell of weed is always in the air, and the dumpster where I take out my trash is always full of beer cans and booze bottles. I stood in the asphalt parking lot and watched Mrs. D drive slowly away over the speed bumps.

I went up one flight, then another to our apartment door. I unlocked it and went in and made sure to lock it behind me. Because it was getting dark I turned on the brightest light, the chandelier over where a dining room table should be. When Jimmy was still here, we'd sit on high stools at the bar counter in the kitchen to eat, but now I just sit on the couch with a paper plate in my lap. I slid open the glass doors to the balcony and went out to touch the fingers of the Douglas fir. The weather had taken a turn, it was foggy and drizzly now. I stood there for a bit, thinking back over the day, the trip to the doctor's, and how Mrs. D has long thin fingers and doesn't wear any rings. She doesn't wear nail polish and I won't now neither.

Since we'd already eaten, I didn't need to fix supper. I usually have a chicken potpie, which has meat, dough, and vegetables, a whole meal and not too expensive, though it takes forty-five minutes in the oven to cook right. I drank a glass of milk like the doctor told me, then I lay down on the couch and fell into a sound sleep. I dreamed I was running up a mountain, running and running and still something was after me, maybe that big ol' snake I told Mrs. D about.

I woke to the hair standing up on the back of my neck. I thought it might be the snake, though I couldn't remember actually dreaming about it—it just all ran together, the trip to the doctor, the story about the snake, the dream of being chased. I had the strangest feeling, like a snake was lurking nearby. But there I was, in my own apartment with the door shut, locked, and chained. Then I remembered clear as day that I'd left the balcony door unlocked. I could lie there afraid or I could make myself get up and go see that all was well, then it would be over. But it wasn't over. It was just beginning.

It was the middle of the night. I must have slept for hours. There was nary a sound nor a light, everyone in the wide world sleeping. I slid the glass door open, my heart thumping to beat the band, and stepped out onto the balcony, into the misty blackness waiting there.

I saw the glow of his cigarette first. I felt my eyes open wide, to try to take in what they couldn't believe they was seeing. He was sitting in one of the lawn chairs Jimmy bought at K-Mart, just sitting there in the dark looking out at the night. He didn't even turn his head to look at me. I could smell him, a kind of animal smell like he hadn't had a bath for weeks. There was fear in that sweaty smell, the smell of the chase. It smelled like the odor possums put out when they're treed by barking hounds. I always felt sorry for them, ugly though they are. He didn't turn when I slid open the door. I knew I couldn't possibly get the door shut and locked if he didn't want me to—he'd be too fast for me. I was afraid any sudden movement would set him off. The smell of smoke floated in the air. I thought of trying to ease back into the apartment or even of jumping over the rail, but it was two stories down. How did he get up here? He must of climbed up one of the trees. How did he know where I lived? He followed us. I knew these things clearly, from some smart part of my brain.

"Do you smoke?" he said into the dark.

When I didn't answer, he said, "Do you mind if I do?"

You'd expect him to have manners, being Mrs. D's son and all.

"It's okay," I said and my voice came out clotted. "Out here," I couldn't help adding.

"Oh, I see," he teased, "no smoking in the house. Well, you're the boss."

We hung there in silence for a few minutes. I couldn't move, and my legs felt the way they did when I saw the snake with Ganny.

He snubbed out the cigarette on the cement floor of the balcony. Now that my eyes had adjusted more I could see that he was smaller than I had imagined, skinny-like, his hair short as a soldier's, not the pretty curls like in the pictures.

"Are you sick?" he asked.

I didn't answer, but with my mind so electrified I could read behind his words. Dr. Dunn's. He followed us here from there.

I thought about saying I'd call the police, but I didn't want to risk trying to speak again, to give away how scared I was. He could stop me if he wanted, leap up and put his hand over my mouth, stuff a scream back down my throat. Tighten his hands around my neck. But I was not like those other girls. That I knew for sure. I knew what they didn't know. About Ben, his evil ways.

"We do have a problem here, don't we," Ben said at last. His voice was low, as if confiding in me.

But he was right, we did have a problem. He was the problem.

"I'm going in now," I finally said in a ragged whisper. "I'm going to lock this balcony door." I spoke slowly and firmly, the way I might talk to a bear on the road. "Then you have to leave."

"They'll kill me, you know," he said. "Electrocute me. It's a ghastly way to die."

Neither of us spoke for a long time.

"You can't imagine," he said, shaking his head. He had the start of a straggly brown beard on his chin, something he didn't have in his graduation picture, where he looked so smart and full of promise. "It's unbelievable. They won't let me explain. They believe what *they* want to believe, and no one will listen to me. Maybe my mother, I don't know. All they want is to kill me. Ask her to come here tomorrow night. Tell her I'll tell her the truth."

I slowly took one step back, my foot feeling for the frame of the door. Then I took another. I moved carefully, hoping he wouldn't notice. I tried to imagine how many seconds it would take to slide the door closed and lock it. One, two. It wasn't open very far, but if he wanted to he could jump up and stop it. It wouldn't even take much strength. He'd be stronger than me, even though he looked like a stray dog. But skinny strays are sometimes the strongest, the meanest. The most desperate.

Once I was over the threshold, back into the apartment, my bare feet on the brown wall-to-wall, I carefully slid the glass door shut. I didn't try to hurry. It seemed important to keep my wits about me. I felt Ganny was directing me, telling me what to do. I seemed to know deep inside what to do, and I trusted that feeling. I felt for the door lock and pushed it down. There, locked! I backed away from the balcony door, my hands leaping up to my mouth.

He was out there, separated from me by a wall of glass. But I was on the inside now. I could still see him, sitting hunched over on the lawn chair, as if he hadn't even noticed I was gone. As if he didn't care. At the end of his rope, that's what he was. That was what his body said. He didn't have it in him to run no more. I could see that. He was all wore out from running and hiding and killing. He didn't look much like a killer now. But maybe that was just a trick. I knew I couldn't trust him.

I thought about calling the police. I played it out in my mind. I could rush to the phone, dial that new 911 like they told us, find my voice if it hadn't disappeared completely. I'd only have to say one word, "Ben," and the police would come, there'd be lights and sirens and they'd get him. They'd get him like a possum up the tree. Maybe he'd try to shimmy down the tree and run off into the woods, but they'd get him. I could see him being marched out of the woods with his hands cuffed behind his back, his shirttail out, his desperate face with its scruffy beard. I tested it in my mind. Yet I stood there. I just stood there. I thought of Mrs. D and wondered what she would want me to do.

It felt like one of those stories we wrote in fourth grade, where at the end you put, "It was all a dream." Was he really out there? Or was I dreaming it? I went into the bedroom, shut the door, and pushed the button lock in. It was just a flimsy door, he could kick it in in an instant. But I knew if he really was out there, if it wasn't just a dream, he wouldn't come in. I didn't know how I knew, I just did. Something about him. There was no murder in him now, at least not tonight. I could just see that with my own eyes.

What would Mrs. D want me to do, that was what I studied. Would she want me to call the police? Or would she want to see him, let him tell her the truth? She had to tell me what to do. I tried to think about those girls, the girls he hurt so bad. But I couldn't call them to mind, not the way I could call forth Mrs. D's face. How could I tell her it was me that turned him in, that let the dogs loose upon him?

The rest of the night I spent half sleeping and too wide awake. When morning came, I tiptoed to the glass door and peeked out. There he was, asleep in the aluminum chair. He was sort of curled up, cold, and dew had made his shirt damp. I wondered where he got that plaid shirt, what he done to get it. I went about getting ready for work, quietly, and I ate my cereal just like usual. The doodlebug was hungry. Then I fixed some toast, but when I looked at it, I didn't want it. Instead, I put it on a tray. I poured another glass of milk and set it on the tray too. It was an old tray Jimmy's mama gave us, one with a big magnolia hand-painted on it, though she was no artist. I looked in the icebox. Cottage cheese. I didn't much like it myself, but I thought the little bit might. I put the carton on the tray, and I poured the rest of the coffee out of the coffeepot into a mug. I crept over to the glass door and pushed up the lock. Then I carefully slid open the door and he didn't even wake up I was so quiet. But when I stepped through with the tray, he jerked awake. I could see the terror in his eyes, until he saw that it was just me, not the police like he must have thought at first. I set the tray down on the cement balcony floor, not too near him. He didn't move. I kept my eyes on him the whole time. I backed up into the apartment. I slid the glass door nearly shut but then I left it open a crack. I grabbed my pocketbook, locked the front door behind me, and ran like a house afire to catch the bus just pulling into the stop on Military Way.

Chapter Eleven

Inga

I was taken aback yesterday when Jean said she wanted to stay here with me. I wasn't sure what she meant but it did touch something in me. I had only agreed to take her to see David because it seemed easier than saying no at the time. But there was something about her when she asked, standing there looking small and fragile in that same damn pink sweater she wears all the time, that struck me as brave. Maybe she got that from her grandmother. I haven't been paying much attention to her at work, preoccupied and troubled as I am over my own problems. But she has been paying attention to me. I saw that clearly when I collected her in the waiting room after her appointment with David.

I could tell she was nervous on the way to David's office. She became a chatty little thing, maybe from nerves or maybe because she's lonely. I sat with her in the examination room to meet David, but I left when it was time for him to give her a pelvic exam. She looked at me then like she wanted me to stay with her, but she didn't ask. She's a strange little thing, that's for sure, the way she says things with her eyes that you couldn't imagine coming out of her mouth. I've known dogs like that, you feel like you're reading their minds or maybe they're reading yours.

David called me back in after he had examined her, pronounced her healthy and fit, and started her on some vitamins. He sent her out to the waiting room and turned to me. "Healthy seventeen-year-old, that's the age females should be bearing young, biologically speaking," he said, looking at me through his thick glasses, his eyes swimming behind the wavy lenses, something I was used to, though now that I thought of it, maybe that had scared Jean. "It's you I'm worried about, Inga," he said. "This latest business about the escape can't be easy on you."

What was there to say. I nodded.

"You have Valium for when you can't sleep. Is that still working?"

I nodded again. Sometimes it was my best friend.

"You shouldn't use it too often, though. You don't want to get addicted."

I shook my head, no. I only used it when I was afraid for myself, afraid of what I might do.

"All right, then," he said and sighed. "I won't try to spoon-feed you that pabulum about people not being given more than they can handle. This is more than anyone could or should handle. People get broken all the time. I don't want you to be one of them."

I stood up quickly and gathered my purse. In the bathroom the tears came hard and fast, I pressed my hand against my mouth to try to muffle the sobs. I would have thought I'd have completely used up my tears by now, but certain things could still bring them up from some bottomless well. Certain kindnesses.

I washed my face with cold water. I didn't really care if people knew I'd been crying. I was used to people stealing curious glances and then quickly avoiding my eyes. A freak was what I'd become, dressed in a print shirtwaist from Nordstrom's.

Jean was looking through a magazine, but she glanced up quickly when I came through the door, searching me out. I read her face when she saw me. It was painted there clear as day—the way she drank me in, now that I'd reappeared. It all came together, the little things she did at work, the way she'd practically bow when she came to get her cart reloaded with returned books, the way she offered to wash my coffee cup, even if I was only half through my coffee! It made me want to laugh, it was so ridiculous and touching. She was like one of those baby ducks that imprints on the first thing it sees when it cracks out of the shell. Thinking it's Mama. Thinking it's love.

I got to work around seven-forty today, per usual. I looked for Jean to arrive, as she usually does, a little before nine, closer to opening than we'd like, but the bus only runs every hour out her way. She didn't come right over to my desk, as she always does. I saw her standing across the room, staring at me. She looked so odd I immediately got up and crossed the room to her. Maybe she was ill, or maybe she'd started bleeding and was going to lose the baby. Neither of us spoke, the strangest thing, but silenced like that, we stared into each other's eyes in a way that gave me goose bumps. I had the weirdest feeling, as if we'd broken through some social barrier that protects one from such encounters. Her eyes are a smoky green, with a dark rim around the corneas, as if outlined with a deep gray eyeliner pencil. She seemed to be speaking to me with her eyes, some complex communication I couldn't read but that made the hair on my arms stand up, electrified.

I suddenly felt sick, as if I might faint. I turned without a word, but as I walked away I heard her say, "The snake is back." It didn't make any sense. I was feeling so shaken that I just kept going, even stumbling a little on the carpet, which caught the rubber sole of my shoe. I sat down at my desk and a wave of nausea passed over me. *Maybe that's it*, I thought, *maybe I'm coming down with something.* I looked across to where Jean was, but she was gone. I shook my head to clear it. I thought about going home, but what was at home? Empty hours, whereas here at the library, the patrons would be arriving in a few moments, and things would sweep me up, take my mind off my own troubles. I felt a little calmer, and wondered at my reaction, and at Jean herself. Maybe the girl wasn't quite right after all. Could she be mentally unbalanced?

When she didn't appear, I gave her cart of books to Margery to shelve. "That's Jean's job," she whined. "Where's Jean?" It's your job today, I snapped, and I began to help patrons find books and articles. For several hours I was caught up in directing people to sections or helping them locate material. We were busy, and it was in my mind to seek Jean out at lunch, but I let the work take over, which is what I like the best. Time passed, which has become my standard of living, my quality of life.

A little before lunchtime, those words floated back into my brain unsummoned: *the snake is back*. I felt lightheaded all over again, that same sort of hit from behind feeling I had when I was with Jean earlier. And suddenly I understood.

I went to look for her, my heart pounding hard and fast. I quickly searched the stacks and bathroom, and then I took the stairs to the basement, where we keep books no longer in circulation. I found her at the end of one of the stacks, just standing there in her blue skirt and pink sweater. She could have been standing there all morning—no one would have found her. It was a perfect hiding spot, the kind a child would know to seek out. She didn't seem surprised to see me but raised her green eyes to me as if she'd been expecting me.

"Where?" I took her by the arm, startling her. My own fright and alarm made me fierce.

"On my balcony."

I leaned back against the stack and slid to the floor. All breath left me. Jean quickly knelt down beside me and fanned my face with her hand. "Are you okay, Mrs. D?"

I grasped both her hands in mine and held them to my cheek, I don't know why. I couldn't read my own gesture.

"It can't be," I cried. "How can it be?"

"He was just there," Jean said. "In the dark."

I took this in. Could she be lying or imagining? I knew where she lived, she'd told me her apartment was on the second floor. What was she talking about!

As if reading my mind, she said, "He shimmied up one of the big fir trees. He must of followed us home from the doctor."

I heard someone open the door at the top of the stairs, but they didn't come down. I slowly stood up, swiped the back of my dress to remove the dust. I took her by both arms, gently this time, and looked right into her eyes. "Have you told anyone else?

"No ma'am," she shook her head.

Then she shocked me even more. "I left the door unlocked—from the balcony. I figured he'd need to get in, take a shower, use the bathroom. Eat."

I stared at her. "You did," was all I could say.

"He wants to see you," Jean said. "Tell you the truth, he said."

I felt a big tear in my heart, as if someone had grasped it roughly and torn it in two distinct bloody pieces. "This can't be happening," I muttered.

"Inga!" I heard someone open the door again and start down the stairs. It was Larry. "Are you down there? Are you all right?"

"I … I was just showing Jean where we keep the old circulation material," I called back quickly. "In case she needs to search for someone."

"That's not her job," Larry said calmly. "But all right. Just checking to make sure everything is okay."

"I'll be right up!"

We were silent as we heard him ascend the stairs, pause, then shut the door.

"You can't go home alone," I whispered. "It's out of the question."

"Then you'll come," she said.

I nodded my head, yes.

I left her in the basement, telling her to come up in about ten minutes and to go about her job as usual. It took every ounce of strength I had to carry on myself, but I needed time to think. I didn't even attempt to eat the tuna sandwich I had brought—but it made me think of Ben. He had access to food, provided Jean actually had something to eat in the apartment. I sat at my desk, pretending to go through the most recent addition to *Books in Print.*

It was then that I looked up to see Ron browsing through a magazine in the magazine section. I felt a bolt of fear, knowing that his visit wasn't about books and magazines. He caught me looking his way and took his time replacing the magazine before he sauntered over. *But why didn't he just come up to me when he first arrived? Why the magazine ruse? Because he wanted to observe me.* I wondered if I'd given anything away, if I looked as flustered and wild as I felt when I came up from the basement. I'd grown adept, I believed, at keeping a poker face, not letting people read what's inside. It had been a necessary protection now that Ben was in the news all the time. Some in the media had described me as cold because of it. But I locked that face on whenever the emotions were the most fierce inside.

"Inga," he said, and I had the strangest sensation that he was going to take my hand and kiss it. He wasn't what I thought a homicide detective would be like, not that I had given that a thought prior to Ben. He was polite and respectful. Serious and calm. Not a jerk. Likable, even.

"Hello, Ron," I said, and tried to smile, though my face felt frozen. "Is there news?"

"Let's go," he said, and I followed him to the conference room. We sat at the long, faux-wood table, and I clasped my hands together on the smudged surface to calm and ground me.

"We think Ben might still be in the area."

I felt him watching me, gauging my reaction.

All I could do was nod. Things were happening too fast, I needed time to think.

"We found a stolen pickup truck with his fingerprints in the parking lot of the K-Mart on South Tacoma Way."

"I haven't seen him, if that's what you're asking."

He studied me, and I felt my right eyelid twitching like mad. *I can tell him*, I thought. *I can just tell him now about Jean, the balcony. It will all be over.*

"What do you want me to do?" I asked.

"Notify us immediately if you have any contact with him. You have to do that, for your own safety. Harboring a fugitive is a federal offense." Then he dropped his shoulders and spoke to me differently, not as a police officer but like a friend. "You have to turn him in if he contacts you, Inga. Even if it's hard. The hardest thing you'll ever have to do. Think of the girls. And there will be more victims, I can promise you that. Please, call me if you hear from him. He may try to contact you. That's probably why he's still here, where it's so dangerous. We'll continue staking out your house and the library, providing protection for you."

"I don't need protection from Ben."

"Call me—I give you my promise that I'll see that he's protected when he's taken into custody. No guns if he gives up peacefully."

"I haven't heard from him."

He was watching me. "I know how hard this must be for you."

I stood up. I was shaking all over, but I couldn't stop it. "No you don't know. With all due respect, you really don't know."

"You have my number," he said.

Back at my desk, I opened the *Books in Print* catalog again, the tiny print swirling before my eyes. I glanced up to see Ron leaving the library, and I looked around to see if anyone was paying attention to me. I noticed a woman I didn't recognize at one of the library tables. She was sitting where she had a clear view of me. I knew she was only pretending to read, because when I glanced at her, she quickly looked back to the book in a way that gave her away. I was under surveillance, of course. Then I saw Jean looking at me, waiting, wanting to know what to do. I scribbled on a slip of paper, "*The police know he's in town. They're watching me. I can't come tonight.*" I quickly took my purse out of the bottom desk drawer and got two fifty-dollar bills out. I always carried a hundred dollars in cash in case an emergency came up. "*Don't go home!*" I underlined it. "*Spend the night in a motel. Destroy this note immediately.*" I slipped the two bills into the paper and folded it over and put it into the first book on the reshelving cart. I motioned for Jean to come over to my desk.

"Here's a new cart of books for shelving," I stood up and motioned to the cart, so that the policewoman could see that everything was normal, routine, I was just giving instructions to staff. "Start with this row, the nonfiction ones." I knew Jean would look through the books as she always did, reading a page or two. "If there are any that you can't figure out, bring them back to me and I'll help you."

We stared at each other for a split second. She had a serious, unflappable look about her. She was so young! I saw how she trusted me, how she put her faith in me. I had a sudden glimpse of the kind of grown woman she would be, grave and dignified. *Please don't let any harm befall her!*

Jean went off with the cart. My mind was racing. *If she didn't go home, Ben couldn't harm her. But Ben wouldn't harm her! I didn't believe it for a moment!* I felt shaken not only by the news about Ben but also from Ron's visit. His words played in my mind. *You have to turn him in.* I knew what the right thing was. And I would. Ron had said he would guarantee Ben's safety. But first I had to see Ben. I had to talk to him, alone, outside of jail. I would figure out some way. Could he possibly be innocent? Why couldn't that be true? He said he was. Maybe it *was* some terrible mistake. I had to know the truth, whatever it was. Jean wouldn't go home, she'd do what I told her. Please, God, just let me have a little time with him. Then I would get him to surrender to Ron. If I was there, he wouldn't get hurt. He wouldn't get shot.

Chapter Twelve

Jean

A hundred dollars! That was a lot of money! I stood in the stacks, rubbing the two bills between my fingers. I read the note over and over. Maybe I could buy Mrs. D a present. A pretty figurine or a soft woolly shawl. She'd look good in purple. I wanted her to come home with me, give me a ride in her Nova the way she did when she took me to the doctor's. But Mrs. D couldn't come home with me, at least not tonight. She said stay in a motel but I'd seen those motels on South Tacoma Way from the bus. You might catch something just from being in them. They looked like places for prostitutes, or people on the lam. Not a place for a girl like me, a girl all by herself. Someone might have a key and come in during the night. No, the known was always better than the unknown.

I wanted to talk to Mrs. D, explain that it would be all right, that Ben wouldn't hurt me right now. I was his hidey-hole. I knew what he was like, what he had in him, but I had some things on my side. It was an even enough match, at least for now. At least until Mrs. D could figure something out. That was how it came to me.

I finished unloading the book cart. I took the note into the bathroom, tore it into little pieces, and flushed it down the toilet. There. No one but us would know about the snake. The snake was our secret. Mrs. D wanted to see Ben, talk to him. I'd help her. I'd keep my head, move slowly, not panic. I'd be brave like Ganny, not like the little girl I used to be who fell to the ground in a heap. I remembered the fairy tales we used to read, Ganny and me. I felt like I was under a spell, a magical spell where nothing could harm me. At least I hoped that was true.

I brought the cart back to Mrs. D. She looked at me closely, worried. I knew we were being watched, though I didn't know who was doing the watching. Everyone was just reading or looking through the card catalog or browsing through magazines. But one of them was the police, and I knew I had to be careful.

"I got 'em all reshelved just fine," I told her. "I understand everything you told me." I hoped I was saying it in a way that she would understand.

"Good," she said. "That's fine, Jean." She squinted her eyes, trying to read me.

"I know exactly what to do."

She paused a moment, studying me. "Well, all right, then," she said. "Are you sure? *Always do exactly as I say.*" She gave me a stern look. "All right, okay then. Goodnight, then." It was almost five o'clock. "See you tomorrow?" She looked like she was about to wring her hands, but she forced herself not to.

"See you tomorrow!" I said brightly, loudly, and I walked away. No one would suspect that I was anything more to her than a library worker. I felt a flush of pride that we'd fooled 'em.

It was already dark when I left work. Ever since Halloween, it felt like spooks and spirits were in the air. I didn't know where to go. I walked down to Wright Park, checking to make sure no one was following me, but I didn't go too far into the park. I sat down on a cold bench and looked around, trying to see in the dark like a bat. No one was around, thank you Jesus. I wondered how Mrs. D would figure out how to come to Ben. She was smart and would work it out. Ben must have got his smarts from her. I wondered what he would say to her. The truth, he said. I felt a little flutter like I'd swallowed a goldfish. Then I remembered what it was. It made me feel less alone; there were two of us now. While we were just sitting there I realized we were hungry. I hadn't had any lunch today. I was thrown off my feed. But now my stomach was grumbling and so I walked back up the hill to McDonald's. I ordered the Big Mac and paid for it with my own money. I didn't want to break one of the big fifty-dollar bills. They were for later, for something special, though I didn't know what yet. As I ate, I tasted the fear, like blood in my mouth, that I had felt with the snake curled on my balcony this morning.

• • •

I got off at the corner of Military Way and walked the five blocks to the apartment complex, my steps getting slower and slower, like I was dragging a big anchor behind me. I wondered if the snake would be gone. Maybe he would have slid back down his hole. Or maybe he'd strike when I stepped in the door.

I unlocked my mailbox. Empty. I wondered where Jimmy was, what was happening to him at this exact same moment. I had trouble remembering what he looked like. Ben had thrown me off writing Jimmy about the baby. I thought about Mama, how she'd probably be at the mill, her thoughts not on me. But I knew Mrs. D was thinking about me. She might be mad that I didn't go to a motel, so I'd have to explain. But what would I say? I didn't always know why I did the things I did. I climbed the stairs one by one, putting both feet on each step as I went up.

When you're in the woods, you make a lot of noise to let the critters know you're coming, so they can get out of the way. I made a big noise unlocking the door. I wanted him to know I was back, so there wouldn't be any surprises on either side. I told myself it was fifty-fifty that he'd be gone, gone for good, but I kinda knew in my heart that wouldn't be the case. Where would he go? And he was hoping I'd have Mrs. D with me. He wanted to see his mama, and he'd wait for that I knew.

I looked behind me. There was no one around, no one on the stairs or the landing. Across from our apartment was K-10, but the door was always shut. I'd never seen anyone come or go from there. I opened the front door slowly, and I left it wide open. I stepped into the entry hall. Dark. The carpet that covered the whole apartment was dark brown, and it made the place black without the lights on. Everything was silent, still. The little galley kitchen was on the right, and beyond that, the space that's supposed to be the dining room, and beyond that, the glass door of the balcony. I flipped on the light and stepped into the kitchen. The balcony door was just as I'd left it, slid open a couple of inches. I couldn't see the whole of the balcony—the part where he was sitting last night was hidden by the curtains. I stepped out of the kitchen into the dining space, turned on the chandelier light, and glanced quickly around the living room. Nothing. No one. Everything the same as I left it. I went down the little hall and turned on the light in the bedroom. The same as when I left. The bed was made. I always make my bed, something we never did at home. I'm not even sure Mama knows how to make a bed. I had to learn that by myself, and now I do it every single day, even this morning. Why we do the things we do. I tiptoed to the closet and with my heart beating hard, flung open the door. There were my clothes—some things hanging half off the hangers and some piled on top of my tennis shoes on the floor. I looked in the bathroom. I could see something was different here. I didn't take a shower this morning. I hadn't wanted to undress and get in the shower. I had slept in my clothes and only brushed my teeth and run a brush through my bed head before going to work. But someone had taken a shower. The towel was damp, folded nicely and hung on the top of the shower curtain rod. Very neat.

I went back in the kitchen and opened the refrigerator. The milk carton was lighter, but at least he didn't drink it all. Two chicken potpies were missing from the freezer—he must of been hungry. The empty cartons and the little aluminum dishes they came in were in the trash under the sink. A plate, glass, and fork draining in the drain rack. Jimmy always left his dirty dishes in the sink.

I crept to the balcony door. I couldn't see to the far side without opening it. I slid it slowly open. He was sitting in the same folding chair he was in last night, but in the reflection from the chandelier light I could see he looked better, he had shaved, and looked less like a possum on the run.

"You don't have to be afraid," he said slowly and carefully, holding his hands up in front of him. "I know you are, afraid, and you have a right to be, but I want to assure you that I won't harm you in any way. You have my word."

All I could do was stare at him. I wanted to say that I didn't think his word was worth much, but I bit my tongue.

"Thank you for your hospitality," he said. "You've been amazingly kind. As you may have deduced, I took advantage of the facilities. I hope you don't mind, but that shower was a godsend. Plus I ate some of your food. Oh, and I used your razor. You'll need a new blade. I hope to be able to repay you, but as you can imagine, right now I'm short on cash." He flashed a jokey grin and he was so handsome it made my heart flutter, even if he was the devil. He seemed in an altogether good mood, not the broody dark hole of last night.

"It's okay," I said.

"I won't rise from this chair," he said. "If that will make you more comfortable. But … my mother? Is she—coming?"

"She can't," I blurted out. "I mean, not tonight. Not right now. The police are watching her. They know you're in town."

His face flushed and for a moment he just looked down, like he was collecting himself. Even with his hair short, buzzed by the prison guards, he still looked like he could pose on a sailboat or walk with a pretty girl along a sandy beach in a fancy magazine. He looked bigger than last night. He got lucky with that beauty mark by his eye.

"You haven't told the police?" he asked, looking right at me. I couldn't stand his gaze so I turned away.

"No," I said. "Not yet."

He took this in in silence.

Then, "I thank you for that."

"I'm going to lock this door now," I said.

"I understand," he said. "But please …" He held up his hands again, palms facing me. "Can we just talk for a few moments? I won't move from this chair, you have my word. But just a little conversation. I'd like to get to know you. I'd like to hear about my mother. Just a few moments. But if you don't want to, I certainly understand."

He talked beautiful, like a prince. And he had nice manners. That was one area I thought Jimmy needed some improvement in.

"What do you want to talk about?"

"Well, you're obviously not from here. That's an adorable accent you have. Let me guess. Georgia? Alabama?"

"Way off."

"I've never been to the South. I hear it's beautiful. Of course the South has a tragic history. But wonderful storytellers and writers. Mississippi? Faulkner territory?"

"North Carolina. We don't talk like people from Mississippi. We're mountain people, not delta."

"The Smokies? Tell me about where you're from."

"Why do you want to know?"

"Well, I haven't met many Southerners. And really, I'd like to get to know you. I mean, here we are, we might as well get acquainted."

"I think you should know I'm married with child."

He didn't miss a beat. "Well, congratulations, then! A baby, that's so great. But you're awfully young to be having a child, aren't you?"

"Not really."

"When's it due?"

"At first I didn't want to have it, but then Ganny said to give life, and I saw what she meant. Give life, not take it." I looked at him pointedly.

He looked away and I saw a strange expression cross his face. A wave of fear passed over me. Maybe I had gone too far, like poking a snake with a stick. But then he changed again, back to his friendly self. "Who's Ganny?" he said. "Tell me about her."

"She's my grandmother and she lives way up in the mountains. A place called Morgan's Hollow. She knows about snakes and bears and mountain lions. She cooks on a woodstove and only has an outhouse. What're you going to say to your mother?"

Again he looked away from me. "I have a grandfather," he said finally. "I don't get to see him often. He lives on the shore of Lake Superior."

"Where Mrs. D was raised."

He nodded. "We used to go visit in the summer. Take the train across the Rockies to the Twin Cities. He'd drive down and pick us up, and then we'd spend a week at the resort. He'd take me fishing in his boat. Herring and lake trout. That lake was so cold you couldn't swim in it. But I did anyway, howling my head off when I first jumped in." He laughed a little at the memory, as pretty as a picture.

"My husband's in Vietnam," I said. "Jimmy Jones."

"Ah!" For a moment he seemed at a loss for words. "That's really tough. We have no business being there."

"The police are watching your mother. They'd follow her here."

He nodded his head slowly. "She doesn't deserve all this. If only I could talk to her! Me! Strangling those girls … It's unbelievable! The police just need to blame it on somebody, get the public off their tails. All this … is an … incredible … mistake!" He laughed, a hollow, forlorn sound.

"Well," I said. "Now we've talked. I'm going to lock this door."

"Oh, okay, okay," Ben said. "But just one favor. Do you happen to have an extra blanket? It got so cold out here last night. I understand perfectly about—the arrangement. But a blanket would really help. If you have one, that is, and if you don't mind. I don't mean to impose so much. You've already been kinder than I can comprehend."

I'd brought several of Ganny's patchwork quilts from home, in a cedar chest in the truck. It wouldn't hurt to lend him one. But I was not going to give him a pillow. I shut the glass door and locked it, then went and got one of the quilts from the chest. It was made from scraps of material that Ganny saved up over the years, old-timey material from making bonnets and dresses back in the twenties and thirties. I took the one that had some gray cotton ticking sticking out, with water stains on the yellowed backing, where the roof must of leaked on it. It smelled like cedar. I hated the idea of anything being cold. I was doing it for Mrs. D. She wouldn't want him to get sick. I remembered how Ganny would come in at night in the winter when we were spending the night at her place and throw another quilt over me and my sister. That was a good feeling, that and having a full stomach. I slid open the balcony door and laid the quilt on the cement in front of the door. Ben didn't move from his chair.

"Thank you so much," he said. "I really appreciate it. I can't thank you enough."

"Well then," I said. "Good night."

"Good night, Jean," he said.

He knew my name!

I quickly slid the door shut and locked it. He must of looked through my stuff. He gave me the creeps, even if he was Mrs. D's son.

I locked the front door and then my bedroom door, pushing the dresser over in front of it. I couldn't sleep at all, my eyes wide open staring into the dark, listening to hear if he was trying to get in that balcony door. Then the next thing I knew, the sun was shining through the blinds, which I forgot to pull, waking me up.

When I opened the balcony door, the snake was gone.

Part II

Chapter Thirteen

Inga

Christmas was fast approaching and I wanted no part of it. Larry had invited me over to be with his wife, Marilyn, and their kids, David asked if I wanted to go with him to his sister's in Seattle, Lorraine tried to talk me into going to Spokane to her family's, but I just wanted to be alone. I had expected to be visiting Ben in jail this Christmas. I was hardly looking forward to that, but now his escape was even worse. Sometimes it seemed like a dream Jean and I shared, Ben showing up on her balcony like that. We had never told a soul, and never discussed it ourselves beyond her telling me that the snake was gone. The snake was gone, that was all. As inexplicable as everything else about Ben.

I was furious with her for going home that night, not staying in a motel the way I told her to, but I was learning Jean had a mind of her own. It was hard to admonish her too much, since she looked so hangdog when I scolded her. She didn't say a word in her own defense. I called a locksmith and had him meet Jean at her apartment to install a security bar on the balcony door. She reported that it had been done.

It gave me hope that maybe Ben wasn't guilty since he hadn't harmed Jean. But did that mean anything? I'd become a crazy person, ricocheting from faith in his innocence to certainty that he was a complete stranger. I tried to consider the evidence, the fact that the police were so certain. The handcuffs, his escape from jail. But the teeth imprint results that Ron was counting on had come back inconclusive. In the next minute I'd berate myself for even considering his guilt.

I hadn't told Ron about Ben being at Jean's. I knew I should have. He'd become a friend of sorts, not just the lead detective on Ben's case. At first it was so shocking that Ben had turned up like that, and then … I didn't know why. I just couldn't, didn't. I never actually lied to Ron, but the sin of omission was just as bad. Weeks passed, and no sign of Ben, and the longer I went without telling Ron, the more impossible it became.

My impression of Ron when we first met was of a family man, someone with a long settled marriage, grown children nearby, grandchildren whom he adored, to whom he played the indulgent, adored Grandpa—letting them ride in a police car, turning on the siren and lights, a hero in their eyes. A happy family life, I thought. Maybe because that was what I myself lacked. As we got to know each other over the months of the investigation, the sunny picture I imagined became shaded. It turned out he was single and had no children, though he'd been married three times. I was a little shocked at that, even though I myself got a divorce—another thing I never would have expected.

The closer Christmas got, the more peckish I felt, as my mother used to say. Cranky, irritable, and hungry. I was turning into the Little Match Girl myself, someone standing outside in the cold, peering into a fantasy of family, food, and warmth. I'd always enjoyed fixing Christmas dinner, all those years when it was just Ben and me. I'd make it really special, so that he … and maybe I … wouldn't feel like we were missing anything, a husband and father, more kids, a bunch of relatives around the table. I loved cooking a turkey and all the fixings, and then luxuriating in leftovers over a long holiday. Those were good times, weren't they? Ben would think so, wouldn't he? It was like one of those optical illusions, where I saw Ben first one way and then another, like that beautiful woman looking in a dresser mirror who with a tilt of your head becomes a skull.

I couldn't even imagine what Christmas would be like for the families of the girls. As torn up as I was, I knew their hearts had been absolutely carved out. At least my son was still alive somewhere. At least I'd get to see him again, god willing. They would never again be able to be with their girls. And having to live with how they died. An accident or natural cause would be devastating enough, but to be strangled to death. It was beyond imagination, at least my imagination.

• • •

On Christmas Eve day, the library was closing at two o'clock. As I watched the time creep past noon, I felt fidgety. There were hardly any patrons, everyone busy with last-minute presents and preparations. The whole world seemed caught up in something I was excluded from. Of course I knew other people had their troubles. I shouldn't indulge in self-pity, when all my sorrow should be on those girls and their families. But eventually your emotions, even your guilt and horror, get worn down, dulled by the quotidian.

A little before two o'clock Jean came up to my desk.

"Well, Merry Christmas then, Mrs. D," she said softly. "See you on Monday, I guess." I could see she wanted to say more but was having a hard time getting it out. When she blushed, two pink roses bloomed on her cheeks. She delivered a wrapped gift from behind her back.

Now it was my time to flush. "What's this!" I exclaimed awkwardly when she put the gift on my desk. It was wrapped in bright green Christmas paper, a hundred red Santas waving merrily and shouting ho, ho, ho. "Jean, you shouldn't have …"

"You could open it."

"Now?"

She nodded, watching me eagerly. I could see she was thrilled by the whole thing; I hoped the gift wouldn't embarrass us both. But when I opened the box and lifted away the tissue paper, I was stunned by what I found—a shiny metallic pink music box, round, with a gold star embossed on the lid.

"See," Jean lifted the lid to show me the powder puff inside, "you put this on your dresser and you can listen to music while you powder your face!" I wound it up with the little key underneath, and it tinkled out "*When you wish upon a star …*"

"Oh, Jean, you really shouldn't have!" But when I saw the look on her face, I exclaimed, "but I'm so glad you did! I love it. It's the nicest gift I've ever received!" In a way it was true. Ben gave me gifts over the years, red roses some Mother's Day or a sweater or pin I had hinted I wanted for my birthday, but gift giving wasn't something that came naturally. I could see that this gift gave as much pleasure to the giver as the receiver. And I had a feeling I knew where she got the money.

"Jean," I said suddenly. "What are you doing tomorrow? Do you have plans for Christmas?"

"I'm gonna have a Swanson's TV dinner. Turkey with dressing and cranberry sauce. Green beans too."

"Would you like to come to my house? Have Christmas with me. It won't be fancy, just the two of us, but …"

"Okay!"

Seeing her shining face, I had to smile. We made plans for me to pick her up at noon. All I could do was shake my head.

Leaving the library, carrying my gift in an extra shopping bag I had on hand, I felt almost lighthearted. It was true my world was grievous ill. And for that matter, so was the whole country. But at this moment, for the first time in a long time, I felt if not happy—at least halfway alive. That was as close to happy as I could come now. I had a mission, something to do. I'd go to the Safeway near my house, where they knew me and left me alone, treating me as if I was just another customer. I'd buy a nice fat roasting hen and some stuffing mix, maybe some pearl onions and a green vegetable, depending on what looked good. I might even get an avocado and a pomegranate, if they had one, for a Christmas salad.

I was in the produce section trying to find a ripe avocado, not too soft, not too hard, when a big man wearing a red plaid shirt and baseball cap caught my attention. He was staring at me, like he was trying to remember where he knew me from. Normally I ignored such people, they got their look and went away. But what with the Christmas music and sense of excitement and bustle of last-minute shopping in the air, I flashed him a quick smile. That's all it took. He was in my face, his own pudgy face snarling with hatred. "You're that guy's mother," he accused, pointing a finger right at me, almost poking me in the chest, so that I had to stumble back against the vegetable rack. "That murderer! What right do you have to be here all la-de-dah when those girls are lying cold in their graves! When they catch … your son"—and he almost spit the word it infuriated him so much—"they ought to string him up by his balls!"

People around us had turned into statues. Far away I heard "Have Yourself a Merry Little Christmas" playing in the background. That was when the store manager, Nick Martinson, a tall, stooped man who was always there, as if he slept in the back room, came rushing up and took me by the elbow, pushing my grocery cart with his other hand. He steered me over to the check-out lane, saying, "I'm so sorry, Mrs. Daudelin, are you all right, here, let me help you with your groceries. On Christmas Eve, of all times!" He seemed outraged that such a scene had occurred in his store.

I mechanically unloaded my frozen peas, my celery and onion, my bag of herb stuffing in a daze. It had taken me so by surprise, I didn't have any defenses up. Maybe he was right, maybe I didn't have any business humming to myself and testing avocados, acting as if I was a normal person with a normal life! I fumbled for the money in my purse. All I wanted to do was to get my groceries and get out of there. I should have just walked out, but some part of me wouldn't abandon that four-pound chicken. I was going to have Christmas dinner for Jean, and no one could stop me! Nick carried the two bags out to the car for me himself, solicitously. "Some people are just cruel," he said, shaking his head. I wondered if he meant Ben.

At home I felt a familiar hopelessness rising inside me. Trying to come up with some distraction, I pulled down the attic stairs and climbed up into that dusty, dark crawl space to get the box labeled in magic marker, "Christmas— LV." Oh Little Village, beloved icon of my childhood! I staggered back down holding the box against my chest. I slit open the masking tape on top with a kitchen knife and began unwrapping. I didn't know where my parents got such a whimsical thing as these little houses with holes in the backs for inserting Christmas lights. Each house was a different color—red, blue, green, silver—with a shiny peaked roof, frosted with "snow," silver white granules that were always shedding, so that some of the houses were almost bald. The houses had little puffs of green bushes in front, and there were six snow-covered pine trees with round red bases for setting around the village. Mother always set up the little village, wadding up newspaper to make hills and valleys, covering it all with white felt "snow" to look like the deep snow that covered the meadow in front of our house. I had continued the tradition for Dad and me after she died, and when Ben was six, Dad mailed the Little Village to me. We'd decorate the tree and set up the Little Village on the mantel, eating store-bought Christmas cookies and drinking hot chocolate. Ben's eyes would shine with excitement. He was a normal child, he didn't grow up to be a killer!

I set the houses up across the mantel. I had assumed that one day I'd give the Little Village to Ben, for his children. I always made a traditional Christmas Eve dinner for us, Ben's favorite, roast beef and Yorkshire pudding. I stopped eating beef after Ben was accused. Seeing raw meat made me sick to my stomach. Maybe I should give the Little Village away, to someone who had young children. Maybe I'd give it to Jean, for her baby. But not yet. Maybe next year. Whenever I was ready. Whenever I was sure …

When I tucked the colored bulbs into the backs and plugged the lights in, each little house glowed with warm light through its colored tissue paper windows. I could almost see the people inside, cozy and safe, the smell of turkey in the air, Christmas music on the stereos, presents under the tree, not grasping how lucky they were.

When I picked Jean up the next day, she was all dressed up, or as dressed up as Jean was capable of. She had on a white, long-sleeved blouse with ruffles down the front, in need of a bit of ironing, and what appeared to be a new pair of jeans, tight against her growing tummy. She had a big grin on her face and looked out the window, smiling, as I drove her to my house.

I'd got the hen in the oven and made some dressing and peas with pearl onions, but I couldn't make the salad I had in mind because I had dropped the avocado when that man accosted me. I let Jean set the table, to give her something to do. I put out Mother's white lace tablecloth. Jean seemed awed by my pretty things, the Wedgwood dishes I collected one by one on my librarian's salary after Charles left, the crystal glasses of which I had only two. We devoured a good deal of that chicken, picking at pieces of the crusty, golden skin. The dressing was especially good, with sage and thyme. Jean told me about Christmases at her house, how her mother made corn bread dressing in crisp patties on a baking sheet, the trick being adding cornflakes, and how there was a ceramic manger scene with little sheep and cattle that Jean loved as a child. When she'd first arrived, she had stood for a long time in front of the Little Village, really taking in every detail. It did add a festive glow to our day.

After dinner, I gave her her gift. I had picked it up the day before, luckily before that incident in the grocery store. I didn't want to overdo it, give her the wrong impression—that I was adopting her, so to speak—so I didn't spend much. It was just a bottle of hand lotion from the drugstore, though later I worried that might be something an older woman would like, not a young girl. Her eyes grew bright and she opened the bottle on the spot, offering me some first and then rubbing it not only on her hands but all up her arms and onto her neck. It did have a nice fragrance, lavender.

I set her music box on the coffee table, and we sat listening to its plaintive melody, played in a minor key. *When you wish upon a star …* I was bemused that I was spending Christmas with this strange young girl I hardly knew, but whom I had somehow fallen in with, even to the point of sharing Christmas. But then nothing in life was as I would have imagined—nothing! Normally I would be spending this Christmas with Ben. But would Ben be who I'd always taken him to be?

Stuffed and sated as we were, we turned on Walter Cronkite on CBS. They were repeating some of yesterday's color coverage of Apollo 8 as it orbited the moon. I had intended to watch but had forgotten all about it the night before. At the library we'd all been following the mission, the first human spacecraft to leave earth's orbit. It had taken them three days to travel to the moon, and the three-man crew were the first humans to see its far side. Suddenly, as we were watching photographs of the moon's cratered surface, there on the screen of my RCA Victor was the most startling image: a small, bright globe with blue and white swirls rising above a barren, bleak moonscape into the blackest space imaginable. A distant sounding voice—one of the astronauts—began reading from the book of Genesis: "*In the Beginning God created the heaven and the earth. And the earth was without form, and void, and darkness was upon the face of the deep. And the spirit of God moved on the face of the waters, and God said, Let there be light, and there was light. And God saw the light, that it was good, and God divided the light from the darkness …*"

A shiver went through me. I stared at our planet, transfixed. How lonely and fragile it looked floating there, yet how brave! For one blinding instant I comprehended all the teeming life it contained, all the diverse peoples, all the creatures of land and sea, all the growing things large and small, all the joy and pain. Jean said, "Is that real? Is that really the earth, the one we're sitting on right now, here in Tacoma, Washington?" I told her yes, we were seeing our whole, amazing planet. We watched in silence until Frank Borman came on, "And from the crew of Apollo 8, we close with good night, good luck, a Merry Christmas, and God bless all of you, all of you on the good Earth." Jean and I looked at each other, her eyes shining. "Wow," she said.

It was dark, and I was fretting about Jean having to go home to where Ben spent those two nights. Of course she'd been staying there all the nights since he disappeared, and it had been over a month. I didn't want to believe that Ben could hurt her—that he could hurt anyone—but I couldn't banish the gnawing anxiety that had settled deep inside me.

I was lost in the usual limbo about Ben when Jean awoke from a nap she'd been taking on the Victorian sofa. Her child's face was creased with the seam of a pillow, her ponytail springing loose from its band. I could see the swell of the baby against her jeans. She was into her fourth month now, past the first trimester, so the pregnancy was probably safe. She yawned and stretched, as natural as a cat waking from a nap.

"You could stay here tonight," I said hesitantly, uncertainly. I didn't want the police to know about Jean, because it might lead to their questioning her. No one had followed me to pick her up this afternoon. At least the police had given up their twenty-four-hour house watch, but I never knew when one of them would drive by, checking, or even follow me in an unmarked car.

"I'm not afraid to go home," she said, as if reading my mind.

I drove her back, checking to make sure no one was behind us. It was dark out and cold. I parked in the lot, facing her building, and insisted on going up with her. I had never been in her apartment, but tonight I just couldn't let her go up alone. The open stairway was cement and smelled faintly of cigarette smoke and urine. It was anonymous and scary going up those stairs to her landing, with not a soul around. She turned her key in the lock and entered as if she didn't have a thought or care in the world. "Don't you worry, Mrs. D," she said, "Ben's not gonna be here."

"How do you know?" I asked, stepping into the entry hall. I was afraid and yet filled with longing. If only I could see him.

"I just know."

Her apartment was practically empty, with no dining room table under the bright chandelier. She showed me around, proud of the place. There was a cheap couch in the living room, the kind you get from rental places, a beanbag chair in a corner, and in the bathroom her nightgown was crumpled on the floor, as if she'd just stepped out of it and left it there. At least the bed was made. The place was sort of a mess; apparently Jean never hung up her clothes, and it smelled of spoiled food. It wrenched my heart to think of her coming home to such a place every night, alone.

I inspected the sliding glass door and indeed there was a security bar in place. "Can I see?" I asked tentatively, and without a word, she unlocked the glass door to the balcony and slid it open. Two folding chairs were tipped up against the cedar shingles of the building, to keep rain out of the seats. Nothing else. So that was where he had been.

"Those are the trees," Jean pointed out. "He shimmied up one of 'em I guess."

All I could do was nod.

When I was convinced she was safe, I drove home. To keep from thinking, I turned on the radio. They were playing Handel's *Messiah*.

I'd finished the dishes and was thinking about getting ready for bed when there was a soft knock on the door. I was startled, and of course Ben was the first thought that crossed my mind. But when I looked out the peephole, there was Ron O'Loughlin standing on my front porch. It reminded me of that first time he came knocking, to tell me Ben was a suspect in the murders. I shivered a little, wondering if he knew about Jean, or maybe he had news. I opened the door hesitantly.

"Merry Christmas," he said. He must have seen my troubled face, because he quickly added, "No news, I just wanted to drop by and wish you … well, I don't know that Merry Christmas is really … appropriate. But …"

"It's okay," I said. We stood there awkwardly. "Would you like to come in for a minute?"

"Oh. Well, maybe just for a minute."

We went into the living room where we'd had so many conversations and took our usual places. He had on his familiar white shirt, no tie, and blue jeans. He'd become so familiar to me. I was pleased and grateful that he cared enough to stop by tonight.

"So," he said, "how was your Christmas? I can't imagine it's been an easy day for you. I was thinking about that … and just decided to stop over. Make sure … you're okay."

"Oh. I had a pretty good Christmas … all things considered. I had a … young friend in." Perhaps he already knew.

"Who was that?"

"A girl I know from work," I said quickly. "Someone who didn't have another place to go. We saw Apollo 8 when they rebroadcast it."

"I watched it last night. Amazing times we live in. I went to my cousin's in Puyallup. Tiring, the way these things are. Holidays aren't really my cup of tea."

"Oh. Would you like a cup of tea? Or coffee? I have a bottle of scotch."

"Not a drink. I'm recovering," he said. "Do you have any Sanka?"

He followed me to the kitchen and sat at the little kitchen table while I put on the water. I felt nervous but glad he was here, glad for the company. I remembered the box of chocolates Larry had given me and retrieved it from the top of the refrigerator. "Here," I said. "Open this while I get the cups."

"A Whitman's Sampler," Ron said, taking off the cellophane. "We used to save all our allowance money when I was a kid to get one of these for our folks. Then us kids would eat them all. Hmm, let's see. Looks just the same. Have one?" I took my favorite, dark chocolate with maple filling.

"Hey, I want that one," he said, so I popped it into my mouth in one bite and then was left to chew it like a cow. He laughed and took a couple, putting them on the paper napkin next to his coffee cup.

"If you don't mind my asking—" I said. "You were an alcoholic?"

"They say you always are. But for me, it's been a long time since I've had a drink. Twenty-five years, if you can believe that. I just prefer not to mess with it."

"You don't seem much like an alcoholic," I said. "Not that I know what alcoholics are like."

"They come in all stripes." He told me how he was married the first time at age twenty-three to a heavy drinker. At first he had joined her, figuring that was the way to handle it. She was in treatment for a little while, but then when that didn't work, he wanted out. "I was just a kid," he said. "I had to save myself. She was like a drowning person about to pull both of us under." That was when he swore off liquor. "It seems like that was another life," he told me. I could relate to that.

"What about your second wife?" He told me she was a stewardess. "The sex was good," he said, "so I assumed everything else was good." He paused and glanced at me. "I hope I didn't cross a line there …" I assured him it was okay, to go on, though it had stirred something in me. "Of course she was away a lot. She met a lot of men flying, both passengers and pilots. One of them, a pilot for Pan Am, turned out to be the love of her life. Believe it or not, no hard feelings." He really seemed to mean it. "Our thing ran its course. It wasn't something I couldn't let go of."

"Okay, that was number two. What about number three?"

"Whoa," he said, "this is entirely too much about me. I know about Charles and your divorce. But why didn't you marry again? Tell me if this is overstepping, but you must have had … lots of …"

"What?" I said, feeling flattered.

"Well, I assume … it's not like … You're …" Now he was at a loss.

"Actually," I said, "I did have a lover once."

"I'm hardly surprised."

"No, you don't understand. It was while I was married."

"Okay then. You had an affair."

"That's why I always felt responsible for the divorce. Not that I ever told Charles. It wasn't even the other man. I didn't want to be with Charles."

"Maybe you needed this lover to show you that. Charles didn't sound like the greatest guy to go through life with."

"He was damaged in the war. Something changed in him. I should have had more compassion … understanding."

"Tell me about this lover."

"Well," I said, embarrassed. "What can I say. I was young, twenty-five, he was fifty, and you know … he knew a lot more than I did … I mean …" I met his eyes briefly, and he was looking at me in that intense way he had. I'd never told anybody about Tony. "It was nothing, really, it didn't even last that long, but … anyway … tell me about your third wife."

He was studying me. I fiddled with my coffee cup, downing the last bit of decaf. I took another chocolate, my hand trembling a little.

"It's nothing to be ashamed of, Inga. Things happen, people aren't perfect. Maybe you needed that other man. That's not so strange."

I didn't know what to say.

"So. Okay, you want to know about number three. My second wife I could let go of but the thing I can't let go of is my third. Lola."

"Whatever Lola wants, Lola gets?" I half laughed. But at the same time I felt let down, pained even.

"They wrote that song for her."

Who can say why one person is like a drug for another, an addiction that is impossible to break? That's the way Ron described Lola—a habit he couldn't kick. "She's long moved on, except for the random times when she'll reenter my life briefly—a late-night phone call begging to see me, to try again, only to grow petulant or bored after a few weeks or even a few days. She just wants to make sure I'm still hooked," he said wearily, disgust in his voice. They were married for less than a year, because she was running around the whole time. "Her addiction is other men. I don't even think she's aware that she's hurting me. She's only able to think of herself."

I'd been looking down while he was talking, but now I raised my eyes and looked at him. His face was sad and open. It was a masculine face, with a cleft in his chin. I must have noticed that cleft before, but not like I noticed it now. I wanted to touch it, put my finger there, bring his face near. I noticed, too, the dark hair poking out of his shirt at the top button. All at once I felt something swift and surging, something that I hadn't felt in a long, long time.

Chapter Fourteen

Jean

I'm drifting in a nap on a late Sunday afternoon a few weeks after Christmas. According to Dr. David, the baby's about five months along now and I've gotten right used to it being inside me. It's delicious-like to curl up just the two of us with an afghan Ganny made from Daddy's old ties throwed over us. She made the back side of it out of the coolest material, bright green with red dragons, Chinese-like. I haven't a clue where she came by that fabric, but it's like Ganny to use up whatever someone gives her, plus she'd fancy something dashing like those dragons spouting fire.

There comes a knock at the door, something that hasn't happened in the months since Jimmy left. Ben, of course, came in the back door, so to speak, up a tree, not the normal way, but then that's Ben. I know it won't be him a'knocking on the front door. Maybe it's Mrs. D! I struggle to wake up, hardly knowing if it's day or night. Four in the morning or four in the afternoon? I stumble to the door and open it, rubbing my hair that must look like a chicken's butt.

Two soldiers are standing there in fancy green uniforms, not the camouflage kind the guys around the apartment complex wear. One is short and muscular, like he's about to pop out of his uniform, with the short, stubby arms wrestlers have. The other is blond and has deep dimples even though he's not smiling. I wonder if they've come to ask about Ben. But when the strong one asks me, formal-like, if I'm Mrs. Jimmy Jones, it feels like he thumped me in the chest. He asks me if they can come in. "No," I say, "you cannot come in." And I go to close the door.

But before I can get it shut, the muscle man reaches out and holds it open, stronger than me. We struggle over the door, me trying to close it, him holding it open.

"Mrs. Jones, please," the cute one says. He looks like he's about to cry. They both look so pained that I feel sorry for them.

"I know why you're here," I say.

"May we come in now?"

"You might as well get it over with." I lead them to the living room. Mr. Muscle tells me to sit down on the couch, but they remain standing, looking down at me. That's when he tells me he is sorry to inform me that my husband, James Blackbird Jones, has been killed in action in Vietnam.

"Your husband died in service to his country," the guy continues, his face full of twitching muscles. "You can always be proud of him."

"I guess."

"We're so sorry, Mrs. Jones," the blond one says. The other soldier gives him a dirty look. It must not be part of their script.

"Okay then." I'm ready for them to leave.

"Is there someone you'd like us to call, ma'am, someone to come be with you?"

"You can go ahead and leave now."

They glance at each other and I can tell they don't know what to make of me.

I stand up. "I'm carrying a load here," I indicate my belly, "and I'm in the middle of a nap."

They look at each other again. I start toward the door, hoping they'll follow.

"Ma'am, his body will be shipped back to the States in the coming days. Do you wish to receive it here or in South Carolina?"

"North!" I stamp my foot. "North!"

They look at each other like fools, not understanding.

"Send him back to his folks in Franklin," I say. "North Carolina."

I listen to their steps going down the stairs, and then I shut the door. I lie down on the couch, and I fall asleep just like that. Like the knock on the door was a knock on my head.

The next thing I know it's dark and the phone is ringing. It's Mama.

"Oh darlin'," Mama is bawling. "Jimmy's folks just called with the awful, awful news. You poor little gal all the way out there all by your lonesome. When you coming home?"

"I'm not coming, Mama."

There's a mean silence on the other end of the line. I know Mama's silences, like she's winding up.

"You're so young to be a widow, honey. Your whole life is ruined, Jeannie! Ruination."

"I know, Mama." But I don't know. I pat the baby and smile a little to myself, like that Madonna in the art book at the library.

"When you coming home, Jeannie?" Like she hadn't heard me.

"I can't leave here, Mama. I got a job. It won't matter to Jimmy now. He's dead and gone."

"Poor Jimmy," and Mama commences bawling again. She didn't even like him all that much. "He died for his country. He's a hero, Jeannie, a goddamn hero!"

"Okay, Mama."

"You're coming home, Jeannie, that's all there is to it."

"We'll see, Mama."

"Don't give me that 'we'll see' stuff, Jean Louise. I'm on to you. You've always been a queer one."

"I have to go now, Mama."

"Oh, honey, I'm so sorry. Jimmy shot in the head. Did they tell you that, honey? Shot in the head like an animal!"

"I know, Mama." Though I didn't.

When I hang up I try to conjure Jimmy in my mind. I can't picture his face at all. I go and get a photo of him, taken back home before we left for here. We're standing by the truck, Jimmy with his crow hair and cowboy boots, looking serious, like he already knows something we don't know. I'm looking off to the side, annoyed by Mama yelling at us to smile. At least now he won't have to know I sold his truck. I stare at Jimmy, and he's just a picture, nothing that seems real.

I squinch my eyes shut and try to bring him into my mind. But all I can see is his arm between his wrist and elbow, how strong it was and smooth, the skin a nice caramel color, almost hairless. I picture his dead black toenail, the one he dropped the concrete block on. But no eyes, no nose, no mouth. I try saying out loud, "He's dead, Jimmy's dead," but I don't feel a thing. It's no more real to me than that foreign country where they say he died.

I think about Jimmy's folks and how they must be feeling. His mother is Cherokee, that's where he got his looks, the black hair and high cheekbones. She is nice enough I guess, but never said much when I was around, maybe because Jimmy's dad, Big Jim, talked too much and too loud, like the rest of us was hard of hearing. Jimmy was afraid of him, I know that much. Big Jim took the belt to him when he was growing up, Jimmy told me once, and then wouldn't talk about it ever again. Maybe his folks was what made Jimmy so silent himself, never revealing what was going on inside him.

At least he knew about the baby. I hope he got the letter before he died, though I haven't heard back from him about it. At least I didn't tell him about his truck. That would have made him mad and sad. Now he'll never even see his little child.

I try to think what to do. I could call Mrs. D but I don't want to bother her at home. She gave me her number, for emergencies she said, and I know what she meant, and this isn't that. I turn on the TV, Bonanza is just coming on, I recognize the theme song. I watch Hoss and Little Joe, resting my hands on my tummy, feeling life there. I wonder if the baby heard about her daddy. I'm pretty sure it's a girl. I'm gonna call her Inga.

The next day is Monday, so I go in to work. When I go over to get the shelving cart, I say to Mrs. D, "Jimmy got killed in Nam."

She just freezes there, like a photograph herself, half bent over with a stack of books. I didn't realize anyone could stop like that, not move a thing, not twitch an eyelid or lip, though there is a funny quivering in her jaw. Her eyes, staring up at me, go big and glassy, funny-like. It's almost like I've shot a bullet into her brain and messed up everything in there so she can't think straight.

Slowly she begins to move again, like an old person, carefully. She puts the books on my cart, not straight up like she always does, but on their sides.

"Jean. Did you just say Jimmy got killed?"

"Yes ma'am. In Nam."

The look on her face makes me feel like crying, for the first time. Like I need Mrs. D to feel things for me, like I can't do it on my own. My own eyes fill with tears, but whether for Jimmy, me, or Mrs. D, I can't tell.

"Come with me," she says, and there we are again in that little coffee room, where she first told me I was pregnant. Jimmy has been killed in Nam, and Baby Inga will never have a daddy. That's too sad to think about, so I don't.

She asks me when, and I tell her about the soldiers coming to the door.

"Oh my god! Jean, why didn't you call me? I'm so, so sorry! My god. Dear god in heaven!" She rubs her face with her hands, as if trying to wipe something away, and she gets choked up, her eyes brimming with tears.

I wait for her to collect herself.

"Have you made plans to go home?" she asks when she's pulled herself together. "I believe the military will pay your way, but—don't even think about it, Jean, I'll take care of it. I'll help you make plane reservations. Larry will understand, of course. Don't worry about a thing, your job will be here when you return. Of course you may not want to come back …"

"I'm not going."

That stops her again. She just stares at me some more, like she can't believe me. But it's me, Jean, she knows me.

"But …"

"I want to stay here with you."

"Oh my god, Jean. You have to go home! At least for the funeral."

"I'm not going."

"But … but … why not?"

"Don't want to. Jimmy's dead and gone now and he won't care. He's beyond caring."

"But … what about … his family … your … Will you at least think about it?"

I tell her I will, but I have made up my mind.

She tells me I could take some time off, I don't have to stay today, to go on home, and she'll come with me if I'd like. But what would I do at home?

"Maybe there are phone calls you need to make. Have you talked to your folks?"

"Mama called. I told her I wasn't coming. There's nothing for me back there. Only Ganny. But I'd have to wade through the whole lot of them to get to her. And I don't want that. All of 'em feeling sorry for me, or acting like they do."

"But funerals are important, they help you understand that the person is really gone."

"I don't need a funeral to know Jimmy is dead, Mrs. D. That's Jimmy's story. Now I got to live mine, mine and this baby's. I can shelve those books there. They're waiting for me."

I leave her sitting there, staring into space. A little later Mr. Reynolds comes up to me on the second floor and tells me Mrs. D told him about Jimmy, how sad that is, how he is so sorry, and I can certainly take off some time, whatever I need. I just shake my head and go on shelving books. Later I can tell the other workers are whispering about me. In the restroom Margery rushes in and puts her arms around me before I can even go in a stall to pee. "Poor baby! What are you going to do now, what with that bun in the oven!"

"I'll just do like I always done," I say, pushing out of her grasp. "Right now I got to pee."

"Poor little Jean. You always were a loser."

I go in the stall, hoping she'll go away. I sit there until she gives up, and I hear the outside door shut.

Mrs. D offers to give me a ride home, but I take the bus like always. I'm not worried about the snake being there, and like always I unlock the security bar and open the balcony door. It's raining lightly now, and there's a light mist that makes things look sad. The Douglas firs seem to be weeping, with their long green needles dripping. I wonder what it's like in Vietnam, in the jungle, and who shot Jimmy in the head. A soldier on the other side, someone I can't even conjure. Our soldiers call them gooks but maybe they're people just like us. I mean, with babies and wives. What is it we're fighting for? What did Jimmy die for? The soldiers said for our country, USA, but why? Why was it for us if he was way over there in Vietnam?

Mrs. D wants me to go home, to go to Jimmy's funeral, like I'm supposed to. Maybe she will go with me. I could take her up to meet Ganny, show her the mountains there, different from the snow-capped ones here. But then I want to come back here with her and take up this life again. Have the baby. Baby Inga. Live in this apartment and go to my job that I'm good at. I'll have to ask Mrs. D if she'll go to North Carolina with me. I bet she will.

But I never have a chance to ask her, because the very next day she gets the word about her daddy.

Chapter Fifteen

Inga

I was trying to find a 1947 *Life* magazine in the archives for a student who was doing a paper about Truman when Larry came down to the basement to find me. "Inga," he said, "there's a call from your father's doctor in Duluth. He's waiting on the line for you."

A chill swept through me. "No!" I exclaimed. "He can't be dead!"

Dad was eighty on his last birthday. He'd led a tough, outdoor life, going out in all elements, doing the work of several men. It made him strong and able for most of his life, so it was a shock last summer to see the muscles in his arms going soft, as if the flesh were softening wax instead of the hard granite of my girlhood.

Larry put his arm around my shoulder and gave me a hug. He smelled of old books and tobacco smoke. "He's had a stroke. The doctor will give you the details. But he's alive."

I took the call in Larry's office. Dr. Husby told me that Dad was paralyzed on his right side, unable to speak. The prognosis wasn't good.

"He's dying," I said flatly, sensing the truth. "How long does he have?"

"It's hard to know with a stroke," he said. "He could have another one at any time or linger for weeks. There's no chance of recovery, I'm afraid."

I hung up the phone and just sat there, trying to absorb this blow. I pictured my father's laughing, animated face. He was always eager to see the good in people, to think the best of them. I couldn't believe he might actually die. Of course I knew it would happen one day. Yet I couldn't imagine the world—my world—without him in it. I wanted whatever time we had left. I wanted to hold his warm hand, the shape and size I knew so well. Those were the very hands that made and then held up the world. Maybe a lot of daughters feel that way, especially ones who have lost their mothers early. How lucky I was to have such a decent father! Such a good man in my life all these years. I used to take it for granted, but now I understood I had been blessed.

I wondered if Ben—the trouble he was in—had caused Dad's stroke. He had never believed that Ben could do such things, refused to even consider the possibility, as if that was what family loyalty—family love—consisted of. Absolute belief in Ben's goodness until there was irrefutable proof, and after that a different kind of loyalty. The standing-by kind, no matter what.

I was lost in these thoughts when Larry knocked on the door. He sat down across the desk from me, and I started to tell him what the doctor said. But the words opened a floodgate. I buried my face in my hands and sobbed uncontrollably. Then I was over it. I had to think, I had to get organized.

"Larry, I have to go to Dad. I have to take care of him." Again the tears came, but this time I fought them until I gained control. He handed me a box of Kleenex, and I grabbed a handful, blowing my nose and wiping my eyes, clearing my clotted throat so I could talk intelligibly. "I'll leave tomorrow, if you can manage without me. Of course you can! All those times when I didn't come in …"

"Do you want me to call the airline?"

"I'm going to drive." I was afraid of flying. I always drove to Minnesota. I couldn't stand the idea of being locked up and helpless so high above the ground. It made my heart pound just to think of it.

"I forgot you don't like to fly. But … really, Inga. That's a long way to drive by yourself. Given all that has transpired. You're not in the best shape. For all I know you'll take a wrong turn and end up sitting on the side of some highway somewhere. Maybe someone can go with you, if you insist on driving. Lorraine could go …"

"Jean!" I exclaimed. "What am I going to do about Jean, Larry? She just found out her husband is dead. I think she's in shock. She doesn't seem to register it."

"It's horrible about her husband," Larry sighed. "We never should have gotten into this war to begin with, and we just keep getting in deeper. I don't understand why she doesn't just go home. But I asked her this morning and she won't budge. She's an odd duck. Apparently she's latched on to you. How would you feel about taking her with you? I can't be responsible for her myself."

I didn't know whether I'd be looking after Jean or she'd be looking after me, but at least there would be two of us. Two lost souls.

"I have to leave right away, Larry," I said, feeling the urgency. "I mean tomorrow. I'll have to pack, take care of some things ... for all I know he'll be gone before I get there." And again the tears came. I wondered if I would be able to make the trip in the shape I was in.

"Let me go find Jean," Larry said.

After Larry left I started to pick up the phone to call Ben, to tell him about his grandfather. My hand suspended in midair over the receiver. I felt confused, as if the world was upside down.

Larry came in with Jean close behind. "It's your dad," she said. "I'll go with you."

She stood there looking composed despite the chaos all around her. My heart ached for her. I felt like taking her in my arms, reassuring her ... about what? I was hardly one to reassure her about life. Maybe it was myself I wanted to console.

"You're sure about not going home?" I asked. There was a long silence. She often pauses before she speaks. "I want to go with you," she said.

Larry said he'd take her home now so she could pack. I told her I'd pick her up at seven the next morning, and to bring any bills she had, including the address where she mailed her rent check. We'd pay them from Minnesota if we had to. I told her I had no idea how long we'd be gone, or what to expect when we got there. I told her to call her mother. I wrote down Dad's address and phone number and handed it to her. "It'll be very cold in Minnesota," I told her. "Colder than anything you've ever felt. Bring your heaviest coat." Then I wondered if she even had a heavy coat, coming from the South. "Never mind. We have a closet full of warm jackets at home. You'll be okay once we get there."

It's amazing how much one can get done in an emergency. My next door neighbor would take in the mail and water the houseplants. I canceled the paper, gathered up my bills, and wrote checks even if they weren't due, to drop in the mail on the way to the bank. I packed pants and sweaters and a black wool dress, not allowing myself to think the word "funeral." I cleaned out the refridge, took out the trash. By then it was almost five in the afternoon.

I had been putting off the last thing on my list. To call Ron.

I had to tell him that I was leaving town. My hand actually shook a little as I dialed his direct line. He had left rather abruptly Christmas night, and we hadn't talked since. Had he felt anything like what I had? No, it was impossible. What was I thinking? No one would ever have to know what a fool I was.

"O'Loughlin." No hello, no nothing, just his last name barked out as if I was interrupting him, which I suppose I was.

"It's Inga," I said. There was a long silence on the other end.

"Do you have something?" he asked rather gruffly.

That stumped me for a moment. "Oh," I finally said. "No, not about Ben. It's just … my father has had a stroke. He's partially paralyzed and may not live." I was stuttering. "I … I thought I should tell you I'm leaving town tomorrow. I'm driving to Minnesota. I don't know for how long. I thought I should … let you know," I repeated dumbly.

Another silence. Finally, "I'm very sorry to hear that," and I could tell he meant it. "About your father. It doesn't get any easier, does it." Not really a question. "You were right to let me know."

I could sense there was something else he wanted to say. It hung in the air, over the line, between us. Maybe something about Christmas night. But of course that was just in my mind, not his, and rightly so.

"What?" I finally said.

"Two young women were killed overnight. In Modesto. Someone broke into their apartment, strangled them to death. Naturally—given his history—we have to consider Ben."

I couldn't speak.

"Are you still there?"

"Oh, uh …"

"Do you want me to come over?"

"No. Yes. No. I don't …"

"Are you sure you're okay?"

I gave him my father's phone number.

"Will you be all right? I mean, with this news. And your dad …"

"I'm okay," I said weakly. "And someone is going with me. A girl from work. Larry insisted," I added. "So I won't be alone."

"Good, then," he said. "I'm not saying it was Ben. We don't know yet but we'll find out."

It couldn't be Ben. Two more!

"I hope things will go okay for your father, Inga. I'll check in."

When I hung up the phone I sat down on a kitchen chair. Two more girls. Why would Ben be in Modesto? They would naturally suspect him but that didn't mean it was him. *But what if it was.*

I felt a deep pain rip through me. What if I had told Ron when Ben showed up on Jean's balcony?

Would it have saved them?

Chapter Sixteen

Jean

We've been in Minnesota about a week now I figure, but to tell the truth I've lost track, the days running together so. We drove across some big open spaces to get here, nary a car nor house in sight. I like that feeling of being between things, neither here nor there. I like the feeling of going over eighty miles an hour, like Jimmy drove, though Mrs. D and I stuck to the speed limit, even when I was dying to put the pedal to the metal. I like feeling that who you are don't matter, because out there on the road, no one knows you, you don't have a snake on your balcony or a husband shot dead in a jungle you can't even find on a map.

At first Mrs. D and I played the radio when we could get a station. Sometimes we'd laugh at the lyrics to the songs, *What would you think if I sang out of tune ... Lucy in the sky with diamonds ...* and once they even played Jimmy's favorite song, *Purple haze all in my brain, lately things just don't seem the same, acting funny but I don't know why, scuse me while I kiss the sky*, with that torn-up guitar riff that sounded like the world was about to end. I remembered how Jimmy would play air guitar like he was out of his mind, and maybe he was, after smoking a big joint. But then the news report came on about two girls murdered in their beds in Modesto, and Mrs. D turned the radio off and we never turned it on again. Most of the time we were silent, comfortable-like, but sometimes we'd talk about what we were seeing out the window, our favorite foods, or the kinds of games we played as kids. Mrs. D told me about how her grandfather came over from Norway to settle on Lake Superior, how he built a two-story frame house right on the shore and the family lived upstairs, because downstairs was where they cleaned the herring and lake trout. Her father learned boat building from his father, and along with the fishing they ran a little summer resort of twelve cabins. Soon I would be seeing it.

Once she asked me about Jimmy, but I didn't know what to say. He was someone I had known all my life though not well, and then we got married. I can't say I really knew him. He didn't let me into his thoughts. But maybe that comes after you've been married awhile, after years of being together you open up. Or maybe not. But now with Jimmy I'd never know.

Everything in Dakota was white. I had seen snow in the mountains near Ganny's plenty of times, but I had never seen it laid out so deep over so much flat, bare land. The wind blew sideways, so fierce it shook the car, not a tree nor hill nor barn nor house to break it. It gave me an eerie feeling, to be out there on those great empty plains, with nothing but white surrounding us. It made me glad the car had a good heater. When we'd stop for food or to use the bathroom, the wind cut through my coat like I wasn't even wearing one, and the little hairs inside my nose froze.

Minnesota was more of the same, just snow everywhere you looked. I couldn't imagine why anyone would want to live in such a godforsaken place, but sometimes you're just born there and don't know any better. By the time we reached Duluth it was dark but also bright, the stars and moon lighting up the snow. We started up Highway 61, which ran alongside Lake Superior. Mrs. D pulled into a scenic stop, and even though it was night, we got out and stood there shivering and looking at a dark, crashing ocean with the moonlight making a bright stripe across it that ran right up to where we were standing. Mrs. D didn't say a word, she just took a deep breath, like she'd been underwater and was coming up for air for the first time in a long while. That's how I knew she was home and that home meant something to her. I knew that feeling myself, though I'd take my own deep breath in the Blue Ridge if I could.

We pulled into her father's place about midnight. The light was on over the back porch, and an old woman with gray hair in tight curls was sitting in the kitchen, her head down on her folded arms on the table, a cold cup of coffee next to her. Mrs. Sve—a name like none I had ever heard before and couldn't get, until Mrs. D explained that it was

Norwegian, that a lot of Norwegians, Swedes, and Finns had settled on the North Shore of Lake Superior. She lived nearby, just up Highway 61 toward Beaver Bay, and had been helping with Mrs. D's dad until we could get there.

Mrs. D went right in to see her father. He was in a hospital bed in the living room but wasn't hooked up to oxygen or any tubes. He was asleep, but as soon as the three of us tiptoed in, he woke up as if expecting us. He reached for Mrs. D's hand with his hand. He only had one that would work now. He looked so strange, one half of him paralyzed, his mouth twisted out of shape and the other side normal. I could see that he had been a good-looking man in his better days. His blue eyes filled with tears when Mrs. D wept, putting her head on his hand, which she held in both of hers. Unh, unh, unh, he tried to say something, shaking his head. I knew he was telling her not to cry, don't cry, and after that initial burst, she straightened up, wiped her tears, kissed him on the forehead. That's when she remembered me, and called me in out of the shadows, where I was lingering with Mrs. Sve, who smelled like coffee and a new permanent.

"This is my young friend Jean," she told her dad, pulling me by the arm closer to his bed. I recognized the smell of someone sick and dying, from my own dad. "She works with me at the library and helped me drive from Washington."

The one side of his face smiled, gentlemanly, and he reached up with his good hand to take mine. I clutched it fiercely and felt his strength in his grip, his warmth, and maybe something a little desperate, like the grasp of a drowning man. His hair was white and thin like a newborn's, sticking up every which way. He had a little paste of white around his mouth, drool from his sleep, so I took a Kleenex from the box by his bed, dipped it in his water glass and wiped him clean.

Mrs. Sve said she'd be leaving then, and Mrs. D showed her to the door, thanking her for her kindness. I heard their voices, murmuring by the kitchen door, talking about Mrs. D's father no doubt. I stood by his bed in the dim light, to keep him company. We just looked each other in the eye, no need to speak. I understood what he was feeling. It was nothing you could ever have put into words anyway. It was his daughter and his stroke, his wife dying too soon, a long time ago; it was the land he had lived on his whole life and loved, it was the lake he could hear crashing on the rocks, and it was Ben. It was what would become of Inga when he died, because he knew he was dying. The body does know. I read all this in his eyes, and I told him with my eyes that I would do my best, that I'd take care of Mrs. D, and it would all be okay. Soft women voices came from the kitchen, murmuring murmuring like mourning doves. I thought I heard Mrs. D laugh at one point, something I had not heard a lot of, but maybe it was crying. They're too close to tell sometimes. I took Walter's live hand, moved closer to the bed, and put it against my stomach where the baby was nestled. I could feel Baby Inga kicking my innards. I told him without speaking about the baby, and I could see by the way his eyes lit up that he understood. A baby was the same as all that couldn't be said. His warm hand rested there against my busy stomach. The baby calmed.

Mrs. D came back in the living room to find me holding Walter's hand. His eyes had grown heavy, and he just stared into space, those blue, blue eyes. I wondered what he was seeing. His skin was smooth and age had dropped away from him. Pretty soon his lids fell, and he slept, his damaged body craving rest. Mrs. D pulled the covers up to his chin, tucking him in, and kissed him on his cheek.

"I don't think it will be too long," I said to her when we were back in the kitchen. She was opening the icebox, seeing all the food the neighbors had brought in. She turned to me, startled, and I could see that I had frightened her but I had to prepare her. I knew what was coming, and it was better if she knew in advance. It would be less a shock that way.

"What …" she started, but then fell silent.

"I saw my own daddy die," I told her. "There comes a point when the body can't keep on. It wants release. It starts in the feet. They grow cool, then cold, and it moves up from there. The extremities first. It isn't bad. The body knows how to shut down."

She nodded, but the tears began to flow.

"I just don't want him to suffer," she managed to get out.

I didn't speak, because I couldn't promise her that. Life was suffering, that was the truth, and we humans didn't have any more control over that than the beasts of the forests and fields.

• • •

We fell into a little routine, and it was all right peaceful and calm. That is until the day I went tromping down through the snow to the cabins. Later I thought maybe something was pulling me in that direction, something beyond my control. But no, I just wanted to see the cabins. Do something different that day. I had no way of knowing it would end our peace forever.

Mrs. D had given me Walter's room, since he wouldn't need it anymore. I figured he must have always gotten up before sunrise, 'cause no one could sleep the way the sun came beaming in your face like a spotlight every morning. Out his bedroom window was the whitest, brightest snow covering everything down to the water's edge, where there was a tumble of big boulders frosted with white ice, piled along the shore, then a whole blue sea stretching to the horizon. The smell of bacon and eggs would pull me toward the kitchen, and I'd usually find Mrs. D there in her flannel bathrobe. I'd go in to visit Walter. These final days he'd be sleeping heavily, breathing in jagged starts and stops. Mrs. D would join me by his bed, and we'd tend to him. After that we'd have breakfast and do what needed to be done around the house.

It became my habit to take a little walk after our chores were done. Mrs. D had given me some winter clothes she wore when she was growing up: wool pants, a soft checked flannel shirt, and a wool fisherman's sweater from Norway. Over that I'd wear a bright blue down jacket, some high boots, and a pink wool stocking cap with a pom-pom on top. I looked right colorful, and even though it was cold out, I liked my walks. Usually I walked up the drive to the road and back down to where the plow had carved out a turnaround circle at the first cabin by the shore. After I'd done that a few times, I'd be hot except for my face, which turned bright red and stung when I came back in the house.

On the day our peace ended, I decided to see the cabins Walter rented out down by the lake. Mrs. D told me they closed them for the winter at the end of October, and they didn't even plow the road to them, just locked 'em up. They sat cold and silent until the thaw in late spring, getting a rest themselves after all the summer people left. The same families came back year after year, so Walter kept a "no vacancy" sign hanging all the time from the big sign that said "North Shore Cabins" out on the highway, because they never needed to rent to strangers.

As soon as I stepped off the plowed drive, I was up to my knees in snow. I got stuck and fell flat-out backwards into a cold drift. I couldn't even get up at first, I just rolled around like a bug on its back. I figured I might die there and not be found 'til spring. Finally I figured if I rolled over onto my knees and gave a mighty push, I could right myself. I was so covered with the white stuff I looked like the Abdominable Snowman.

I began clomping through the snow on what must have been the drive toward the first cabin. I heard a chickadee calling "dee-dee-dee." How could such a little critter live in such a cold, snowy place? It was fun to break through the crust and sink down a foot or so. I was getting the hang of it and leaving deep foot holes in the snow.

The cabins were made of logs painted a creamy yellow, with dark green trim, probably nothing extra inside, just a bed, a stove, an icebox, a table, a chair. All a person really needs. I could live in a cabin like that just fine.

The first cabin had a porch just big enough for one metal lawn chair. I tried the door—locked. For a moment I could see a July day, the sun warm, leaves on the now bare trees, the lake laughing and splashing water up on the black rocks. Mrs. D had told me how people had bonfires in the fire pits Walter built on the rocky lakeshore. You could sit out there at night with the cool air on your back and the warm air in your face, and maybe see the Northern Lights, great sheets of colored light that sometimes danced across the sky. I had never heard of such a thing before.

I kept tromping down the line, determined to visit every cabin, but I was starting to shiver, and my legs had grown weary from lifting the boots out of the snow. It took a lot of effort, but I was going to finish the job, just like Mrs. D taught me.

The last cabin was buried in a little grove of fir trees. As I got closer, I could see two long tracks coming up to the cabin from the other side. I wondered what kind of strange, northern animal could make two tracks side by side like that. Then I saw two skinny skis propped against the wall on the little porch. I stood stock still and stared, trying to puzzle things out. Instead of the red curtains like the other cabins had, someone had draped an army blanket up inside to cover the front window. A little smoke was coming from the metal stovepipe on top.

Suddenly a stinky leather hand clamped onto my mouth from behind. Something gripped me around my shoulders hard, like talons. I tried to squirm away with all my might, but he had me in his claws. He began dragging me through the snow, me kicking at his legs, trying to twist away from the arm that had slid up around my throat. I tried to bite him through the leather glove, but I couldn't get my mouth open. I was afraid he'd smother me. My heart was trying to break out of my chest but more than fear, I felt determined. He was not going to pull me into that cabin, not if I could help it. But I couldn't even get my feet under me the way he was jerking me along so strong, all of it happening too fast.

He kicked the door to the cabin open with his foot. When he had me inside, he pushed me hard so that I fell forward onto the floor, trying to break my fall with my hands to protect the baby. I thought I'd pee my pants. I pulled my knit hat over my face, as if I could hide that way, but he jerked the cap off roughly. I turned to look at him, though I already knew who it was.

"God!" he exclaimed, once he saw my face. "Jesus! Jean!"

I stared at him. He looked different, with his curly hair grown back in and dyed black. He had a bushy brown beard, and he'd put on weight. But it was him all right.

The overhead light was on, the double bed scrambled with a blanket and spread. Even though I was shivering, I was surprised to feel warmth—he had the space heater turned on. There were cans of beans and chili on the Formica table by the front window covered with the army blanket. There was a black pistol lying next to a can of sardines. The place smelled of wet wool and bones, like an animal's den. I tasted blood where he'd made me bite the inside of my lip.

"God, Jean, what are you … ?" He looked dumbfounded, rubbing his black head all over, scratching his bushy beard. There was an odor about him, like Jimmy's sweaty jockstrap used to smell. He pulled out one of the two straight-back chairs from the table and sat down, looking dazed.

I scrambled for the door on my hands and knees, but he leapt up and blocked my way. "For Christ's sake, get off the floor," he ordered.

I staggered to my feet, feeling helpless. *What was Ben doing here? He must of followed us! Why couldn't he just leave us alone!* I felt sorry to my soul that I had gotten Baby Inga into a fix like this.

"Sit down," he ordered. "And don't look so scared."

I eased down onto the other kitchen chair. When he saw my eyes go to the gun, he took it and put it in the icebox. I glanced around frantically, but I could see no way out.

"Please don't kill me," I pleaded. "On account of the baby."

He frowned so fierce, his eyebrows almost met in the middle. "No one's going to kill you, Jean. For God's sake!"

"You're not?"

"You're not my type."

"What do you mean?"

"A joke, Jean. A bad joke. Now shut up so I can think." He propped his elbows on the table and rested his head in his hands. His black hair looked weird. He certainly wasn't talking now like a gentleman the way he had when he was hiding on my balcony. But he hadn't killed me then when he could have, so maybe he wasn't going to kill me now.

After we sat there in silence for a long time, I couldn't hold my tongue any longer. "What are you doing here! You're not supposed to be here!" I held my mittened hands out, exasperated, palms up and open, as if he could just put the answer right in them.

"What are *you* doing here?"

"What do you mean? Didn't you follow us here?"

"Is Mother here too! What's going on? Granpa ..."

"He's dying, Ben. He had a stroke. That's why we came! He's dying ... I'm sorry ... but ... what the fuck!" I sounded like my daddy when he went to cussing 'cause of the glass chewing him up inside. I learned a mess of bad words from him, and now they filled my mind and mouth. "Fuck!" I said again, bending over the baby, putting my head as far down as I could get. I was getting overheated in my down jacket. "Fuck, fuck, fuck!" My legs were jumping and I felt out of breath, like I'd run a hard mile.

"I didn't know you talked like that. Fuck this and fuck that."

"I don't! I mean, not usually. Not unless I can't help it. And you don't know me!"

"Okay, okay, don't be such a hothead."

"*You're* one to tell me—or anyone—what to do!"

"Jean," he said, and he looked at me in a way that made me snap to. "Tell me about Granpa. When did it happen?"

"Why did you come here!"

"Where else could I go?"

I just stared at him. It really was Ben. He wasn't a monster with fangs, blood dripping off them, like in those vampire movies. He seemed like most any other dude, only better looking. I wondered what he had been like when he took those girls, if they had pleaded with him to let them go. Had he told them to shut up? I waited to see what would come next.

"I want to see him."

"No, no, Ben," I said quickly. "Not a good idea. I mean, going up to the house and all. There are people there ..."

Ben was silent. His jaw was clinching and pulsing like a piston.

"I have to see Mother. Talk to her."

Now I was silent. Mrs. D had her hands full with Walter dying. The last thing she needed right now was Ben. I was sure Walter would have a gun. Probably several. A shotgun for sure, a pistol probably. Daddy taught me about guns when I was ten years old. I could shoot as good as the next fella. I could just bring a gun down to this cabin and shoot him. Take care of it myself, once and for all. I slipped off my mitten, and tested the inside of my lip to see if it was still bleeding, but it had stopped on its own.

"I've gotta go now," I said. "Your mother will be worried about me." I eased out of the chair and edged toward the door, afraid he might jump up again. But he looked lost in a world of his own, hardly aware of me.

"You should leave here," I said. "You should just go."

"Where would I go?"

Straight to hell, the words rang in my mind, but I left them unspoken.

Chapter Seventeen

Inga

Reverend Sjoblad and I sit with my father, me holding his hand, wishing I could ease his labored breathing. It seems he has lost his cough reflex and can no longer clear the phlegm that is gathering in his throat and lungs. He's slipped into unconsciousness. Now it's just a matter of waiting and trying to make him as comfortable as possible. I believe he can still hear me, even though he can't respond. I whisper softly that I'm with him, that I love him, that all is well. His hand feels cool, unnaturally so. I remember what Jean said about the extremities going first. His body is drawing in on itself, sending its flagging resources to the core. He's dying, I tell myself, but I can't believe it. It's too big a thought or feeling to hold on to. Every now and then a flash of realization comes over me, then closes up again. When I was little, Mother told me that lightning was a glimpse into Heaven. I marveled at how dazzling bright Heaven was in the split second when we could see into it. We would never be able to stand the sight of Heaven for any longer than that. Now I can only stand a dazzling split-second realization that he is dying, before the black sky closes over again.

Reverend Sjoblad is a new—at least to me—minister at Dad's church, Our Savior Lutheran, but he has gotten to know Dad in the three years he's been here. He's been good to come around every day, to offer whatever support he can, though sometimes I wish he'd take a day off. Dad, of course, is beyond our grasp, suspended between life and death. When Jean comes in from her walk, face flushed, the minister suggests we all stand around his bed and pray for his soul, that it make a swift departure from his body and ascend to heaven. Jean surprises us by singing "Amazing Grace" in a pure, light soprano. When I compliment her on her voice, she says she used to sing in the choir back home.

Just as the minister is leaving, Greta Sve stops by, bringing a tuna hot dish. I ask if she'll stay for lunch, but she says she's on her way to the Super One in Two Harbors. After the others have left, Jean and I have grilled cheese sandwiches in the kitchen, just a few steps from where Dad is doing his dying. It seems strange that we can eat, but we're both hungry. The warm melted cheese and toasted bread are simple and comforting.

Jean has been awfully quiet since coming in from her walk. When I ask her if she enjoyed the snow, she just nods. Maybe she's thinking about Jimmy being killed. Maybe the news is finally sinking in. I wonder if she regrets not going home for his funeral. She never talks about home, her mother or father, or even Jimmy for that matter. I can't read her, really, but then I've given up trying to decipher other people.

While I'm standing at the sink doing the dishes, Jean says, "Can I ask you something, Mrs. D?"

She's still sitting at the table, and there's something in her tone that alerts me that this is not just casual conversation. I purposefully keep my back to her, so as not to scare her off. "Of course, Jean," I say.

"If you could see Ben again, would you want to?"

I hold the griddle pan in midair. Why is she thinking about Ben instead of Jimmy! Or Dad? Why would she even ask such a thing, now? I plunge the pan into the soapy water.

"You know, like when he was on my balcony and wanted to see you. You said you'd come. You really wanted to see him then, didn't you? Talk to him."

"Jean," I turn to look at her. "Why are you asking me this? Now—with Dad the way he is!"

"I'm sorry," she mumbles miserably. When I glance at her, tears are glistening in her eyes.

I sit down at the table and think about taking her hand but then don't. Occasionally I'll pat her shoulder, but we never touch. Just more of my Norwegian reserve. "Jean, Dad is dying. It will probably be tonight. Do you understand?"

She nods, silent, observing me with her serious green eyes.

"I don't want to talk about Ben right now. Not tonight." Then, as if I can't help myself, as if the words have a life of their own, "But he's still my son. He'll always be my son."

Around nine I get a call from Ron. He's been calling every day. A part of me lives for those phone calls, for the sound of his voice. I tell him how Dad is doing, what has happened that day, small stuff, and he listens and tells me a little about his day. Nothing about Ben, because there is no news. There's something sweet and caring about our conversations. I wonder if he looks forward to them as much as I do. It does feel as if something subtle and delicious is going on, made easier no doubt because of long distance. I tell myself it's only my imagination. But then I think how he doesn't have to call.

After we hang up, I take up my vigil at Dad's bedside. Jean goes to her room, and at about ten the light under her door goes dark. I sit in the semi-dark with Dad, who tosses and turns, restless in his dying. I wonder how long it will be. I'm glad that I have this time with him, his last hours on earth. I talk to him in a low voice about the good times, the memories that I know would make him happy—when Mom was still alive, and how we'd go fishing in Canada in the summer, and cross-country skiing in the winter. About his good life, how people respected him, how I love him dearly. I feel I have moved into a different dimension as the night wears on. It's as if nothing else exists, we're in our own separate bubble of time and space, my father still alive, still with me, but slowly passing. At some point in the night I put my head down on my forearms on the side of his hospital bed and doze. *I won't leave you*, I either say or dream. I'll be right here with you until the end.

I don't know what time it is—but it must be two or three a.m.—when I wake suddenly to the sound of the back door opening. We never use the front door, we come and go through the back, where Dad has a reception desk for the resort guests, with a phone, booking calendar, and his records, such as they are, in a spiral notebook. We never lock that door—there's no reason to way up here on the shore. I'm startled though not particularly alarmed to hear the familiar sound of that door opening deep in the night.

I rouse myself to see a figure standing in the doorway to the living room, where we have Dad. It takes an instant for my eyes to adjust, but when they do, my heart jerks wildly. Ben, in a heavy wool overcoat and yellow pigskin gloves. He has a horrible beard, and his hair is black, but I know his face, his eyes, his mouth, his nose, the way he stands, the way he holds himself, as familiar to me as myself. I jump up and go and hug him hard, embracing his warm, live body. He puts his arms around me, patting me awkwardly on the back with his big gloves. He's alive, he's here, and for a moment nothing else matters.

He laughs a little and cups my head in his gloved hands. "Hi, Mom," he says in that wry way he has. "How's Granpa doing?"

"Ben, my god! What are you doing here? You can't be here!"

He just shrugs, avoiding my eyes. "Granpa?"

"Ben, what are you …" Just then Dad gives a long, low moan, but whether he knows Ben is there or not, I can't say.

Ben and I rush to his bedside. "He's had a stroke, and now he probably has pneumonia. There isn't anything else to be done."

Ben leans over and kisses his grandfather on the forehead. "Hi, Granpa," he whispers. "It's me, Ben."

Dad seems to be trying to get out of something. He twists and turns, as if tangled in the ropes of life, which he longs to break. He wants to be released. I think of all those fish he caught over so many years, gasping for breath in the bottom of the boat. His breathing is labored and stops for long periods, frightening me. I have to remind myself that this is the necessary part. He wouldn't want to be saved now.

Then he takes a long last breath. I stare at him. This is it, I think, and it is everything and nothing. Ben and I stand there on opposite sides of the bed, frozen by what we're witnessing. Then he is still, stiller than I've ever seen him. His visage immediately changes, his eyes half-open and half-shut, but empty. I can tell the spirit has left his body. There is a definite sense of absence.

"Mother?" Ben looks at me uncertainly. But I can't speak. I lay my hand on Dad's small forehead— it seems to be shrinking under my hand, Dad seems to be shrinking, as if when life left, the body immediately began to recede. It is a strange sensation, how small and absent he looks. I close his eyelids with my fingers, for his half-shut eyes have gone opaque. A loneliness I've never felt before suffuses me, an emptiness that scares me.

Ben sits down in the chair I used in my vigil, still wearing his coat, and drops his head into his gloved hands. Then I realize he's crying, his shoulders shaking. I start to go to him, but something stops me. He looks like the most alone person in the world. My heart aches for him, but it also stands back. I try out the word "murderer" in my mind. It's hard to attach that word to my son, who is crying softly beside my father's body.

"We have to talk," I say finally, after Ben has sat there, sunk in the chair, in a daze, for many minutes, just staring at his grandfather's white, vacant face. "We don't have much time. I'll have to call the minister at the church when the sun comes up. People will come." I can hardly think. My mind feels as windswept, cold, and empty as pictures of Antarctica.

When Ben looks up at me, he looks so young, younger than his twenty-five years—like a boy again. It seems at that moment I see him at every age, from when he was just a laughing baby through his boyhood and teen years, all at once, all together, telescoped into this one moment. It frightens me how much I love him, how I have done wrong for him.

We go in the kitchen and Ben takes off his coat and gloves. I crack four eggs in Dad's blue bowl, which I remember from childhood, the one with the spout on the side. Dad loves—loved that bowl, and for a moment, I just stare at it. *Oh what am I going to do!* A wave of grief sweeps over me. I sink into a kitchen chair, and put my head down on the table and sob my heart out. *Gone, gone! I'll never see Dad alive again!*

Ben has the sense not to touch me. He lets me have my cry, and in the meantime, he melts butter in the cast-iron frying pan and scrambles the eggs. By the time they're done, I'm through, for now. I sit up and wipe my eyes, ready to deal with business. I wonder, briefly, what it would be like to just give up myself, give in, fall apart, refuse to move, to speak, to live another moment, really. But that isn't an option, is it? Ben puts Dad's chipped Fiesta plates in front of us and divides the eggs, though I scrape most of mine onto his plate. There is toast, and I become aware of fresh coffee brewing on the stove. I wipe my eyes with my shirttail.

"Where do we start?" I say.

"I don't know."

"Those girls in Modesto," I say.

"I wasn't in Modesto. Ever. It wasn't me. They think it's me because they want to pin everything on me."

"Because I would never forgive myself."

"You don't have to worry."

I just look at him. "Not worry?" I hold his eyes until he looks away.

The air around us is dense and heavy, as if we're on another planet. One with different gravity, lacking oxygen. I struggle to take in a breath.

"Please believe me. It wasn't me. Not Modesto." I look at him, and I want to believe him. There's nothing he can say or do to convince me. Yet I do believe him.

"But the others ..." I say slowly. "What about the other girls, Ben? The four at Alpine Lake. We don't have much time. Tell me the truth."

He gets up and puts his plate in the sink. He exhales a long sigh. "I'm not going to ask you to believe me. Because obviously you believe *them*. But police lie all the time. They cheat, they plant information, they make things up. There are a million maniacs out there. You have no idea. Rapists, murderers, pedophiles, psychopaths, the works. But for some reason the police think *I'm* responsible for those four girls. There's no evidence! No real, physical evidence. Think about that. Why wouldn't people say they saw me with those girls, when my picture's been plastered over every newspaper across the nation! All these so-called sightings from people who came forward after the fact—after they'd seen my picture everywhere. That's why I had to escape. It's a setup so they can fry someone—even if it's not the right guy."

I stare at him, wanting to believe him. I have never wanted anything in my life so much as I want to believe Ben. My whole body strains to believe him, the way it strained to push him out into the world.

"But that massage girl identified you. She said you left that night with Angela Cruz. Before your picture was even in the paper! And the handcuffs found in that stolen car, Ben. How do you explain those?"

"You don't believe me, do you!" I see an ugly look come over him, an anger that frightens me. I am silent. Would he kill me too? Do I care?

We stay that way for what seems forever. Just suspended. I don't move. Time must pass, but somewhere else.

"Okay," he says at last. "Okay." He begins pacing back and forth, as if something has shifted. "I get that you want to understand. Everybody does. I do too! What a person who could do those things is like. And why. I want to understand too. I'm not saying I have any idea. But I can speculate—if that will help you. Let's just say that if a person did do things like that—there might be … we can't even call them reasons … but forces, let's say, that drove him. That he was not in control of. Maybe there was a period in his life … a few weeks, let's say, when he was out of control. Things seemed … things were … Most of the time this person is normal … maybe even more than normal … Or maybe it's that he passes for normal, I don't know. Maybe everyone does. Anyway, pressure built up. Like an obsession. The need to do something, to … It's hard to understand. Not that I'm saying I know. But I can imagine. I can speculate. Okay? Okay?" He seems to have forgotten I'm in the room. He's pacing faster, back and forth, his features contorted, his face grimacing.

"This person wouldn't really understand himself why he did those things. But something … I don't know. Maybe it started as a game. A challenge. To pick up girls, get them to do things they didn't want to do. Not really hurt them. But make them do things they were ashamed of. To make them cry. Maybe one of them wouldn't go along with … do those things … and that made him very angry. Pure rage, from somewhere deep inside—that had been building, maybe for years. And the thing is, that rage made him powerful! The power was amazing, irresistible. To be the one in power … not the powerless one, not the one crying and ashamed! It would be an incredible high …" He gives a shudder, takes a deep breath, turns and looks out the window. I'm swallowing and swallowing, involuntarily, as if I'm choking back vomit.

After he's calmed himself he turns back and looks at me. "He would be sorry afterwards. But it was done. What could he do? It was done. But then in a few days, maybe he'd find he had to do it again. To achieve that feeling of power and excitement again." He paused. "Of course I don't really know. That's just what I'm thinking."

I must have stopped breathing. A reflex takes over, I gasp for air. "You talk like it's in the past, Ben. Like it's all over."

"It is," he said. "Like a storm that passed."

We stare at each other for a long moment. "Oh Ben!" I groan.

"It's not me, that's the thing. Not me! You have to believe that."

"Why wouldn't this person seek help?"

"Help. Oh, great. Like there is help available. They wouldn't believe him, Mother, they wouldn't care that he couldn't help it, that it wasn't

… his … fault. Anymore than a crazy guy can help hearing voices in his head. They'd *execute* him. Put him in prison, take away his freedom! Do you know what they *do* to guys like that in prison, Mother! Think about it." Sweat has broken out on his forehead. I have to look away, sickened.

"Tell me, Ben," I finally say. "When did it start for this person? Why did it start?"

"How would I know! I'm not saying I know what this person is like. I'm just guessing! Theorizing."

"Well theorize, then!"

"Look, we don't have to have this conversation at all. I didn't know you were here. I came because I didn't have any place else to go. To hide. Because they're after me. Mark my words, they will hunt me down like an animal! They'll kill me one way or another. They won't stop until they do."

Suddenly he's by my chair, kneeling down, laying his head in my lap like he's five years old again. "Help me, Mother. Please, help me! I'm so afraid! I don't want to die."

I want to push him away, but I can't help stroking his hair. Soothing him, the way I did when he was a child. My heart aches and burns, but I feel dry as a bone, beyond tears.

"I'll arrange for the sheriff here to take you into custody, Ben. I'll make sure everything is handled correctly. I'll be with you, Ben. We'll explain everything to them. I'll get help for you, I promise." I lift my hand from his head.

He stands up, moves away. He has shut a door, retreated back into a place I can't go.

Out the window, I notice the sky brightening. Night is giving way to day. Soon the sun will be coming up over the lake. It's a day I wish did not have to come.

"How is Walter?" comes Jean's voice from the hallway. She crosses quickly, ignoring Ben, the blue down jacket I loaned her over her night-gown, and goes into the living room to his bed.

I come out of my trance, jump up and go to her, putting my arm around her thin shoulders, the first time I have ever done so. "He's dead, honey. He died during the night."

She stands silently looking down at him. She pulls the sheet up over his face. "I'll miss him," she says.

Then she turns and looks at Ben.

"Ben's here," I say idiotically.

"I know."

"She found me. In number twelve. That's where I've been staying."

Now I understand Jean's misery when she came in from her walk, and her questions over dinner.

"If you ever lay a finger on this girl, I'll kill you myself," I say to Ben. I go over to where he's leaning against the counter, and gather his wool sweater below his throat in my fist, pulling his face toward mine. I feel an animal violence in me. I actually growl out the words through clinched teeth. "I gave you life and I can take it back. Do you hear me?"

He pushes my hand away, releasing my grip. "I very much doubt that, Mother. And why would I hurt Jean?"

I turn away. The image of my father's gun in the hall closet crosses my mind. It seems to hover in the air, as if I could take it in my hands, a mirage that I could grasp. There would be a supreme satisfaction in putting a bullet in his head. Just killing him now, quickly and purposefully. The one answer that would end all the questions.

We all hang there in silence, as if both of them can read my thoughts. Waiting. Then I take a deep breath and exhale.

"He has a gun, Mrs. D," Jean says.

We all consider this for a long moment. "That changes things somewhat," I finally say. "You have to give me the gun, Ben. Before someone gets hurt."

"You have to do better than that, Mother. It won't matter if I have a gun or not. Those cowboys will come roaring into Dodge, looking to be heroes. Taking me out will give them something to talk about at the local bar on Friday night. I might as well do the job for them."

"I know someone," I say quickly. "A detective back in Tacoma. I'll call him right now. He'll talk to the sheriff here, he'll tell him …"

"What? How to do his job? I tell you what. You call that policeman in Tacoma. Get him here by tonight. Can you do that one thing for me, Mother? I'll turn myself in to him, this 'friend' of yours. But only him."

"I can't trust you, Ben. How do I know you'll even stay put until he gets here?"

He looks down for a long moment. Then he looks right in my eyes. "I can't run anymore. But it has to be done right. None of these gun-happy local hotdogs. I do trust you, Mother, even if you don't trust me. I trust that you'll do right by me this one last time." He can't speak for a moment. He comes over to me, puts his hands on my shoulders, and holds my eyes with his. "Mother? That person we were talking about? He is normal, most of the time. He is the person people think he is. He is the son you think he is."

Then he grabs his coat and is gone, just like that. Without a word, Jean and I go to the picture window, and I pull the heavy curtain open. The sun is just clearing the cloud bank to the east over the choppy blue water. We watch Ben tromp through the snow back toward the cabins. I stare at his retreating figure, lost in a place I have never been before.

I don't know how long we stand there, until Jean says, "We have to prepare Walter." That breaks my breathless reverie; it brings me back from wherever I had gone. I remember to breathe again. She speaks calmly, taking command.

"We'll wash him and dress him. We'll have him ready when the undertaker comes."

I see that things have to be done. Dad has died and attention must be paid. I'll need to go through his closet, find his newest suit. I remember how we buried Mother in a coffin Dad made from a black ash tree. He made another coffin ten or so years ago, preparing for the time when we'd need it. It's in the shed by the garage. How like Dad to take care of things, even his own burial.

But first I have to do the hardest thing I've ever done in my life.

Chapter Eighteen

Jean

There was something Ganny used to say when she'd hear of a particularly disgusting act on the part of a human being: "For this the flesh grew tall?" She got it from some preacher man passing through during a revival. Those words came to mind when we watched Ben slink back down the drive to number twelve at the end of the road. He had his neck scrunched into his coat, his hands jammed into his pockets, and his bare, curly head bent low, the way Judas must of looked after he betrayed Jesus. He must of felt like the lowest of the low, Judas, and so did Ben from what I could tell. It wouldn't have totally shocked me if we found him dead by his own hand. He knew how to kill, plenty, so why not kill himself? But I knew he probably wouldn't, couldn't, because he'd seen pain and death up close, and what he had enjoyed in others he would not find so pleasing for himself.

Mrs. D had gone and sat down at the kitchen table and was just staring off into space. I could tell she was thinking the most serious thoughts of her life. It scared me how she looked so far away. Though she sat perfectly still, I could see she was wrestling, like Jacob with the angel. I wanted her to come back to me.

Outside the sun was lighting up the lake. It was going to be another clear, cold day. Across the meadow, between Walter's house and the first of the cabins, lay a carpet of unmarked snow, sparkling where the morning sun touched it. I could see a path at the edge of the woods that the deer made. They'd eaten the bark off the trees and stripped the lower branches they could reach. The lake was a sparkling dark blue as the sun climbed higher. It was windy, the waves slapping against the rocky shore. I shut my eyes and saw Walter's white boat moving out over the chop, the way Mrs. D had described it to me. I thought of Mrs. D growing up here. To have a father like Walter, that would be a good thing. Someone who would never dream of raising his hand to you. Now he was gone, and Mrs. D was an orphan.

I decided I'd just stand still as a deer myself. I didn't want to interrupt the thoughts Mrs. D was so lost in. Lost in thought. That was a fine expression. Like your own thoughts were a tangled wood you couldn't find your way through. The woods at home were like that, full of briars, underbrush, kudzu vine, and dense, scrubby pine. I knew that kind of lost and that kind of thought, which didn't even come to you in words. Deeper, from some part of you too deep for words. That was the kind of thought Mrs. D was lost in. And when she found her way out, she would be a different person.

After I don't know how long, she just stood up and went in to see her father's body. I followed after her and took my place by her side. Walter looked peaceful now, after his trials. There comes a time when a body is ready. But what about the young ones, I couldn't help thinking, like those girls of Ben's, who were taken by surprise, who hadn't had a chance to prepare? Hadn't even had their lives, the way Walter got to have all of his. The way Jimmy didn't get to have his. A horrible sob broke from my chest and flew out my mouth, though I tried to stop it with my hand.

Mrs. D gasped. Then quick as a flash she threw her arms around me, saying, "Oh, Jean! Oh, Jean!" She patted my head like I was a little dog, and we cried in each other's arms, both just broke down to nothing but wet tears and awful sounds. I didn't even know what I was bawling so about. Whatever it was, it took me over, like I'd never done my rightful share and now I was making up for it. Mrs. D, too, she shook and wept and held on to me like she was going down for the third time, until I feared my spine might snap. My neck was soaking wet where she buried her face. Between us the baby kicked. It must have got her in the stomach, too, because she jumped back. When we both realized what had happened, we started laughing. She grabbed onto me and said again, "Oh Jean, Jean, oh Jean," but in a different way.

She let go of me and began pacing a little, going to the window and looking out, then coming back to where I stood. After a moment she spoke. "I'm going to do what Ben asked," she said, looking at me in a fierce way that scared me. "I'm going to call that detective I know in Tacoma to come here to take Ben into custody. I have to take that chance. I know what'll happen if I call the sheriff's office. He'll kill himself. Or they'll kill him or he'll kill one of them."

"What if Ben cuts and runs, Mrs. D? Before that man gets to us?"

She was silent a long time. I broke her spell when I handed her a Kleenex. "I have to take that chance," she said. "I believe if I do what Ben asks, he'll do what he says. I may be the biggest fool on earth. But I'm his mother. I don't want him shot like a mad dog. I can't let that happen."

I nodded solemnly. "You remind me of this chicken I once knew, Mrs. D. One time our dog Blaze came upon her with her chicks out by the shed. You should have seen the way she spread her wings and lit out after Blaze, chased him all the way back to the house, and him a big old boxer. She would rather die herself than let anything happen to those chicks. You have a lot of that hen in you, Mrs. D."

She smiled a small, sad smile, shook her head and sighed. "I feel so alone," she said. "Like Robinson Crusoe, shipwrecked and washed up on some desert island."

"You're not alone, Mrs. D," I said. "I'm here. I'm your Friday."

She looked at me in surprise and then she cried a little. When she wiped her eyes she squinted at me. "You've read *Robinson Crusoe*, Jean?"

"We had to read it in ninth grade."

"Well," she said, snuffling. "Oh. Well, then. Did you … like it?"

"It was in-ter-esting, I'd say. More than some …"

Mrs. D nodded. Then she held her head in her hands, her elbows splayed out on Walter's bed. She moaned and groaned. I figured maybe this was the worst of it. She had to get it out.

"Come here," she finally said. When I moved over to her chair, she put her hands against my stomach over my flannel nightgown, where the baby had quieted down. Her hands felt warm and soothing. I thought of Baby Inga growing inside me, still a weird thought if ever there was one, but mostly I'd gotten used to it. I still didn't want to think too far ahead, to the moment when it had to come out. It must of felt Mrs. D's hands against it and wondered, "*Who is this? What's going on? Hello out there!*"

"I can remember when Ben was in me as clearly as if it were yesterday. All that secret life brewing inside you. Just the two of you, so close.

It makes you feel so special, so alive. Not that it isn't uncomfortable at times."

"Heartburn and piles."

Mrs. D snorted. "There are things you can do for those, you know."

"Like give birth." I frowned. "Well, it's morning time. You go get dressed and make your phone call. I'm gonna make pancakes and Jimmy Deans. It's gonna be a long day."

She sighed, and still she sat there. "All right," she finally said. "Would you call the minister for me. Sjoblad—he wrote his home number on that church bulletin by the phone. He'll take care of the arrangements. What time is it? I have to call Ron—it's two hours earlier there."

All at once she said, "I still love Ben. But love is no excuse, I know that. There are things bigger than love." She cried a little more. Then, "I just hope I'm not making a mistake." She got to her feet. "We need to tend to Dad. We only have today … before everything else takes over."

I wished I could tell her her dad was in a better place, the way you're supposed to, but I couldn't. Was Walter in a better place? Was Jimmy? Those girls? Where is such a place? I had a feeling heaven for Walter was heading out to his fishing nets on a fine summer day in his little white boat. A day when he didn't even think about dying and going to that "better place" someday. What was heaven about it was that Heaven was the farthest thing from his mind.

I found the preacher's note just where Mrs. D said, and I dialed the number. "Walter finally died," I said as soon as he picked up the phone. "Can you come over here and make the arrangements?" The preacher said he'd be right over, like he couldn't wait to be around death.

I didn't quite know what to do with myself. I heard the door to the bathroom shut and the shower starting up, probably to hide Mrs. D's crying. I decided to tidy up the place. People would be coming around, and Mrs. D would want things to look nice. Truth was, there wasn't much for me to do except gather up the Two Harbors newspapers and put them in a trash bag. I decided I'd cook, that was always a good thing to do. People have to eat. I started the sausages in a cold skillet and poured some Aunt Jemima into a bowl. If only we had some buttermilk. Plain water would have to do.

I wondered what Ben was doing right then, down at the cabin. Maybe he was having his own breakfast, out of one of those cans. Like they said, this was the first day of the rest of his life, or maybe it was the last day of his life. We'd have to wait and see. Mrs. D was going to call that policeman. It would all be over by this evening and I was glad.

While Mrs. D was still in the bathroom there came a knock at the back door. I knew it wasn't Ben 'cause he was not the knocking kind. Reverend Sjoblad. I let him in and he took off his snowy boots in Walter's little hall office. I hung his parka on a hook. He had that preacher look I didn't much care for, earnest and yet watching for something, maybe sin. I knew he wondered about my belly. I made a point of flashing my left hand around, so he could see the ring Jimmy bought me. It was more like a chip than what you'd call a stone, but I was a proper married woman, so he couldn't get me there.

Then I remembered that Jimmy was dead. So I must be a proper married widow. It didn't seem real that Jimmy was dead. It was just a word, dead. Sometimes I tried to make myself cry. "Jimmy's dead," I'd say to myself, but nothing came, no feeling, no tears. I was amazed at that flood of them earlier, how they came up suddenly when I wasn't even expecting it, took over, then disappeared. Sometimes I felt my way in the dark, tentatively, toward the jungle, toward Nam, toward a bullet ... But no. Not now. I had plenty of other things to deal with.

The preacher had a big nose with hair sticking out. Those black-rimmed glasses made me think of masks you buy at Halloween that look like Groucho Marx. In my experience preachers were not normally handsome fellows.

He followed me into the kitchen. I offered him some coffee, which he immediately drank down in a couple of big gulps. I poured him another mug. We sat in silence, waiting for Mrs. D, but she didn't come out. How could she make that phone call now that this guy was here? The only phone was right there in Walter's hall office and the preacher would hear her.

"May I see Walter?" he nodded his head toward the hospital bed in the living room, where Walter was lying dead to this world.

"Help yourself," I couldn't help saying, though I blushed because it sounded so sassy. Sometimes you just take a dislike to someone and you don't know why.

He got up and went in to stand over Walter, praying, I suppose. I sulked in the kitchen, resentful. I loved Walter, though I didn't really know him. But then again, I *did* know him, the true him, the him that put his hands on my baby belly. Some people you just know. Seeing his face I knew everything about Walter I ever needed to know to love him. I didn't think the preacher loved Walter the way I did, or Mrs. D, who loved him the most.

When he came back in the kitchen, he sat down and looked at me hard. "I don't suppose there's any news on Ben," he kind of whispered, not wanting Mrs. D to hear but unable to stop himself, the way vultures can't help picking at roadkill. It's their nature, and I could tell it was this preacher man's nature to want to draw near our pain and suffering. Mrs. D was like a bad accident on the highway he couldn't help but gawk at.

I just shook my head, no. He thought he could lure some gossip out of me, but I didn't open my mouth. He looked around, his eyes narrowing, snoopy, taking in everything. Suddenly my own eyes opened wide. There on the kitchen counter were gloves, men's big gloves, yellow pigskin ones, not like any gloves me or Mrs. D would wear, dark on the fingers where they were wet. Ben wore them here and then forgot them when he slinked away at dawn! I saw him again, the way he had his neck all hunched down into his coat, and his hands bare. I felt the preacher man's eyes bore into them and hold. I saw a lightbulb come on in his head, the way you pull a string in a dark closet. I tried to think what to say, to make the light go out again. I went stupid with fear.

"Whose are these?" he said, going over and picking them up.

"Mine."

"Yours! They're awfully big for you, aren't they?"

Something in the preacher had changed. He was in a hurry to leave, before he'd even spoken to Mrs. D, told her how sorry he was about her father. He had a hunch, I was sure of it, and I knew it had to do with Ben. He couldn't wait to snoop around outside. He'd see the footprints, he'd follow them all the way down to cabin twelve. Then all hell would break loose.

Chapter Nineteen

Inga

"Mrs. D, come quick!" Jean was calling to me from the kitchen. "He knows!"

I hurried down the hall to find her backed up against the sink, her hand to her mouth, her eyes wide and worried. "What? Who knows? About Ben? How?"

"He was here," she told me. "The preacher. While you was getting dressed!" Jean cut her eyes toward the pigskin gloves on the Formica counter, next to the toaster oven. I stared at them, confused. Those were Dad's gloves! What were they doing here? Ben must have gotten them from the workshop shed. They were a soft aged yellow, palms up, like hands making an offering, or beseeching, dark from melted snow. How often had I seen those gloves, and now here they were, where they shouldn't be.

I started to ask how she could be sure, but then I'd learned that Jean was not one to speculate. Sjoblad would notify the police. If Ben didn't shoot him or himself first. I felt my knees give out, I sank down hard on the kitchen floor. A dull, hot pain exploded in my chest. The day darkened, closing in on me.

The next thing I was aware of was the office door banging. On rubbery legs I pulled myself up and lurched to the picture window. There was Jean, in only her socks and nightgown, chasing after Reverend Sjoblad, who had just reached the first cabin. She grabbed his arm, padded in a gray down jacket inflated like a float, and pointed back up to the house.

I ducked out of sight. What was she doing, what was going on? My heart squeezed like a fist. Maybe I was having that heart attack Ron had thought I was having that first night he showed up at my house. Maybe it would all be over, finally, at last.

I found myself sprawled on the living room carpet, not quite sure if I was playacting or not, just as they came crashing through the office door. I felt strangely limp all over, not real. It was just that it was so comfortable there on the floor. I didn't have to struggle anymore, I wouldn't have to feel anything ever again. I smelled Honey, Dad's old yellow lab who'd been dead for more than a decade. She used to lie here by the picture window, where the sun fell in a patch on the rug. I felt that same blackness overtaking me I'd felt the night Ron told me about Ben being a suspect. This time I gave in to it willingly, the way Virginia Woolf must have felt when she was sinking into that river, her pockets full of stones.

"It's her heart!" Jean shouted, the loudest thing I had ever heard come out of her mouth. It startled me, for there was real panic in her voice. I struggled to rise up, to reassure her, but my whole body felt heavy, as if a big boot were pressing down on my chest, pinning me there on the orange shag rug that had been there as long as I could remember.

Reverend Sjoblad was kneeling over me. I hoped he wouldn't try artificial respiration! I would die for sure if his big Swedish lips came within ten inches of my own mouth.

"I'm all right," I murmured, trying to prove it by sitting up. But I felt too dizzy and weak. The pain seared again.

I thought of the girls, Michele, Sissy, Monica, Angela, and those girls in Modesto. The pain squeezed in my heart again.

"You have to get her to the hospital!" Jean was screaming, pulling on Sjoblad's shoulder. "She might die at any moment! She's had a heart attack before."

Well, here was an unsuspected talent of Jean's: actress. Or was she right? And why couldn't I tell? I'd figure it out later. Right now I just felt so tired—dead tired. I had never fully appreciated that expression before.

Oh how I wished everyone would just go away, so I could curl up in a ball and sleep. I wanted to sleep and sleep, and when I woke up, things would be the way they used to be. Mom, Dad, and I cozy in the kitchen with the snow coming down outside, the view of the lake obscured by a whiteout, Dad repairing his fishing nets, getting ready for summer. We'd have the radio on, the station in Duluth that told of items people had for sale, church socials, VFW bingo nights. Mom would get out the cast-iron skillet and cook whitefish I had gotten for her out of the freezer in the shed. It was before she got cancer, before Charles, before Ben, before I ever left home. I'm just a girl in my parents' house, and all is well… .

I felt myself being lifted by those inflated arms. I was surprised by my dead weight. I could feel Sjoblad's heart beating against my side; he was frightened, poor man! I was not too heavy at least, only 115 pounds, and he a big young Swede, well over 200. It might not seem like it, but we were doing him a favor. We were saving him from finding Ben.

Soon I was rattling down Highway 61 toward Two Harbors in Sjoblad's truck, slumped against the passenger door like a sack of groceries that had fallen over. Maybe it was the cold air that revived me, but the pressure in my chest—the boot that had come down on me on the living room floor and pinned me there—had let up. I rested my head against the pillow Jean had run out to the truck with, and snuggled in the blanket she'd tucked around me. Sjoblad told her to stay at the house, that someone should stay with Dad's body, and I hadn't been in any shape to argue. But now I realized I couldn't just leave her back at the house, not with Ben so close.

"We have to go back!" I said. "I'm okay. It's passed."

Sjoblad gave me a look. "I don't think heart attacks pass."

"But it can't be a heart attack! Look, I'm talking, I'm alert, I'm fine. We have to go back!" In my chest, a deep burning ache.

"Not before you're checked out by a doctor," he said, and I could see he meant it. Oh lord, what now?

Not for the first time, I had no idea what was going on. How had I gotten into such a mess? I was about to call Ron, but then Sjoblad showed up and things veered out of control, more than they already were. And now here I was speeding toward Two Harbors and Jean back at the house, alone, with Ben down at the cabin. Now my heart was trying to escape, throwing itself against the walls of my chest. The boot came down. Ben wouldn't hurt Jean! I mean, Ben … But what did he say, about power, about rage, about something taking over … I felt the blackness closing in, fast, and I shook my head, willed myself to stay conscious.

"You doing okay?" He was driving a little too fast, skidding on places where the snow from the cliffs alongside the highway had melted and run down on to the road, refreezing overnight.

I pulled myself straighter in the seat, ordered my heart to calm down. "Well, it appears I'm alive. But I won't be if you don't slow down, Reverend."

"Call me Spike."

"Spike!" I sat up straighter. A pain jabbed through my chest, but this felt more like a muscle strain. Maybe I had pulled something in my chest when I sank to the floor. "I thought you were Swedish!"

"Ya, Swedish," he said in an exaggerated Scandinavian lilt. "My parents named me after a friend up dar on the Range. Had a reputation for adding a little something extra to da coffee."

"Please, can't we turn back? I'm sure I'm okay."

"You've had heart trouble before?"

"No! Well, yes—once. I had to go to the hospital the night I first learned that Ben was a suspect." There. I'd said his name. "But there was nothing really wrong, not a real heart attack, they said. Just ... stress."

"Heartbreak," Sjoblad said solemnly.

I looked out the window. I didn't want pity from him, or anyone. Sympathy was the way people tried to get in, to get close to a murderer's mother. A cold wind off the lake was shrieking outside the car window as we barreled toward Silver Creek Cliff. Down below, the lake beat against the hard black rocks of the shore. The girls. I'd read how adrenaline kicks in when you're in mortal danger, how your endorphins surge. You don't feel pain at those moments when you're struggling for your life. I hoped it was quick and painless, though of course it wasn't. It was just the opposite.

"Why in the world do you believe in God?" I asked. "You're a man of God. And you know what happened to those girls. How they suffered. How do you reconcile that with God?"

He glanced over at me. He had a big, open face, with those thick lips that made me think of a duck. He'd taken off his knit cap, and white blond hair was pressed against his skull. Ugly black glasses. He couldn't be more than thirty, thirty-five. I studied his face. He looked as if he had never entertained a bad thought in his life, as if *What you see is what you get*. But no, that wasn't right—not anymore. I no longer trusted my impressions of others. For all I knew he was a murderer on the side. In his spare time. We rode in silence for a few miles.

"It's not so much that I believe," he said at last, long after I'd forgotten I'd asked. "I mean, I do—believe. But it's more like I just *know*. The same way I know you and I exist. I know God exists, and that He is love."

I wanted to slap him! Anger roiled in me, a mocking, sneering anger that wanted to smash his innocence! I looked out the window at the steep precipice of Silver Creek Cliff. Way down below, the lake beckoned. For a mad moment I thought about grabbing the steering wheel, taking us both over that cliff. Was I losing my mind?

Oh, what in the world was happening back at the house!

"Your dad and I talked about Ben, you know," Sjoblad said, looking over at me. "He came to me for spiritual guidance."

"No, I didn't know."

"Not that your father was a big talker, of course," Spike said. "But he was deeply troubled—spiritually—like we all were. Are. Your father was a fine fellow. And for something like Ben to happen … in the family. Well, he didn't understand it, and none of us up here did either."

I nodded. A deep sorrow filled me. A deep ache all through me, and I thought, *this is all I can stand. This is as far as people can go.*

"What did he say?"

"He wanted to know why God would allow such things. And he was worried about you. But he still loved Ben. He had a hard time believing it could be Ben. Like all of us."

I stared out the window. Wasn't it funny—silly, really—how we expected things to make sense. To understand things. We wanted answers to our questions, when in reality we were surrounded by mysteries too big and deep to ever fathom. We rowed the little boats of our lives out across a deep, cold, dangerous ocean, pretending that we were going to make it to shore.

"So what did you tell him?"

"We don't understand God's ways. His plan. We aren't able to see the big scheme of things."

"You can't believe that those girls being murdered is part of God's plan!"

He sighed. "We struggle to understand His ways. But all will be revealed someday. It's not for us humans to know."

"You know," I said hesitantly, more to the lake, the waves, than to Sjoblad. "Some say it's the mother's fault. A lack of love, bonding. But I loved Ben and I love him now, if you can believe that."

"He's still a child of God, no matter what," Sjoblad said.

In spite of myself, I found some comfort in this.

"Do you believe in evil? Like the devil. That kind of evil?"

"I don't know," Sjoblad said thoughtfully. "I've known some mighty mean people. But usually they were hurting bad. Something in their lives made them the way they were. But I wouldn't consider them evil. But then you've got your Hitlers, your Mussolinis. So evil does exist. But do I think Ben is evil?" He took a deep breath. "That's not for me to say."

We were coming into Two Harbors. We passed the fish shop on the left, and the Super One on the right. The clinic was up a hill off Highway 61 in about a mile. When we got there, Sjoblad would call the police.

"Are you married?" My heart hammering. "Do you have kids?"

"Ya, you bet," he said, and I couldn't tell if he was joking with the accent or not. "One of each. Boy and girl. Married my high school sweetheart."

He glanced over at me. The closer we got to the clinic, the more desperate I felt. The police would come, Ben wouldn't surrender, he'd kill himself, or someone would get killed, maybe Jean. I couldn't let it happen, I had to be there. I could make him surrender without anyone getting hurt.

"How old are your children?" I was stuttering now.

"Eric is seven, Cindy four. Great kids."

"You must love them very much!"

"Oh they're not angels, I'm not saying that. But they're pretty good kids. I can't imagine life without them."

"Exactly! It's only natural to want to protect your kids," I gasped. "I mean animals will protect their young with their own lives!"

"But we're not animals," he shot back. "We have free will."

"I know! But you would try to stand by them—no matter what. I mean, regardless."

"I wouldn't do wrong for them," Sjoblad said sternly. "I mean, I hope I wouldn't. I wouldn't harbor them if they were fugitives. I would try to show them the way. Sometimes love is doing the hard thing. Sometimes that's the best test of love."

"It was cold in the house this morning! I sat up all night with Dad, and I thought I'd maybe start a fire, bring in some wood. I got Dad's gloves and hauled in logs from the pile. Wet logs—wet from the snow …" I was stumbling.

He looked over at me with what I thought was pity. How could he not despise me? I despised myself. I couldn't meet his eyes.

"I'm sorry," he said.

We were silent as we pulled into the clinic's circular entrance.

"Just stay with me," I begged. "When I see the doctor. Don't leave me for awhile. I'm afraid! Please!"

"Just remember, Inga," he said, turning off the truck and cupping his hand gently on my shoulder. "God is with you. He's always with you."

"No," I cried, putting my face in my hands. "No, please, no, no, don't … Wait …"

Chapter Twenty

Jean

Mrs. D and the preacher man hadn't been gone five minutes before I heard the office door open. I'd just had time to strip off my snow-packed socks and stuff my fifty-dollar bill down a pair of dry ones. I ran into the kitchen where I grabbed a little no-count paring knife. At least Walter kept his knives sharp, what you might expect out of a fisherman. I stuffed it quickly into the pocket of the down jacket I had put on over my nightgown.

"What's going on?" Ben came busting into the kitchen like he had every right to know. "I saw that guy carrying Mother out. She looked unconscious!"

"That guy is Reverend Sjoblad and he knows you're here," I said. I pointed to the gloves still lying on the kitchen counter. I felt some satisfaction when I saw Ben's face, how he looked like he'd been socked.

"What's happening?" he said again, his eyes darting everywhere. "Tell me!"

"Your mom may have had a heart attack." I turned my back to him and began washing the skillet I'd cooked the pancakes in. I figured if he wanted to kill me, let him. There was nothing much I could do about it now. I couldn't stop my heart from pounding, but at least he couldn't see that. I certainly didn't want to give him the satisfaction of knowing I was afraid. I'd treat him the way you do a mean dog, don't show fear, don't make eye contact.

For a few minutes the only sounds were me clanking the pan in the sink. Then Ben said, "I have to leave. Right now."

I was silent, taking my time scraping the burned parts off the pan with a steel wool. *So go*, I thought. *No one's stopping you.*

"You're coming with me."

My hands froze in midair.

"No way," I said. "I'm staying right here."

He came up and took me by the arm, firmly, but it didn't hurt through Mrs. D's jacket. I wondered if he had the gun with him. "Shut up, Jean. Get dressed. Right now. Wear the warmest clothes you got. Get your stuff together. Pack it up."

I thought about resisting like a cat you can't force into a box. But I didn't want to press what little luck I had left. I went in Walter's room and put on an extra pair of dirty underpants that were lying on the floor, my ugly beige maternity pants and the red turtleneck Mrs. D bought me, which I tugged down to try to cover my belly. I slipped the little paring knife into my bra, where it immediately nicked me. I'd have to carry it in my jacket pocket and hope he didn't find it. I threw my stuff into the duffel Mrs. D loaned me, making sure I got the lavender lotion she gave me for Christmas. I struggled into the fisherman's sweater and put the down jacket back on, immediately feeling overheated, like I might croak.

When I came back in the kitchen I said, "Ben, leave me here. You don't need me. I'll just slow you down."

He came up to me and I shrank back. "We're leaving. Now." I stumbled against the duffel bag at my feet. He put both his hands on my shoulders and looked me right in the eyes. Whatever was in his soul, his eyes weren't the way to see it. Or maybe they were.

"You do what I say, and nobody will get hurt." Then he gave me a look.

"Let's go," I said.

Goodbye, Walter, I whispered as we went out the office door. He died at the right time. And where was Mrs. D? What was going on with her? Maybe the sheriff was on the way. I suddenly thought of bullets zooming all around me, a shoot-out like in cowboy movies. Ben would use me as a human shield. I quickened my pace.

We trudged through the snow down to Ben's cabin. He was breathing heavily, sweat beading his forehead. He quickly threw his stuff into a backpack, sweeping the cans of food right in on top of everything else. I asked if I could pee before we left. He grimaced but nodded okay.

The bathroom was tiny, with a big water heater taking up most of the space next to the little shower. I sat on the cold toilet; I really did have to pee. That was the baby sitting on my bladder all the time. I considered the window, which opened inward from the top for air. Too small to ever squeeze out of, especially in my new big shape, like I had a pillow stuffed down my britches. It had a pretty red calico curtain on a rod across the top. I wondered if Mrs. D sewed it. For a moment I rested my troubled mind on it.

"Hurry up in there!"

I came out pulling up my stretch pants. I felt in the pocket of my jacket for the little knife. I put both hands on Baby Inga, trying to reassure her. *We'll be all right*, I told her inside in that special way I had of talking to her, and she answered right back, *Of course we will.* Who was reassuring who?

We trudged up the driveway to Highway 61 and started walking backwards north on the shoulder, with Ben holding his thumb out. "Okay, here's the story," Ben said. "We ran out of gas. We need to get to Grand Marais because you have a doctor's appointment. For the baby and all."

"Why don't we just take Mrs. D's car. Or Walter's truck?"

Ben just rolled his eyes.

"Okay, then, but what exactly are we supposed to do for money?"

"I have money."

I stared at him. I didn't want to know. I pulled my knit cap further over my ears and covered them with my mittens. "What if your mother really has had a heart attack? I ought to be there to take care of her—"

My words were lost in the noise of a big truck almost blowing us into the ditch. A few cars passed us by, without the drivers so much as glancing our way. We looked normal enough, like regular folks, though we weren't, neither one of us really. I just didn't want him to hurt whoever picked us up. That would be so rotten. Not some unsuspecting good Samaritan. I'd always been impressed with the good Samaritan in the Bible. That was one thing about the Bible, it had some good stories. I figured I was okay as long as he needed me.

We got a couple of short rides, folks who lived up there in the woods and were friendly souls who took us as far as they were going. They asked us questions, nice-like, where we was from and what we was up to hitchhiking on the highway on a winter day. Ben could lie like the devil, telling them how we'd run out of gas and had to get to Grand Marais. He was so convincing and charming he almost lulled me into believing his tale. I felt so tired from the cold I just wanted to put my head against the backseat window and fall asleep. I was not about to say anything that would get anyone shot, myself included.

We got picked up by a gentleman who looked like someone's grandpa. He talked a lot, all about how he was a retired professor. He did look brainy, with his mane of white hair, nicely trimmed gray beard, and those little rimless wire glasses that hippies wear. He had lived in the Twin Cities, he explained, until he retired and moved to the north woods with his wife. She had died last year, and now he was alone.

Ben talked about where he went to college, University of Washington, and how he majored in English, liked writing, and got a job as a journalist right out of college. None of this was true, I knew from the newspaper articles about him. I wondered if the professor might recognize Ben from the news, but he looked so different with his big beard, and of course there was me, his pregnant wife. Ben knew how to use words I didn't even know. He and the professor had a great old time talking about writers they both knew. Ben laughed at the professor's jokes and kept right up with him tit for tat.

"'If a writer has to rob his mother, he will not hesitate,'" the professor said. "The 'Ode on a Grecian Urn' is worth any number of old ladies."

"Old men too," Ben laughed.

What the heck did that mean? I didn't get it but I didn't think I liked it.

"Listen, you kids could spend the night at my place," the old guy finally offered as we approached Grand Marais at the bottom of a steep hill. "Got plenty of room. I haven't anything special to do. I could wait for you until you get finished at the doctor's. It'll be awful late in the afternoon to be hitchhiking home." He proceeded to tell Ben where he lived—eight miles up the Gunflint Trail, turn left at the mailbox that has the number 26309 on it. So trusting, he was, and so lonely. A perfect sitting duck.

"Gosh," Ben said, smooth as silk, "that's awful nice of you. We *will* be finishing up late here—what with the doctor and all."

"Absolutely not!" I said fiercely from the backseat. "Mama and Daddy are coming to get us. Don't worry about us, sir. We've got it covered!" I'd done my share of lying in my life. You kinda had to, around Mama. I got good at it, so it came easy to me just now.

Ben and the old gent looked at each other, raising their eyebrows.

"Pregnant women," Ben finally managed to say. "Pickles and ice cream and needing to nest in their own bed, I guess."

The old guy chuckled. I leaned back, my arms crossed over my chest. I felt in my pocket. Walter's little paring knife was there, like a friend.

He drove us down a long hill into Grand Marais, a frozen little town that hovered on a curved bay of the big lake. A spit of land cupped the toy harbor, with a lighthouse on the far edge. When the old gent let us out, he got misty-eyed when we said good-bye. I could tell he liked Ben, thought he was a fine young man. Ben seemed to have warmed to the old guy, though maybe that was just an act. It was hard to tell with Ben. Maybe the part of him that was nice was true too, just like the murdering part. People aren't black and white, though it would make things simpler if they were.

I watched everything, wondering in my heart about human beings, the mess they managed to make. In another life, it could all be true. I could be Ben's wife, we could be living on the North Shore of Lake Superior, he could be a good man, a good son, a good father. We could be heading to see the doctor, who would check out Baby Inga. For a moment I wanted us to hurry up, we were late for that doctor's appointment.

We went in the one drugstore and sat at the soda fountain. Ben asked me what I wanted and when I refused to speak, he ordered burgers, fries, and shakes for us both. At first I wouldn't eat, but then I forgot what the point of that was, I was so hungry. I had to admit those fries were the best in the world. He pulled out a wallet and paid with a hundred-dollar bill. I thought of my own fifty-dollar bill that I had never returned to Mrs. D. I had spent the other one on her music box. I kept that bill in the bottom of my right sock all the time, so I'd never lose it and would have it in an emergency, which surely this was. I wondered if there was a bus station in town and where it might be. Maybe I could escape and catch a bus back to Mrs. D.

But Ben had other plans. We had to keep moving, we didn't have much time. We both knew that as soon as that preacher man could, he'd call the police on Ben. I wondered what was going on with Mrs. D. If she was okay, she'd come home to find us gone, and *that* might give her another heart attack. We walked north out of town in the gathering dark and stood on the highway again, freezing, and this time I put my thumb out. Cars just passed us by. Soon it would be pitch black. I wondered where we'd spend the night. Maybe we'd freeze to death, just turn into ice on the side of the road.

I gave Ben the silent treatment for as long as I could stand it. Then I said, "What the hell are we going to do out here in the dark at night!"

"Just shut up," he said. "I hate a whiner."

"And I hate ..." I said it under my breath, "you."

Finally an old beater stopped. When he opened the passenger door, in the overhead light the driver looked crazy, with long hippy hair and a crazy-ass beard braided into a pigtail below his chin. He and Ben might as well have been brothers. *Out of the frying pan, into the fire.*

"Where you guys heading?" He had on one of those red-and-blue smelly wool ponchos that come from Mexico. He was just a kid, couldn't be more than twenty-one, twenty-two.

"Well, you know," Ben said vaguely. "Up the road." I wondered what cock-and-bull story he'd make up this time.

"Hop in."

Ben opened the back door, threw his backpack in, and I shoved my bag against a guitar case and got in. Ben shut my door firmly and got in the passenger seat. "Sure appreciate this," he said. "I'm Travis and this is Jenny."

Travis! What kinda fool name was that?

"Folks mostly call me Stevie." The kid chuckled. "Steve, Steven, Stevie, Stevo, I answer to about anything. You folks live around here?"

"Jenny's folks live in Two Harbors. We're staying with them till we get on our feet. I lost my job in the Cities."

"Oh man, that's tough. What kinda work you looking for."

I stared out the window. *Guys*, was all I could think. *Who needs 'em.*

"Oh, just about anything," Ben said. "What with the baby on the way and all."

"What're you all doing out here on the road at night?"

Ben was silent a beat too long. "Well, we ran out of gas—"

"Ohhh," Stevie said knowingly, "I get why you're out here at night hitchhiking." He turned to look over at Ben. I saw a subtle movement in Ben's shoulder. Maybe he was getting ready to pull the gun. I wondered if they could hear my heart up in the front seat.

Ben, who was normally such a smooth talker, didn't say a word.

"Relax! You're safe with me."

Oh great, I thought. *We're safe with him.*

"We haven't done anything wrong," Ben said, in his most innocent voice.

"No!" Stevie hit his hand against the steering wheel. "You're doing the right thing!"

No one said a word while we all thought this over.

"Believe your luck, man! I'm part of the underground," Stevie said.

Again, dead silence.

"Ohhh," Ben finally exclaimed. "Well! My god. I mean, I can't believe it. Our luck, I mean."

In the backseat I kept quiet. What was going on? I thought the underground went out with the slaves. We studied that in school, how they passed them from safe house to safe house until they got up North. There wasn't really anything under the ground.

"We have safe houses, you know, on this side of the border and across. We help deserters like you. Canada is cool, man."

"God," Ben was exclaiming, over and over. "God, I can't believe this."

"Where were you stationed, man?"

"Fort Lewis. They wanted to turn us into killing machines. You have no idea, Stevo. They teach you to ram your fucking bayonet into a dummy's belly and then pull up to tear the guy's guts out. And for what? To 'save' a country that never asked for us to interfere in the first place!"

"Right on, man. Those fucking pigs."

"If we could just get across the Canadian border, to raise our child in peace, away from the madness of America, the madness of this war!"

He sounded like one of those draft dodgers I'd seen on TV. It made me mad. Jimmy died fighting that war, though I still didn't know what we was fighting over. I wondered if Jimmy was buried in the ground by now. No one at home had told me, because they weren't speaking to me. I knew the cemetery well, Lima Baptist, where Jimmy and I had gone all our lives. I knew his family plot, 'cause we went there to put flowers on his grandparents' graves. For a moment I wanted more than anything to put flowers on Jimmy's grave. But here I was out on the highway with Ben, stolen like a moon pie from the corner grocery store. Like the song said, I felt so lonely I could die.

I unzipped my duffel and rooted around until I found the lotion. The feel of the bottle was a cool comfort. I squeezed out a dollop the size of a dime into my palm, not wanting to use too much up. I rubbed it in good and then covered my nose with my hands, breathing in lavender deeply.

"Here's the deal," Stevo said. "One of us will take you across the border. You're just visiting some friends for a few days. Then you have to find a job, man, and have the employer write a letter telling that you have the job. Then you have to cross back over, and go over again, only this time you apply for landed immigrant status. Canada is pretty cool on all this. They'll treat it as an immigration issue. But if they ask you if you've deserted, you have to tell them the truth, man. If they find out you lied, they'll boot your ass back out."

"Yeah," Ben says softly. "Back to the U.S. Straight to jail."

"Right on. Something you definitely want to avoid."

Chapter Twenty-One

Inga

Everything happened so fast once we entered the clinic. The first thing I knew I was forced to sit in a wheelchair, even though I insisted I could walk. It was just that my legs felt useless, like appendages without bones. As soon as I was in the hands of the medical people, Sjoblad gave me a soulful look and then strode off with a determined set to his broad shoulders. Endgame. After the doctor had checked my vitals, which were fine, no heart attack, I begged him to let me make one phone call before they hooked me up for the EKG he had ordered. He looked reluctant but said maybe that would help calm me down. He let the nurse wheel me to a phone in the visitors' waiting room, where I dialed Ron's number at work.

It was a little after seven a.m. back in Tacoma. Ron picked up on the first ring.

"O'Loughlin."

"He's here," I blurted. "You've got to come! The sheriff will be there any minute. I'm afraid they'll kill him!"

The line was silent.

"Try to calm down. Where, Inga? Where is he?"

"At the house, Ron. Dad's place. I was going to call you. Dad died last night. I didn't know Ben was there. The preacher came and now the sheriff is on the way!"

"Take some deep breaths. It's very important that you tell me a few things clearly. Where are you now?"

"You've got to call them, Ron. The sheriff's office in Two Harbors. Ben has a gun. He won't let them take him alive. He might kill himself. Jean is there."

"I'll take care of it. I'll be there as soon as possible. By this evening. Where are you now? Is Ben with you?"

"With me? No, I'm at the hospital."

"Did he hurt you?"

"No! It's just the same thing as when you first came to the house."

"Are you sure you're okay, Inga. Who's with you?"

"The sheriff will listen to you. Tell him to wait for you. Tell him no gunfire. We're twenty-seven miles up Highway 61. North of Duluth. North Shore Cabins. There's a big sign."

The nurse returned then and took the phone from my hand, wheeled me into an exam room, and helped me lie on a hospital bed, where she hooked me up to an EKG machine. I begged her not to give me a sedative, I had to get home, there was an emergency at home. But I felt a small prick in a vein on my hand and I drifted off in spite of myself.

Later the doctor came in with my EKG results: normal. He said what I had was a panic attack, though I think Sjoblad named it better. He talked about stress and ways to cope, meditation, exercise, but all I wanted was to get out of there. I had to get back to the house! He agreed there was no reason I had to stay. When he signed the papers for me to go, Sjoblad was waiting for me in the reception area, with a sheriff's deputy.

When the deputy questioned me, I felt trapped, afraid to say too much. Whatever had happened back at the house had already transpired. It was out of my hands now. I had to get home to find out if Jean was safe, if there had been gunfire, if anyone had been hurt. I wanted Ron here before I said too much. He'd told me harboring a fugitive was a federal offense, and they'd think I had known Ben was there all along. I begged the deputy to please let me go home.

We followed the sheriff's car back up to Dad's, Sjoblad and I riding in silence. I saw myself as Sjoblad must have seen me—a thin, middle-aged woman with pursed lips, something out of American Gothic perhaps. He probably thought I was responsible for Ben—that I made him the way he was, and maybe I had. But I didn't think so. What made Ben Ben I didn't know. God, maybe. I could lay it on Him, then. Sjoblad said Ben was still one of God's creatures, so let God take the blame. Sjoblad couldn't really see me—the me that was inside this tight, closed surface. It occurred to me that maybe only Jean really knew me. I was not the cold woman who stared out the window now and didn't speak, her face a mass of worry and fury. I sensed, the way you do these things, that the Reverend was a little afraid of me.

When we arrived at the house, it looked like a cop convention was being held there in the yard. There were cars from the state patrol, DNR, Tribal Police, Two Harbors sheriff's office, and the county sheriff's. Men in various uniforms stood in little groups, all turning to stare at us when we pulled in. I leapt from the car and ran toward the house, only to be stopped at the door by an officer who wouldn't let me enter until his chief came up from the cabins. I asked him if they'd found anything, if Ben was there, but he wouldn't tell me a thing. No sign of Jean. It was twenty agonizing minutes later before the chief sauntered up, told me they hadn't found Ben but had found evidence that someone had been hiding out in one of the cabins. He gave me a nasty look and let me in my own home.

In a panic I called for Jean, but there was no answer. Maybe the police had taken her in for questioning or even into custody. In the living room I was shocked to see that Dad's body was gone. One of the police explained they had brought a hearse from Two Harbors and taken him away to a mortuary there. It seemed like a lifetime since I sat with him at his passing, though it was only last night.

I couldn't stop the trembling that had started up, making my legs jump and my knees knock like in a cartoon. Where was Jean? What had become of Ben? Fear was making me stupid, as if I'd been clubbed in the head.

The officer in charge, Finlayson, the one who had sauntered up and let me in my own house, was the one I had to approach. He was maybe sixty years old with a broad Finnish face, guarded and hostile. I figured Sjoblad had told him about Jean. I was incredibly anxious that no one here had mentioned her and I had to be the one to bring her up. We were in a cat-and-mouse game, and I was the mouse. I had to come out with it: "Where's Jean?"

Finlayson just looked at me.

"Jean, the girl who's with me. Have you taken her somewhere?"

"Would you like a cup of coffee while you tell us about Jean?" the chief said. Playing with the mouse. We sat down at the kitchen table.

"Just tell me where she is!"

"You tell us. And for that matter, where is Ben?"

I tried to make sense of things. Jean must be with Ben. She would never go with him voluntarily.

"Why don't you just start at the beginning," Finlayson said. He leaned back in his chair, sipped his coffee, crossed his legs, and prepared to take notes. I explained as best I could how my father had had a stroke and Jean came with me to Minnesota to help. When I got to the part where Dad died, I stopped. Finlayson looked at me with his cool blue eyes, as if he had all the time in the world. Eventually I'd come clean. I told him how Ben showed up, how I hadn't known he was here. Then I skipped to where Sjoblad picked me up off the floor and drove me to Two Harbors.

"We got a call from Detective Ron O'Loughlin this morning, shortly after Spike Sjoblad called."

I nodded.

"Why didn't you call local law enforcement as soon as you were aware Ben was on the premises?"

"I … I don't know," I said. "I was afraid. I thought if …"

He shook his head in disbelief or disgust. "Is there anything else you want to tell me?"

"He's armed," I said. "That's all I can tell you, I don't know anything else."

"There'll be an officer outside to keep an eye on things," Finlayson said. "Our people are getting forensics down at the cabin. I'm sure we'll have more questions for you, so don't take off anywhere. Have O'Loughlin call me when he gets in. Here's the number."

After he left I didn't move for a long time. Eventually I got up and made coffee. I drank a cup fast, to try to revive, then ran out in the cold to take a mug to the policeman in his squad car in the yard. He was a young man about Ben's age. He eyed me shyly—the murderer's mother. I gave him a weak smile. Why did I care whether or not he had a warm drink? I just did.

That left more time for me to sit at the kitchen table, nothing to do but think about everything that had transpired in the past twenty-four hours. What did Ben mean when he said that the person he described was the son I thought he was? How could that possibly be? What was he talking about! He was just trying to manipulate me. My head felt like it would explode.

Where could Ben and Jean possibly be? They didn't take the car or truck, so they must have hitchhiked. Finlayson said they had an all-points bulletin out for them. They'd be found, hopefully alive. Ben wouldn't hurt her. I couldn't believe that he would, even now. How was it that I knew Ben, and didn't know him? He was both the son I knew and someone capable of murder.

Ron was actually here. It was so strange to see him on the North Shore, in Dad's kitchen. It was well after midnight, and he had just arrived—exhausted from the trip, grim looking. He had caught a flight out of Sea-Tac to Minneapolis this morning, then driven the four hours straight here, without even stopping to eat. There were several casseroles the neighbors had left this afternoon, good people who came because of Dad. Of course they'd heard Ben had been here. I could tell they were shocked and frightened but they didn't say a word about it. I offered to heat something up but Ron just spooned cold hamburger, gummy rice, and canned mushrooms, all bound together with mushroom soup and topped with soggy Ritz cracker crumbs, onto his plate. There was a green, congealed salad of some sort with what looked to be Cool Whip, marshmallows, and pineapple pieces. My stomach turned. I hadn't eaten all day.

Outside it was dark and quiet. All the action was long over. There was just one lone sheriff's car left in the yard.

I glanced across the table at Ron. He looked right at me. I met his eye, then looked away, unable to face him.

"So start at the beginning," he said. "Tell me everything."

I told him how Ben showed up in the night, how we had watched Dad die. I described how Jean had found him in the afternoon but hadn't said anything to me because people were here. "She doesn't always do the logical thing," I said. "Not that I do either," I added weakly. I told him about my conversation with Ben, how it had chilled my blood, and the plan to get Ben to surrender safely.

"Did Ben say anything to you about the murders?" Ron asked.

I told him how he never actually admitted anything but had "speculated" about what the killer was like, what he had felt and done.

"Then what happened?"

"Jean woke up—this was early this morning—and came in to where we were. She told me Ben had a gun. I told Ben I'd call the sheriff, I'd make sure he could surrender safely."

"Why didn't you call the police right then? Were you afraid of him?"

I tried to explain my thinking. I was afraid if the local police came, they'd shoot him, or he'd kill himself.

Ron took this in in silence.

"I told Ben I'd call you and you'd come and make sure. He said he'd go peacefully, but only if it was you."

Ron waited to see if there was more.

When I couldn't stand it another moment, I said, "I know I should have called the sheriff here. Now it seems so wrong, the way I handled it. But at the time … it seemed to make sense. I can't explain it any better than that."

"Sometimes there's no explaining," Ron said.

I ached all over. I wanted him to come closer and put his arms around me, reassure me that everything would be all right. But how could he? "It's my fault that he took Jean."

Ron pushed back from the table and stood up. "It's late," he said. "We're both exhausted. You've had a hell of a day. So have I. We can talk more in the morning."

"You can sleep in Dad's room. Jean was staying there. The bathroom's right down the hall. There are clean towels in the chest in there, if you want to take a shower."

While Ron was showering I looked around Dad's room. His absence commingled with Jean's absence. Ben's too. They were all gone.

I looked through the closet. Jean hadn't brought many clothes to begin with and I could tell what was missing. At least she wore the fisherman's sweater and the down jacket. I wondered if she was cold. Where could they be out on this freezing night? My head pounded with tension. The room was a mess. The police had rifled through everything.

Ron came in while I was turning back the bed, his hair wet from the shower, already in his pajamas and plaid robe.

"Thank you for coming," I said. I looked into his face, stress and fatigue etched there. I wanted to ease the worry lines with my fingers.

"Inga," he said. "It's not that I don't understand how you feel about Ben. We don't really understand people like him. Someday we'll know more, maybe about abnormalities in the brain itself that create violent impulses or uncontrollable desires. Regardless, we have to contain them. We have to protect the innocent from them."

I sat down on the bed. "Where could they possibly be, Ron?"

He sat on the end of the bed, a distance away. "We figure they got rides, either up toward the Canadian border or back toward the Twin Cities. They could be hundreds of miles from here by now. Do you have any idea where Ben would go?"

"None." I looked at him beseechingly. "Jean wouldn't have gone with him voluntarily."

He sighed. "Let's hope for the best. He knows her. He actually needs her, at least for awhile. It's quite likely that he won't harm her, unless she crosses him or is no longer needed."

"I have to tell you something, Ron. I should have told you at the time."

A muscle jumped in his cheek. "Tell me now."

"Ben showed up on Jean's balcony, back in Tacoma. He spent two nights there after he escaped from jail."

He looked stunned. "We could have taken him into custody!"

"I … I know. But I wanted to talk to him first. I wasn't sure, I still thought maybe …"

"I can't believe this, Inga."

I couldn't look at his face.

"You're so angry at me, aren't you?"

He wouldn't look at me. "How could I not be?"

Chapter Twenty-Two

Jean

I don't know how long we've been riding in this old car, 'cause I must of fallen asleep. It's warm in the backseat, and I'm curled up with my head on Ben's backpack, my legs draped across the guitar case. I wake when we start bouncing down a gravel road, and when I sit up, feeling grumpy and groggy, Ben turns from the front seat and tries to put his hand on my arm.

"Don't touch me!" I bark. "Just keep your paws to yourself."

That pushes him back. He turns around and says lamely to Steve, "Guess she's not too happy about this little trip."

"How far along is she?"

"Going on a lifetime," I say from the backseat. "You see how you like having a pumpkin inside you sometime."

Both men chuckle uneasily. "Pregnancy does something to their hormones," Ben says. Even in the dark I can still see how he twirls his finger round and round pointing to his temple. As if *I'm* the crazy one!

He and Steve have a good ol' time cutting up President Nixon and General Waste-mor-land as we bounce along, me trying to hold the baby from jouncing and keep my back straight. Someone attached anchors to the small of my back while I was sleeping. Weights are pulling on it, and it feels like my bladder's about to pop. "Hey, take it easy!" I yelp. "Are you trying to shake this baby out of me?"

"Oops," Steve says. "Sorry. I can slow down. We're almost there."

Where? I lean between their heads to look out the front window. Up ahead I see what looks like a snow palace, a big old gingerbread house in the middle of nowhere almost buried up to the windowsills. In the bright moonlight I can see huge icicles hanging off the roof. Snow is piled so high on either side of the walk that it would be like burrowing through a tunnel to get to the front door. The first floor is glowing with golden light from within, but the upper two stories are pitch black.

When Ben opens the back door for me, I won't look at him. At least he has the decency to offer me a hand as I struggle to push my belly out the car and then get to my feet. I feel stiff all over, and those anchors pull at the small of my back, fixing to drag me down. I have never been so tired! It seems a mighty trek up to the front door, but I know if I don't make it I'll pee my pants and freeze to death out here. Ben carries my duffel, slinging his backpack over his shoulder.

We all stomp our boots in the entry hall, setting off a big dog inside that barks deep bass warnings. When Steve opens the oak door to the inside, a whoosh of warm air envelops us. A fat black Lab about floors us with its wagging and licking. Ben grabs my arm to keep me from being knocked over, and this time I don't swat him off. When the dog calms down and I look up, I'm met with a sight to behold. Patchwork quilts everywhere, hanging on the walls, draped across the sofa, a stack of them on a big plywood table and folded ones laid across the bottom of the stairs banister. There's a whole wall of open shelves holding material, each bolt a different color and arranged from dark to light, solids, bright prints, patterns, florals, polka dots, and stripes—and all this in the mellow light of kerosene lanterns. As I look closer I can see what wants to be jars, bowls, and vases sitting on the floor. They are crazy looking, twisted-up things. Whoever made them didn't know how to make a pot.

I feel for a moment like I'm back in the mountains at Ganny's. Ganny herself made patchwork quilts, only with old scraps of dress material and this and that—Periwinkle, Log Cabin, Double Wedding Ring. These quilts are like nothing I ever saw at home, not any of the old designs. One has ten or twelve panels of hands, women's hands, doing women's things—stirring a pot, hanging clothes on a line, kneading bread, threading a needle. Another is a crazy quilt made from pieces of fancy materials—satins, velvets, lace, silk—in jewel tones of ruby, sapphire, jade. It won't hold up over time, but it sure is pretty.

"Come in, come in," a woman with frizzy brown hair sprouting out of her head every which way comes rushing out from one of the back rooms. "Who have we here?" she asks Steve and doesn't wait for an answer. "Welcome!" She holds her hands like prayer hands in front of her, bowing a little. "Namaste." She has on one of those granny dresses the hippies like to wear—no waist or bodice, down below her knees. Old mountain women wear shapeless dresses like that. I don't see why any young woman would ever be caught dead in one. I wouldn't be.

"This is Travis and Jenny," Steve is introducing us. "They're on their way to Canada," he giggles. I wonder if maybe he's had a little nip or toke.

"Bless you for not participating in that immoral war," the woman comes over and gives Ben a big hug that makes me shudder. "Hell, no, you won't go! We won't let you!" She laughs heartily. "I'm Lizzy."

Then she turns to me. "And you, you precious thing. Sit down, here, let me clear a place. These quilts are about to take over the joint."

"Could I use your facilities, ma'am? *Now!*"

For a second she just looks at me funny. "Oh. Of course. Only, it's outside. Let me show you."

"Just point us in the right direction," Ben says. "I'll go with her. You don't need to come out in the cold."

Lizzy takes us down a dark hall and opens the back door, pointing out the little shed at the end of another snow tunnel. I trudge toward it, feeling I may not be able to hold it any longer. Why does *he* have to come? I struggle with my pants, sit down on the cold wood hole, and pee loud and long like a horse. I'm embarrassed that Ben is waiting outside and can hear.

When I come out Ben says, "You wait," and he doesn't even bother to go in the outhouse, he just turns his back and pees into the snow. Does he think I'll take off running if he leaves me alone out here in the cold middle of nowhere?

"We won't cause any trouble here," Ben says to me. "Not if you keep your head. Do you understand?"

I understand about the gun. I nod.

"Hey," Lizzy says when we come back in, "take off your coats, stay awhile! Oh my," she says when she sees my shape, "you've got a pie in the oven. Well, I bet you two are famished." The dog comes rushing up to sniff our crotches. "Stop that, Clancy," Steve tries to push him away. But I like him, I like burying my fingers in his stiff hair.

"Boy, I know I am," Ben says to Lizzy, giving her a saucy grin, turning on the charm. He can switch it on just like that. "We'd be ever so grateful. We'll pay you for your kind hospitality."

"Oh, stop that," Lizzy says. "We have food. Sit yourselves down."

Lizzy stokes up a wood-burning stove, just like Ganny has back home. There's an open cupboard with jars of jellies and preserves, green beans, beets, tomatoes. She heats up a big pot of vegetable soup and dishes us each a generous bowl. I'm famished. We haven't eaten a thing since those hamburgers back in Grand Marais, and it's nigh on midnight.

"We're vegetarians," Lizzy says. "We just don't feel right eating our fellow creatures." She smiles at Ben in a flirtatious way, arching her back, sticking out her boobs. What's with her?

"Oh me too," Ben pipes up, though that's a lie. She should have seen the way he wolfed down that burger at lunch. I wouldn't mind a chunk of cow right now myself. Lizzy pours me a glass of milk and Steve and Ben have a beer. Lizzy pours herself a big glass of red wine.

"Did you make all them quilts?" I can't help asking.

"I'm afraid they're my little handiwork," Lizzy says. "Keeps me out of trouble on long winter nights." She winks at Ben. "Then in the summer, we sell them at art fairs. Along with Steve's pots. We're artisans. We make beautiful objects that people can meditate on and use. It's not about money, obviously. It's about process … color … shape, form. Beauty. Creativity. The human spirit."

"There's nothing more important to the world than art," Ben says. "Art can save the world. If only our leaders in Washington made art, not war."

"Make love, not war," Lizzy grins.

"My Ganny makes quilts," I say. "But I never seen quilts like yours."

"You're obviously from the South," Lizzy exclaims. "Appalachia?"

"I reckon so," I feel shy. I'm not sure what she means.

"How special. I'm from Pennsylvania. That's where I learned quilting. In another life I was a schoolteacher. Elementary art." She flips her frizzy hair back with her hand and sticks out her breasts again. Big bra-less ones under her shapeless dress.

"So ..." Ben says when he has eaten his bowl clean and scraped it with the homemade bread Lizzy cut for us, "have you folks been living up here in the woods long?"

"My grandfather owned three hundred acres of these woods," Lizzy says, getting up from the table. "I inherited this house when he died last year." I see now in the light of the lantern on the table that she isn't young the way I first thought, she just looks young in the way she holds herself and the way she acts. She must be thirty-five if she's a day. "Steve and I moved up here in August. We met at an art fair in the Twin Cities. I robbed the cradle."

Steve comes up behind her and puts his hands on her shoulders affectionately, giving them a good massage. "Honey cup," he murmurs, kissing her on the neck.

"How 'bout you love birds," she smiles. "How'd you meet?"

Ben and I look at each other stupidly.

"Don't tell me you can't remember," Lizzy laughs, to fill the awkward silence.

"Oh no," Ben says, grinning, and I can see he's getting his footing. "I was just trying to think where to begin," he says. "Well, we met at Fort Lewis. Jenny is from a military family. Her father was in Nam. Helicopter pilot. I met Jenny at the commissary one day. I just knew across those aisles of chips and dip that she was the one. Right, hun?"

I refuse to speak, staring into the lantern's light.

"It's all a little hard on her," Ben goes on. "Her father went down ..."

Lizzy and Steve stare at me. "And ..." Lizzy prompts gently.

"Killed," Ben says.

"Oh honey, I'm so sorry," Lizzy says, and she reaches over to touch my face.

"That's when I decided I wouldn't go. I didn't want Jenny to have to go through that twice."

"Not to mention wanting to save your own skin," Steve cracks. "Hey, want another one?" Lizzy delivers two more beers to the table. "Why should we let those assholes get us killed. Let *them* go. Fuckers!"

"How come they haven't gotten your ass," Ben asks.

"Four fucking F," Steve says. "Flat feet, man. Can you believe it. Flat fucking feet saved my sorry ass!"

Steve goes into the living room and comes back with his guitar and a little leather pouch. "You wouldn't be opposed to a little toke, would you?" he asks.

"That would be mighty welcome," Ben says.

Steve rolls a joint like Jimmy used to do and lights up, passing it to Ben, who takes a long hit. When I pass, Lizzy murmurs, "Probably a good idea," then takes a long drag herself.

After awhile Steve begins strumming his guitar. "*If I had a hammer …*" he croons, while I slump in my chair, exhausted. How innocent Steve and Lizzy seem, like children playing at life. Having a hootenanny for a killer, I can't help thinking, what a hoot!

"So," Lizzy says, "What do you do?" She sits down again, putting her elbows on the table and resting her chin in her hands, gazing at Ben as if he's the most fascinating thing she's seen in a long time.

"Writer," Ben says.

"Really! What do you write?"

"I have a novel coming out in the fall," Ben says. I just gape at him. "But mainly I do photojournalism. *Time, Newsweek*, things like that. And I just had a thing in *National Geographic*. Maybe you saw it. Grizzlies in Yellowstone."

"Wow," Lizzy says. She passes another joint around. "So you'll probably be able to get work in Canada. Are you going to Toronto?"

"Yeah, probably," Ben lets the smoke out in a smooth stream. "I hear there's a big community there of resisters. It's a happening place they say."

"It's cool, man," Steve says. He's looking a little glazed, like one of his pots. "Let's go too, Liz."

"What's keeping us?" Lizzy says. "Only what would I do with the quilts? Someone might break in and steal them."

"Put them in the bank," Steve laughs crazily. "Like in a vault."

"I guess we should turn in," Ben says after all of them have been sitting around in a daze forever. "We have a long day ahead of us tomorrow."

"You aren't planning on leaving so soon?" Lizzy says. She reaches over and lays her hand on Ben's wrist. "You don't have to go tomorrow. You could stay here a few days, rest up. You're safe here." She leaves her hand on Ben's arm.

What kind of woman is she? Maybe she's lost her mind living up here in the woods all winter.

"Are you and Jenny ... exclusive?" She looks at Ben.

He leans back, tipping his chair up, and takes another deep toke, blowing the smoke toward the ceiling.

"'Cause Steve and I aren't. We agreed from the start that monogamy is a hang-up."

I stand up, knocking my chair over. "What are you even thinking about?" I screech. "I have to leave. I have to get out of here right now!"

Clancy comes up and nuzzles into my hand by my side. I grip his nape and steady myself.

"Okay, okay, don't get excited," Ben says. "She was just joking."

"I'm warning you ... Travis!"

"It's okay, honey," Lizzy says. "No big deal. I mean, I can imagine you feel pretty possessive right now, what with a baby on the way and all. Just relax. We're cool."

"Man," Steve says. "I'm wiped!"

"So," Lizzy says, "are we all. You all take our bed. We'll use the futon."

I wouldn't sleep in that woman's bed if she paid me, but Ben pipes right up, "Oh no, we won't hear of it. Putting you out of your own bed, would we, honey."

Don't honey me, I want to say, but I think better of it. I know what Ben is capable of, so why take chances.

"Well, the futon's not too bad," Lizzy says. "And with a couple of quilts you'll be perfectly warm. The stove tends to die down to just embers overnight."

I could sleep standing up like a horse I'm so tired, though I noticed my legs don't want to push me up out of the kitchen chair.

When I finally make it to the living room, she has what looks like a flat mattress open on the floor. I'm going to have to sleep next to *him*. I feel for my knife. What if I told Steve and Lizzy about Ben—but they might not believe me and if they did, no telling what Ben would do. They seem so defenseless, like sparrows pecking in the shadow of a hawk.

I manage to get down to the floor without toppling over. My center of gravity is all wrong, Baby Inga threatening to pull me forward. Once I'm finally flat, my whole body aches with relief. Lizzy spreads two quilts and pulls one up to my chin, tucking me in, kinda sweet. "I'm sorry, baby," she says. "It wasn't personal. You let me know if you need anything."

Ben waits until they've left the room. He turns off the kerosene lantern and then he slips under the quilts beside me. Our faces aren't but a foot or so apart, and I feel a cold dread come over me. I lay still, not moving a muscle.

"Jean," he whispers in the dark. "Jean?"

I don't say a word.

"Jean, I just want to thank you. I know this is hard on you. I'm sorry, really I am. But I appreciate your, uh … cooperating. Tomorrow we'll get to Canada. It's our best hope."

"Our?" I can't help blurting.

"Okay, whatever," he says testily. "I'm trying to be nice here."

"Why take me with you, Ben? You can get to Canada on your own. You don't need me. I'll just slow you down."

"I don't think the police will be quite so trigger-happy with a pregnant girl beside—or in front of me."

If I was a crier, I'd cry.

"Jean?"

I'm silent, waiting. I try to turn on my side, away from him, but it's hard to do with the baby.

"Jean, do me one favor, okay? Just think about this one thing, will you? What if all this is a mistake? What if I didn't do all those horrible things? What if they have the wrong guy? The wrong guy, Jean. Just think about that."

I don't move, but in my mind I put my hands over my ears to block out his words. He's trying to trick me. *I won't think about it,* I say fiercely inside, *I won't, I won't!*

"Okay, then, goodnight, Jean." He kinda leans up and looks at me, maybe to see if I'm asleep. I smell his breath, foul like old hamburger, but at least he took a shower sometime back in cabin twelve. I keep my eyes shut. After a moment, he turns over, away from me.

I try to think what to do. I'm afraid of what he might do, to me or to Lizzy and Steve. I don't want to see them hurt. We have to leave here tomorrow, before they suspect anything. I feel so wrought up I sit straight up. "Listen," I say, poking Ben in the back. "I won't say anything to Lizzy and Steve—but here's the deal."

He rolls over on his back and I can see in the dark that he's staring up at the ceiling.

"You don't hurt me." I pause to let it sink in. "You don't hurt the baby." I give it a few beats. "You don't hurt Lizzy and Steve. If you agree, I'll help you get to Canada. Much as I can. Then you cut me free."

He's quiet for a long moment, like he's thinking it over. "Done and done and done," he finally says, as if he means it. "You got it, Jean."

"Don't speak my name! You don't know me. And one little slipup, that's it. Those are my conditions."

"I understand."

"All right then." I lie back down. We are silent for a long time. Finally I can't help myself, it's just manners. "Goodnight, then."

"Goodnight."

But I can't sleep. My mind is on fire. What's going to happen tomorrow? Is Ben going to kill me? What's going on back at Walter's? How's Mrs. D doing?

A picture of Ganny comes into my mind. Little Ganny, tough as a banty hen, scrawny and no nonsense, but sweet, too, like the drop at the end of a honeysuckle blossom. I want to go home. I want to see Ganny. I want Ganny to make everything okay. I want her to hold Baby Inga. I want to be with her. The urge is suddenly so strong that if we wasn't out in the middle of nowhere in the middle of winter, I would rise up and start walking home, right then and there.

I try to sleep. I take some deep breaths. But Baby Inga crowds my lungs and makes it hard. Beside me Ben is snoring. How can he possibly sleep? I feel like poking him awake, out of meanness. Jimmy used to snore and keep me awake, and now he will never take another breath and let it out. Something tightens my throat and chest.

I put my hands on Baby Inga, who is sleeping and not kicking me for once. She is off to a rough start with her mama running around with a murderer. I'll make it up to you, I tell her, when we get out of this mess.

Then, just before I drop off to sleep, a little thought worms its way into my brain: *What if… ?* Like he said … *what if… ?*

Chapter Twenty-Three

Inga

Ron offered to drive me back to Tacoma after Dad's burial and after the police had finished questioning me. I didn't see how that would work, given how he felt about me. I couldn't imagine mile after mile of silence, judgment, and condemnation. I had that covered myself already. I didn't need fifteen hundred miles of Ron's disapproval to remind me.

I can drive myself, I told him. I'll take some extra days, it's just driving! We were out in the yard. I was pacing back and forth across the packed snow, my arms hugging my body in my winter jacket. I just wanted to be left alone. I had so much to think about, so much to be sorry for, and I didn't need company for that. I felt sick over Jean. She had trusted me and I had betrayed her with my stupid mistakes. "You fly back," I told him. "I'll drive you to the airport tomorrow, and you can be back in Tacoma by evening. You have work to do. I'll be fine, Ron. Really. I'm not your responsibility."

He didn't try to argue with me. "It's fricking cold out here," he said. "God, how did you stand growing up in a climate like this. I'm going inside. I'll be ready at six in the morning."

Ron pitched in that night to prepare the house before we left. We did the necessary chores together, talking only about what was at hand: cleaning out the refrigerator and cabinets, putting out mousetraps, arranging for a neighbor to stop in every day to make sure the furnace was still working. I touched all the familiar things of Dad's, of our lives together when I was growing up. I couldn't bear to open his chest of drawers. I would come back in the spring and deal with things then. I didn't know how I could ever sell the house and resort. How could I part with them? I would just have to figure it all out later.

For dinner we ate the last of the leftovers in silence, and then while I packed he cleaned the kitchen thoroughly, took out the trash for the last time, swept the linoleum floor. I just threw the things I'd brought back in my suitcase. So much had happened it floored me. I packed Jean's few clothes to take—a few blouses and her pink cotton sweater, useless in a Minnesota winter, the white ruffled blouse she had worn at Christmas. Touching her things, I felt a sadness and fear that was almost unbearable. I had grown accustomed to her steady, calm presence and now I had no idea if she was dead or alive.

Some vicious creature had taken up residence in my stomach, gnawing away night and day, until I half expected it to eat its way out into the light of day. I got down on my knees in the bedroom with the door shut and prayed to a God I hadn't believed in since my mother died, prayed that Jean would be okay, that I could make it all up to her somehow. I wanted to pray for Ben, for his soul, but I didn't know how.

When we left the next morning before daybreak, Ron insisted on driving to the Twin Cities. I had brought along the last of the dinner rolls and cheese, which we ate in the car, stopping to fill up a thermos of coffee. But when we got near Minneapolis, instead of heading south to the airport, Ron took I-94 west. "I've made an executive decision," he said. "You're not driving all that way yourself. You're exhausted, and given all you have on your mind, you may not even be thinking straight. We'll be back in three days, if we don't dawdle." And with that he hit seventy as we cleared the western ring of suburbs.

That first day we rode for endless stretches in complete silence, not the easy silence of people comfortable with each other, but a kind of anxious, strained silence, too courteous and polite, as if a fragile pane of glass between us might break at any instant. I stared out the window a lot, and when I drove, I kept my eyes straight ahead, afraid to look over at him in the passenger seat. Sometimes he'd nap, and I'd surreptitiously steal glances at him. His mouth would fall open, making him look more vulnerable than when he was awake, his jaw set, his expression tense. I had violated his whole sense of right and wrong. I had made a mess of things, proving myself complicit, untrustworthy.

We stopped for the first night in Bismarck and ate dinner at the truck stop near our motel that was just off the highway. I said I wasn't hungry, but he insisted that I try the special he was getting, spaghetti and meatballs. I discovered that I was famished. Eating together after the long drive eased some of the tension. I knew he would probably never relinquish his true judgment of me. But at least we began to make small talk and relax a little. In our rooms that night, I could sense him on the other side of the wall. I knew that I had spoiled what might have been just beginning between us. But maybe he had never felt anything anyway. Besides—it—us—could never have worked. It was just not possible given everything else.

Somewhere deep into Montana we began to talk more to pass the endless miles.

"What do you think is going to happen, Ron," I finally asked. We had been avoiding the elephant in the room.

"Best scenario, Ben and Jean will be found soon. Jean will be okay. Ben will stand trial and then, well … we'll see."

I looked out the window at the passing mesas and distant mountains. "They'll give him the death penalty."

Ron looked over at me. "It's possible he'll get life."

"I still can't believe he could actually kill anybody. I know it must be true, given his 'speculations.' But it's just too big a leap."

"When we catch up with him, he'll have his day in court."

"But you believe he's guilty."

"I do."

I already knew that but it still hurt somehow to hear.

"What about an insanity plea? Because anybody who could kill like that must be insane."

"He's not the victim here, Inga."

"I don't expect you or anyone to understand. I just can't …"

"That's because your desire to not believe is so strong. You can't stand to believe it."

I was silent.

"They'll want his life," I finally said. "An eye for an eye."

"Until we figure out something better," Ron sighed. "As for me, I'd prefer to see him locked up forever. Maybe we'd learn something from him. I don't see the point of taking another life. Especially knowing what it will do to you."

Really, kindness was the hardest thing to take. I stared out the window at the passing emptiness, blinking back tears. Nothing for miles around.

"This will be over for you one day, Inga."

"It'll never be over for me. How could it be."

"I don't mean over, like you can go back to what was … or the way you thought things were … before. But it will resolve one way or the other. And then what? You have the rest of your life. How will you live it?"

"I've been thinking about Jean," I said. "If—when she comes back, I want to make this up to her if I can. I'll do whatever she needs. Give her money, help her raise the baby, if she wants that. She'll need a lot of help."

"That's good," he said. "But what about you? Your own happiness. You can't let Ben ruin the rest of your life. Don't let Ben kill you, too."

I didn't know what to say. It felt like he already had. We rode in silence until Ron said, "I'm thinking about retiring myself. After this case is resolved. I'm tired of all this. All this criminal crap. Lives taken, lives ruined. I've been in law enforcement for what, almost thirty-five years. I'm fifty-seven and feeling it. I don't have to do this forever. I'll have a good pension, I can do something different."

"You're a good man, Ron. You should do that. Retire. Do something easier. Something you'd enjoy."

"I'm thinking about it."

"You know, I haven't really thanked you for all you've done. All you've tried to do for me and for Ben. I'm sorry I let you down." My voice cracked a little.

"We all make mistakes. That's what it was. A mistake. A bad one, I admit, but no one's perfect. He's your son. I get that more than you realize. I get you."

I went back to work at the library. I found solace in the routine, and Larry made it easy for me, treating me as if I was just like everyone else. It seemed important to get up every day, to get dressed, to go to work. For seconds and sometimes even a few whole minutes, it took my mind off things.

Days passed and still no sign of them. How could they have disappeared so completely? That's what I couldn't understand. Their pictures were in every post office and police station in America, and the story had been covered extensively on the news. It didn't seem possible that no one would recognize them. There had been possible sightings, tips, anonymous calls to the police, but nothing had panned out.

A week after we returned, Ron flew to North Carolina to meet the local police with whom he'd been in contact, and to see Jean's family, in case he could stir up any new information or leads. When he got back he came over to the library, we went into the conference room and sat across from each other the way we'd done so often.

"Jean's mother didn't seem too perturbed that she was missing," Ron said, shaking his head in disbelief. "I asked her when she had heard from Jean last, and she couldn't remember. Her comment about what had happened to her daughter was, 'Well ain't that just like Jean Louise to go get herself into some fool situation.' Can you imagine having a mother who criticizes you for being kidnapped by a serial killer?" He ran his fingers through his thinning hair. Something sharp pinched my heart.

"What was the house like?" I asked. "Tell me everything."

"Just a little red brick house out in the middle of nowhere," Ron said. "Everything kind of worn out and run down. Dirty, to tell you the truth. Red dirt and cats everywhere, inside and out. I bet there were twenty cats there, and Big Mama picking them up and talking baby talk to them the whole time. I swear that woman was more interested in those damn cats than her own daughter."

Oh Jean! No wonder she had latched on to me. Ironic, really, given my own "success" as a mother.

"Did you talk to any other family members?"

He sighed. "I interviewed the sister. Very little reaction at all there. When I tried to talk to her about Jean, she just sort of winced and murmured, 'oh dear,' or 'golly gee,' something along those lines. Like I had told her Jean had a bad cold. She obviously never heard from Jean when she was in Tacoma. The only news was through mama. I asked mom to see Jean's letters, but of course there were none. She hadn't kept them. I tell you that girl might as well have been an orphan."

"She must have raised herself," I murmured. "What about Jimmy's family?"

"They're still mad as the dickens that Jean never bothered to come home for the funeral. They have their own troubles, and of course, they're mourning their son." He paused, staring into space. "The mountains around that area really are blue. I never got that when I heard about the Blue Ridge Mountains. But they're all these waves of blues." He looked wistful for a moment. "It'd be a nice place to live someday. Chop wood, take hikes, maybe volunteer for some environmental group there. Like I said, I don't plan to do this forever." His face softened, and the normal grimace he wore loosened. He looked over at me, studying me. I had to look away.

A week or so after that conversation, Ron stopped by the library again. I hadn't heard from him in between.

"Do you own a gun?" he asked in his most official police voice the minute we sat down. All business.

"Of course not. Dad had several but he never taught me. It wasn't a 'girl' thing."

"You should have a gun, Inga."

I swallowed hard, took a moment to compose myself. "No, really."

"You need one." He was looking at me intently.

"You don't believe Ben would actually try to hurt me, do you?"

"I just think you should have a gun and know how to shoot it. It's the great equalizer, as they say."

"No. I can't imagine."

"I don't want to debate with you, I just want you to have a gun and know how to use it. Do this for me."

"I wouldn't know how to shoot it."

"I'll teach you."

"I don't think I'd make a very good student."

"Leave that up to me."

The next Saturday Ron took me to get a license and to a gun store, where he helped me try out various pistols. I found a small one that fit my hand, a Chief's Special Smith and Wesson revolver, for ninety dollars, almost dainty looking, though Ron assured me it would do the job if I ever needed it. I liked the feel of it in my hand, how solid and hard it was—like it meant business. I could see why men liked guns. I felt more powerful just holding it, and Ron was obviously pleased that I was going along with what he wanted me to do.

The lessons began. We went back to my house and sat at the kitchen table, where he taught me all the parts of the gun, how to load and unload it, how to take care of it. We had to go over these things many times, until he was convinced I had them down. I hadn't realized shooting a gun was so complicated.

He began coming over some evenings, and we'd go to the "classroom" for the night's lesson. I looked forward to my training. We never talked again about the reason for the gun, we pretended it was just teacher and student. He showed me how to grasp the pistol high, because if your hand was too low on the handle, a straight rearward pressure on the trigger would tend to pull the muzzle down, placing the shot low. There were a million ways to miss, it appeared.

Then he taught me how to do a "crush grip," where I gripped the gun as hard as I could. Tremors set in in my arm when I gripped it hard like that for long, but Ron said not to worry about it, because in a real situation, you're going to tremble anyway so you might as well get used to it now. He was impressive as an instructor, patient, thorough, and he even began to lighten up, maybe let me off the hook a little. Sometimes I'd fix us a coke after our lesson, and he'd actually stay a little while. Sometimes we'd speculate about Ben and Jean again, both mystified about their whereabouts. Ron figured they'd vanished into Canada, probably the war resisters' community in Toronto, but the police there hadn't turned up anything either.

We moved on to keeping the sights in a straight line, even if your hand was quivering, the way mine usually was. "If the sights are in line," Ron explained, "they'll quiver in the center of the target, and when the shot breaks, the bullet will strike the center of the target." He told me to hold the gun as hard as I could, for each and every shot. That way no one could ever knock or snatch it away. None of this was real to me but I went along. It was like a game at the fair, unconnected to what was too unimaginable.

Next he had me just pretend I was holding the gun, relaxing my hand and moving my index finger as if rapidly pulling the trigger. Sure enough, my other fingers contracted reflexively along with it. "What you've just seen and experienced is called 'milking,'" Ron said. "You know—like a cow. When one finger closes, the other fingers want to close with it."

"So what's wrong with that? And when do I actually get to shoot?"

"This is not a game, Inga."

His words caught me up short. "It is to me, Ron. I could never shoot anyone."

"I want you to take this seriously. You don't know what you're capable of until the situation presents itself. But if it does, I want you to be ready."

I tried to take in his words, but I couldn't imagine any scenario where I would shoot this gun at another person. "So what do I do about milking," I said.

"Okay, now pretend you're holding the gun, but this time with all but your index finger closed as tightly as you can hold them. As you pull the trigger—pretend—you'll feel the tendons trying to tighten the grasp of the other fingers, but you'll see they actually can't. That's because the tight grip has already hyperflexed the fingers, and they can't tighten anymore. The milking action has now been eliminated."

"Oh."

"Now," he said, "stand up. I want you to take a power stance, like a boxer."

I felt awkward, ridiculous even, mimicking a boxer's stance. I'd never stood like that in my life, but I could feel how it balanced and strengthened me to plant my feet apart.

"You'll be shooting two-handed and are right-hand dominant," Ron said, putting his hands on my hips and shifting them a little. I wished he would leave them there. "So the pelvis wants to be at a forty-five degree angle vis-à-vis the target, in this case your refrigerator, with your left leg forward and your right leg back." Again, he gently positioned my hips. I glanced up and met his eyes briefly and thought he flushed a little.

"Guess that's enough for tonight," he said, removing his hands. "You practice what we've gone over." And with that he was gone.

Finally the day came when he was actually ready for me to try shooting. He offered to take me to a shooting range, but I said I'd be too embarrassed with people around. So we drove out to some property a friend of his owned in Gig Harbor, where Ron practiced shooting sometimes. It was an open space carved out of the woods, bordered by a high bare bank, with some big barrels you could move to varying distances. Ron brought some bull's-eye sheets from the shooting club and taped them to one of the barrels about five feet away. He had me load my gun, watching carefully.

"Isn't it too close?"

"Trust me," Ron said. "Go ahead. Do the best you can."

I took my power stance, extending both arms and gripping the gun high and hard.

I fired six times and never even hit the barrel, let alone the bull's-eye. I had thought I'd be a natural.

"Where were you focusing?" Ron asked.

"Well, on that far bank, of course. To the right, left, above and below the bull's-eye, Ron! What do you mean, where was I focusing!"

"Well, here's what I mean. Human vision being what it is, you can't focus on the sight and the target at the same time. You can't even focus on the front and rear sights at the same time. Once you've identified the target, you no longer need your primary visual focus on it. Focus this time on the front sight. Watch the front sight. Hard. Apply your primary vision there, until you can see every little scratch in the machining on its surface. That hard."

Again, I missed every shot. I screwed up my face in frustration.

"Okay, this time I want you to try this." He came and stood behind me, close, and put his hand over mine on the revolver. My heart was beating hard, and I knew I'd never hit the target now with Ron so close. "Take your stance," he commanded, and I did, pointing the gun toward the target, trying to focus on the front sight. "Let your finger barely touch the trigger," he said near my ear, "and let that finger go limp." I felt his trigger finger over mine. "You don't do anything," he said, "just feel what my finger does. We're going to sque-e-eze the trigger. A smooth, consistent pressure. What you've been doing is pulling the trigger in a way that pulls the muzzle off target. You need to pull it back straight. Like this."

I felt my finger come straight back smoothly, I felt the recoil of the gun and I saw that Ron—we—had nailed the bull's-eye! "Amazing." I turned and smiled at him, wanting to say *do it again, put your hand on mine again.*

"You try it now," he said, "but this time anticipate the recoil." Again, I was way off, which I didn't really mind, because again he stood close behind me, he put his hand on mine, his finger on mine, and showed me how it felt to pull it straight back, a smooth, even, uninterrupted pull. Then he had me pull the trigger, with his finger just lightly resting on mine to monitor the progress. This time I at least hit the cardboard. Then he watched as I shot a few more times, never getting closer than the outer circle. But I felt I'd come a long way.

All the way back into Ron's good graces.

Chapter Twenty-Four

Jean

We've been at Steve and Lizzy's for several weeks now. Ben and Lizzy have kept up their little dance, flirting and flitting around each other, but every night he's there beside me on the floor, not that I want him to be. At least I know where he is. He never bothers me, and you couldn't tell for the life of you he's a killer. He's just like any other guy, what with his farts, burps, and snoring. I mean, it's hard to hold the murder part in my mind when I'm around him all the time and he acts okay. But I make myself go over that part a few times a day, like the prayers I used to say when I was little. "Now I lay me down to sleep," only now I say, "Ben is a killer, Ben is a killer." I'm not about to let his "what if" snake its way into my brain.

We have settled into a routine, with Ben and Steve toking up all day and complaining about Vietnam, like they have all the answers, and making their plans to get us to Canada, while I help Lizzy sew her quilts on her big frame. I've let go of the notion of telling her who Ben is, what he is. It'd be like telling her he's a Martian. I'm afraid she wouldn't believe me nor know what to do, especially about the gun. They don't have nary a radio or TV, or even a phone! They scorn the things that most people value. People up in the mountains where Ganny lives would give anything for those things—to be in touch. But Steve and Lizzy are too pure and maybe poor for such modern conveniences. They keep all their worldly cash in a mason jar on the kitchen counter, the money they got from selling their wares during the summer.

While I'm sewing I think about Mrs. D and things back home at the library. I miss Babe and even Margery. Sometimes I long just to shelve some books, like none of this ever happened. One day I'll be back there doing my job again. I wonder how Mrs. D is getting along. I know she worries about me, but I'm okay. I wish I could tell her that. My best chance right now is to go along to get along. It's important to keep things peaceful, so no one gets hurt. I hope when we get to Canada, he'll let me go.

Then one night, way late, when everyone is sound asleep, Ben gets up from the bed on the floor Lizzy made for us. I come instantly awake. Before I can say a word he grabs me by the arm and this time it hurts. It'll leave a bruise. "Shhhh," he whispers fiercely. "Do what I say and no lip. Get dressed, get your stuff, wear your boots. We're leaving."

"Leav ..." but he clamps his hand right over my mouth. That puts the fear of God in me. It makes me remember how he clamped that horrid hand over other mouths, including my own when we were back at Walter's. It leaves a sour, nasty taste when he lets go.

While I'm dressing, he creeps away, in the direction of Lizzy and Steve's room. Surely he won't hurt those kind and gentle children! Well, actually Lizzy is no child by a long shot—but still! I feel Baby Inga kicking me, I feel for the little knife in my jacket pocket, the fifty-dollar bill in the bottom of my sock where I keep it. Three things I can't do without. While I'm standing there, frozen in fear, Ben comes back with their car keys and hustles me out the front door. I haven't heard anything bad, no struggle or screams, no gunshot, so maybe he has just taken the keys. I barely have time to give Clancy a rub on the nose. He looks at us questioningly. *Is it time to go out? Can I go? What's up?* But he's so used to us—he trusts us! I can't help thinking—that he doesn't bark.

"You are stealing their only means of transportation, after they've been so nice to us," I can't help whisper-screeching at Ben as he pushes Steve and Lizzy's old rattletrap of a car down the snow-packed drive.

"We're borrowing it," he growls at me, huffing and puffing as I march alongside him. I'm not about to push. "They'll get it back."

I don't even bother to reply to that.

Once we're out to the main road, Ben tells me to get in. He turns on the overhead light, pulls a bunch of bills out of his jacket pocket, and begins counting and ordering them by twenties, fifties, and hundreds.

"You stole all their money!"

"They loaned it to me. I'll repay them before too long."

He starts the car and glances over at me before turning off the light. "Why would I hurt them, Jean? They're our friends."

I turn my face from him and stare out into the dark woods. Some of the trees have white bark that looks ghostly in the night. "Where're we going?"

"That's for me to know and you to find out."

"Just drop me off somewhere. You don't need me."

"Ah, but I like you, Jean. I would miss you too much." I hadn't realized I was going to cry, but suddenly I'm wailing like a baby. It's all I can do not to suck my thumb. I curl up in a ball against the door as best I can, cradling Baby Inga. I cry until it's over, like a sudden rain squall. Then I determine that I will escape. I will look for an opportunity. He isn't going to let me go, so I have to get away on my own, that much is clear.

"Mind if I turn on the radio," he says when I've straightened up and pulled myself together. He flicks it on without waiting for me to answer, which I wasn't going to anyway. Far away and staticky comes a song like none I've heard before, "*Jennifer ... Juniper ...*" and Ben sings along. He has a pretty good voice.

In some little no-count town we switch cars. Ben goes up and down the quiet, peaceful streets until he sees what he wants. A white van, parked on the main drag, which is no more than two or three blocks long. There's a big Ford dealership and a café advertising smorgasbord on Sundays. Everything is quiet and deserted, a ghost town. Ben pops open the van's hood and hot-wires the engine. The boys in high school knew how to do that. Jimmy knew how, before he got himself killed. Where is he when I need him!

I wait in Steve and Lizzy's car. When Ben comes back, he says, "Get in the driver's seat, you're going to follow me."

"You can't make me." Then I remember the gun. I haven't seen it in all this time we've been together, but I figure he still has it.

He grabs me by the upper arm again. "Jean, I can make you. I will make you, if it comes to that. I'm not going to let them get me. Do you understand?"

I have to get out and walk around the car to get in the driver's seat. I can't slide over under the steering wheel because of Baby Inga. My heart is beating so bad it hurts my chest, but I try to keep my cool. I'm still alive. I'm breathing, though not too good. I feel Baby Inga stirring, and I put a hand over her as I punch her down to get behind the steering wheel. We barely fit, we're so big now. Why does he want me to follow him? Where are we going?

We drive out to the main highway, where no cars are traveling at this time of night. The sky is beginning to brighten just barely in the east. Maybe when daybreak comes, we'll be caught. The owner of the white van will report it stolen. The police will find us, and it will be over, one way or another. I comfort myself, sort of, with that thought.

When I see a side road ahead, I wait until he's just past it, then I floor Steve's old car as I make the turn. I take off like a bat out of hell on that dark county road going who knows where. There isn't a house or store to be seen, just woods and a creepy darkness. And then—I can't believe my eyes—gaining on me in the rearview mirror is the white van. He must of done a u-ey right there on the road or backed up at sixty miles an hour to get back to that turn. I hope a cop will be out here in the country, will see us speeding like two maniacs. I've never wanted a ticket so bad in my life! I take a curve fast and almost skid off the road, my whole body electrified. That's when I pull over and stop, my heart jack-hammering in my chest. I'm afraid I'll flip the car or run off the road into a tree and kill Baby Inga. I can't get away from him. Not this time at least.

He screeches to a stop no more than a foot behind me, the van's lights blinding me in the rearview mirror, and comes running up to my window, his face knotted into a fury. I try to lock the door, but he jerks it open while I'm fumbling for the lock. I cower with my head down, afraid he's going to hit me. He yanks me out of the car, too rough for Baby Inga, and I stumble and fall onto the hard pavement, holding my belly as best I can. He has aholt of my arm and pulls me up and shakes me hard, so that I bite my lower lip and taste salty, warm blood. But he doesn't hit me. Not yet.

"Don't … ever … try … that … again." He speaks slowly and deliberately, as if I'm a child. "Do not provoke me, Jean. You don't want to provoke me!"

"Okay," I whimper. "I'm sorry. I didn't mean it." I will say anything.

A car appears at the top of the next hill. It slows when it gets to us, and a man rolls down the passenger window. "Need any help?"

"No, we're fine," Ben waves. "Everything's fine."

"Okay then," the man says. I have my lower lip sucked into my mouth, trying to stop the bleeding. I don't look at the man, I just keep my eyes cast down. I'm still alive, for now. For that I am thankful.

After the man drives off, Ben gets busy changing the license plates, and then we're in the van, speeding back to the highway. By morning we're in the Twin Cities, blending in with the rush hour traffic, and by that afternoon we're heading into the sun, going west instead of north to Canada. That night Ben steals another car, and then the next night another. We drive continuously, stopping only for gas and fast food. We never say a word. I can't tell where we are. Sometimes the sun is setting in front of us, sometimes to the right and sometimes to the left. Crooked as a dog's hind leg, that's the way we go. He listens to the radio, and I stare out the window, a feeling of hopelessness like a big emptiness inside. I think of animals in cages and traps. I've never liked zoos, the way the animals look out with that same hopelessness I'm feeling. I think of the people I love, Mrs. D, and Ganny, and I even think of Mama. *Mama*, I wail inside, but it doesn't really work. *Jimmy*, I try, but about him I just feel mad. It's only when I think of Mrs. D and Ganny that the weight lifts a little. And Baby Inga, sleeping peacefully now inside me.

"So promise me one thing," I say one day as we're riding through a mountain pass on what seems the top of the world. A month and more has passed with us on the run. I haven't tried to escape again, and he hasn't hurt me. That is the unspoken deal we have struck. We are nigh into California, going over the Donner Pass, where Ben tells me people ate one another to stay alive. I figure I'd do just about anything to stay alive myself. "Promise me when it's time—you know … for the birth—that you'll get me to a hospital. Because I can't have this baby on my own." It's well into April now, and I figure I'm about due.

He glances over at me. I feel miserable and ridiculous, like a balloon about to pop. I'm swoll up in my ankles and legs, and even my face and hands are bloated. Sometimes when I sneeze or cough, some pee leaks out. The baby will have to come out pretty soon.

Ben sighs, as if this is a problem he hasn't foreseen. "How near are you?" he asks.

"How would I know! I've never had a baby before."

"Don't women just instinctively know these things?"

Just as he says that, I feel what I think might be … it's a weird squeezing inside. Baby Inga stirs. It goes away and doesn't really hurt that much, the way I had reckoned it would.

"Soon," I say. "Real soon."

He is silent, driving around some hairpin curves.

"Take me to a hospital, okay? Please, I have to go to the hospital to have this baby. Just this one thing. Please!"

"Okay," he says. "Just hang on. Do you think it's imminent?"

I don't know what he means.

Another squeeze. I feel something wet between my legs.

"I think the water broke." Or maybe it's pee. I'm definitely scared enough to pee my pants.

"Okay," he says. "Not to worry." Though he looks as worried as I've ever seen him and I've seen him worried a plenty. He has a scowl on his face that chills my bones. Maybe my usefulness to him has come to an end. Maybe he'll just leave me by the side of the road, to have this baby by myself. I'm shivering with fear now. The pain grips me again, a little more insistent.

"Don't leave me," I say. "Just get me to a hospital. Please!"

We're coming down the other side of the mountain now, zigzagging like a ride at the fair. I have no idea how far to the nearest hospital. The contractions have let up. Maybe it was false labor—my sister Gloria had that with both her babies.

We ride along in silence, each lost in our own thoughts. All I know is I have to get to a hospital. If wishing could make it so, I'd be there now—white sheets, a kind nurse or even a mean one, a doctor who knows what to do.

"What's going on now," he asks after some time has passed, I'm not sure how long. I've shut my eyes, just focusing on Baby Inga, telling her to wait if she can. I'm not ready!

"Not much," I say. "It seems to have stopped."

"Good," he nods.

"But I still have to get to the hospital!"

"I'll take you when the time comes. I promise."

But he doesn't. That night we stop in another of those cheap motels like we've been staying in outside some dusty little town. And that's where I have the baby. No hospital, no help. Just Ben.

I hadn't realized such words could come out of my mouth. I know how to cuss, sure, but once the pain really starts, I say things I never even knew I knew.

We pull in about dusk. The contractions have let up, and so I let Ben convince me—not that I have much choice—that we'll go to the hospital in the morning. There we are, piled up on that sagging double bed, me big as the mountain we have just come over, Ben snoring away. His hair is so long now he wears it in a bushy ponytail, and his beard looks like a raccoon tail stuck on his face. He made me dye my hair red as Lucille Ball's somewhere along the road, I forget where, because I never even knew what state we were in. He dyed his jet black again. I had wanted black. But actually, now that I'm a redhead, instead of the mousy brown I've always been, I feel more—bolden. I'm not even that afraid of Ben anymore. We are like a snake and a pig, which is how I feel, big and pink and round, in the same pen, not exactly friendly like, but how would you say? Accustomed.

The pain is like nothing I have ever imagined. At first it's okay, like my belly just got tight and hard, and I think, *What's the big deal.* But an hour or so later, I know what the big deal is.

"Take me to the hospital," I beg, "while there's still time. Please, Ben, please. What have I done to make you hate me like this!" By then I'm moaning and crying, down on my hands and knees on that dirty motel carpet, trying to ease my back, and stop the pain from gripping me like a vicious claw every two or three minutes. I feel like I am going to poop and pee at the same time. Before I can get my huge self into the little bathroom, I get the runs. I'm hurting too much to be embarrassed. "This baby is not going to come out," I wail, "it's too big, Ben. Help, help, help!"

He puts his hand over my mouth and I immediately shut up. The last thing I want is our air cut off.

"Someone will hear," he says. He's pale and sweating on his forehead. The mole by his eye seems to be pulsing. "I'm here," he says. "I'll help you. Women have been having babies since … It'll be all right."

"No it won—" That hand again. I'm sitting on the toilet, and I bite down on the little bit of palm I can get my teeth into. He jerks his hand away and backs up.

"God," he says. "What should I do?"

It's too late. I'm going to have this baby here and now, and nothing is going to help or stop it. "I'm freezing," I say. "Help me back to the bed and turn up the heat. Turn on the damn overhead light, you motherfucker." I can say anything I dang well please now. This baby is in control.

He lifts me off the commode and even helps clean me up with a warm, wet towel. I cling to him because I can do no other. We waddle together like something joined back into the little bedroom, and he does as I say. I lie on the bed, my knees up, and he props the two thin, no-count pillows behind me. I pant and bite down hard on a wet washcloth he's used to wipe my red hot face. But I'm still shivering, with fear and cold and pain.

"AGGGGGG," I half scream as a bigger contraction grips me. They come and they go, come and go, come go, come go, for how long I don't know, an eternity, until I feel down between my legs. A big round ball right there between my legs! "It's coming," I say. "It's about to come out!"

Ben gets down near my bottom on the bed. "Wait, wait, wait," I hiss. "Are your hands clean? Get a clean towel. Hurry!"

Another big pain sweeps over me, until I am the pain itself, swallowed by the pain, tumbling through its dark tunnel, ass over teakettle. I'm dying, I think, I'm gonna die right here. This baby is gonna split me open, and not all the king's horses and all the king's men can put me back together again.

"AGGGGG!"

"I see it!" Ben exclaims. "I see the baby's head! It's got hair!"

"Hair?"

"It's red!"

Our eyes meet in surprise. It's the first time I can remember when we've actually looked direct at one another. I have never wanted to look him in the face, in the eyes, but I am caught off guard. His eyes move up to my red hair.

"AGGGGGG!"

"It's coming ... more of the head—the ears—are here."

I am giving birth to an elephant. A grown one.

"AGGGGG!"

"The head is free! It just popped out! A whole baby head!"

"AGGGGG! Help me, you idiot!"

He must do something, maybe pull on the baby's ears for all I know, but suddenly there is another enormous pain, and then it's over. I may black out a moment, because the next thing I know, Ben is laying a slimy pink baby on my chest. Its legs are scrunched up, its little hands in tight fists, its face screwed up and awful looking. This birth was no fun for it either. It has a funny-shaped head with a tuft of copper hair, and while we both look on, it huffs and puffs and lets out a mewing cry. I reach down and wipe the mucus off its nose and mouth, and then it lets out a heartier bawl. I pull it up closer to me, still connected by the pulsing cord, cuddling it in my arm with my eyes staring into its dark blue ones. It stares back intently and calms. I hold it there against my heart, resting, safe, out, my cheek pressing against its head.

We stay that way for a blissful eternity. Then Ben is saying, "Shouldn't we cut the cord?"

The cord has stopped pulsing and we both look at it, mystified.

"Get your knife."

"What? I don't have a knife."

"Never mind. I do. In my jacket pocket. Light some matches, sterilize it."

There are matches in the bathroom and he does as I say. When he comes back, I balance the baby on my chest. I pinch the cord in two places about five inches apart. "Cut between here."

"I don't think I can."

"Wash your hands good with soap and water as hot as you can get it. Then cut the cord, dammit, Ben!"

He comes back from the bathroom and squeamishly begins sawing. At least the knife is good and sharp. Good ol' Walter, thank you.

"God, it's tough as gristle."

"Do it do it do it!"

Suddenly the cord splits. We are two separate human beings. My heart breaks a little at that.

"Something is coming out … I feel it. Hold something down there, a towel or something!"

The afterbirth slips out, a blue-and-red glistening sack that seems to be dying before our eyes. Ben looks like he's about to throw up. I know cats eat the afterbirth, but I'm not about to do that. "Put it in the trash can in the bathroom," I say.

When he comes back, I'm resting with the baby cuddled up in my arm, my face against its fuzzy, copper tuft.

"Can I see it?" Ben whispers.

I hesitate a moment. Then I hand it over. He takes the baby in his hands carefully, his face flushing. "That was just amazing!" he says, and at that exact moment, it pees straight up into the air. We both look down between its legs. Baby Inga has a tiny perfect penis.

Chapter Twenty-Five

Inga

February turned to March, March to April. Our days of winter, so foggy and chilly, began to brighten toward spring, lifting spirits, even mine. In Point Defiance Park the early wildflowers, trillium and youth-on-age, brought a sense of renewal, and by mid-April the daffodils and rhododendrons were in bloom. On my days off I washed windows and floors, losing myself in physical labor, my mind blank except for the task at hand. I practiced my shooting, sometimes with Ron at Gig Harbor, sometimes alone in my kitchen, gun unloaded, trying to coordinate all the things I'd learned. Sometimes he and I would go to a movie or out to dinner, careful to be totally casual about it, just two people getting to know one another better.

There was still no sign of Ben and Jean and nothing to do but wait. They'd been gone almost four months. Jean would have had the baby by now. I had to believe that she was alive, that I'd see her again and hold the baby one day.

As for Ben, I kept having a recurring dream about him. He was about thirteen or fourteen and had run away. In the dream, just like in life, I was both angry and bereft. He'd been gone a long time, or at least long enough for me to know he was serious, that he wasn't coming back anytime soon, if ever. I knew he was in trouble, that he was hurting, and yet there was no way I could help him. At the same time I was watching the dream, watching myself and watching Ben, who was himself watching from the woods. I knew I couldn't reach him, talk to him—he'd run away from whoever the me was who knew he was there. I was both the distressed mother in the house, and the watching one who was nowhere and everywhere. In the dream I always wrote the same note on a piece of paper and nailed it to a tree where he'd find it: *Please come home.* That's when I'd wake up.

One beautiful May evening Ron showed up unexpectedly at the house. I was surprised and a little alarmed; we always made plans ahead of time for shooting practice or going out. It was so unusual my heart raced—*maybe they'd been found.* But Ron shook his head before I even let him in the door, signaling without speaking that there was no news.

It was almost eight, and I'd taken off my work clothes and put on my mother's old housecoat I'd kept all these years because it reminded me of her. It was a floral cotton print, worn thin, with snaps down the front, big pockets, and a silly ruffle around the hem. I needed to wash my hair, and I was wearing fuzzy wuzzy bedroom slippers.

Perplexed, embarrassed, I showed him into the living room. He took the wing chair and I sat on the edge of the sofa, nervous and excited at the same time. He was wearing a polo shirt that wasn't tucked in—I was so used to seeing him in a white tucked shirt, leather belt, pants with crisp pleats. Now he had on jeans, as if he were trying out a new style or self even. He certainly looked ill at ease.

"Excuse my appearance," I said, trying to pat down my hair. "I wasn't expecting …"

"You look fine," he said brusquely.

"You look … different," I couldn't help saying.

"Yeah, I guess," he looked down at himself, frowning in appraisal. "I'm trying to loosen up. Relax," he slurred a little.

I stared at him. "Ron—you've been drinking?"

"So it shows that bad."

"—I thought you didn't drink anymore."

He moved over to the sofa, his hands in loose fists resting on his blue-jeaned knees. "I'm not starting up again, if that's what you think. I just needed a little help—to get my courage up."

I waited, my stomach full of flutters.

"I've been seeing Lola again," he said at last. "I hadn't heard from her since last fall, when I hung up on her, and then suddenly, out of the blue, she called again. And there we were, just like before."

I was silent. I remembered how he had said he wasn't ever going to see her again. I felt deflated. What did he want, for me to counsel him?

When I didn't say anything, he raised his head, which had been bowed, and looked right at me in that direct way he had. "Aren't you even going to ask me about it?"

"What do you want me to say?" I raised my eyebrows in a questioning look. I hoped my face didn't reveal the way I felt.

"I told her tonight I was seeing someone else."

A flush rolled through me.

"I always knew Lola was bad for me. I shouldn't be with her. But there I was, back in her bed."

I waited.

"I know where I really want to be. I just don't know how to get there. Here."

"But … You were so mad at me."

"You're right, I was," he said. "I still am." He laughed a little ruefully. "Obviously there's more to this … than that. I just really want you. I can't help it."

I nodded. I couldn't conjure a single, coherent thought. We sat there, both frozen for a long moment.

Then, as if beyond my will, "I want you, too."

We stole a quick glance at each other. I longed to touch his arms, his blue-jeaned legs, to take his face in my hands.

"What do we do now?" I sounded so miserable we both laughed.

"If we were in a movie, I'd carry you straight to the bedroom."

"We're hardly movie stars." Something was making me feel electric. He moved closer to me on the sofa and began massaging my neck.

We were both silent, absorbing everything that was happening. He kept on rubbing my neck.

"I kind of want to," I said finally.

"You're an easy mark."

"Don't tease me. I'm afraid."

"There's nothing to be afraid of."

"There's a lot to be afraid of!"

"Like what?"

I paused. "Life."

"Tell me what you're afraid of."

I wanted to tell him but it was hard. "Loving. It hurts. You lose people. They aren't who you think. They disappear."

"I'm right here."

I took that in.

"And another thing," I said after a moment, making us both laugh a little again. "I haven't ... you know ... in a long time."

This made him laugh more. "It's like riding a bicycle. It'll come back."

"God!" I buried my face in my hands, overcome.

He put his arms around me and kissed me. He kissed me slow, sweet and good. "How did that feel?"

"Good I think."

"If you're not sure I better try again."

Now we were half lying down against the armrest of my mother's old Victorian sofa. "I'm going to get a new sofa," I murmured.

He was nuzzling my hair, running his finger around my ear. It had been so long! So much of life had passed. I had lost so much! I kissed him back passionately, certain now of what I wanted, my body taking over for my mind, sure of things.

He led me down the little hall to my bedroom. We passed the shut door of Ben's room. It was on both our minds, but we ignored it. This was about us. Ben wasn't going to spoil this for us.

My pretty white bedroom. Ron transformed it. He was ravenous, and so was I. So much had built up for so long, so much had to be released. I moaned and emitted sounds from a primitive and remote area of my being. When I came hard and fast, I felt him explode inside me, then a sensation of us dissolving together, which I had never felt before, even with Tony. We were almost obliterated, at least I felt that way. Washed up on shore. When it was over, all I could say was, "Oh ... my ... god!"

"That was definitely an 'Oh my god,'" Ron said, leaning back against a pillow, stroking my hair where I lay against his furry chest. "How come we waited so long?"

I started to cry.

"It's okay, Inga," he said. "You're not alone anymore."

Chapter Twenty-Six

Jean

I have to admit it surprised me that Baby Inga turned out to be Buster. I named him that because he looked like his name already *was* Buster, and I was just meeting him for the first time the day he was born. I wondered if I'd be able to warm up to him, since I had already fallen so in love with Baby Inga. But after Buster started sucking on me, looking up from my breast so sweet-like with his bright eyes, I fell for him right fast. I couldn't see none of me or Jimmy in him, he was just a whole new person, and about the cutest baby there ever was.

For a long time after that first time, I wouldn't hand him over to Ben. If he had tried to talk me into it, I wouldn't have done it. But he never asked. I watched how he was fascinated by Buster, studying him when he slept, making silly faces at him to make Buster grin. When Buster would cry, Ben would ask me anxiously what was wrong, was he getting enough milk, was something hurting him? I'd put Buster over my shoulder and explain to Ben about burping. Maybe seeing Buster come into the world like that had gotten to Ben.

Right after Buster was born, we hit the road again. Ben was hell-bent on getting to San Francisco, to the end of the continent out there near that golden bridge. Maybe it reminded him of home, of Tacoma or Seattle, or maybe it was just that we could disappear into the crowd there. Now that I had Buster, I had my hands full. I figured I would stay put until I got my strength back. I had been with Ben long enough to know he wasn't interested in killing me. Being together all the time like we were, I was used to him. He took right good care of Buster and me, paying for a motel room when he could tell I was done in, shoplifting groceries so we could eat good, and we held up ever now and then in some small town so he could take an odd job for gas money.

Once we got to San Francisco, we hung out in a big park for a few days, making do with some other lost souls who had a camp like hoboes. The fog would roll in sometimes and almost cover us up, and the nights, even though it was May and ought to be warm, could freeze your blood.

In just a few days Ben talked his way into a hippie house. We got a yellow room upstairs with a rainbow painted on the wall. It didn't have a lock on the door, so Ben couldn't lock me in at night. He had to stay put to keep an eye on me. He still had his pistol, of that I was sure. Not that he threatened me with it. But after a few weeks, since I didn't seem about to bolt, he began to let me go down the hall to the bathroom by myself. I knew eventually he'd get kind of careless with the gun. I was just biding my time, making my plans. The best word in the Bible is "watch."

I began to let Ben hold Buster sometimes, which was a big help to me. I could take a bath by myself, leaving the two of them back in the room. Ben was careful with Buster, and careful with me, as if he knew I would take Buster away if he didn't do right. Sometimes I couldn't help but laugh at the way Ben would play peekaboo with Buster, making him giggle with surprise when Ben would reappear from behind his hands. At night Ben would lie down to sleep next to us on the mattress on the floor, though always on his side of it. He never tried anything, and I had stopped thinking about it. We settled into a right peaceful routine, him and Buster and me.

When we'd hang out with the others in the kitchen, I could see that the girls liked Ben and the guys admired him. He was quick with the jokes, had a winning smile, and he knew stuff about most every subject—movie stars, politics, the history of Vietnam, how to make vegetarian lasagna. He made laughin' come easy when he had an audience, though I wondered how he could even crack a smile given what was on his conscience. But maybe it wasn't on his conscience, that was the thing. Maybe he had forgot, like I sometimes felt in danger of forgetting.

Whenever I came close, I recited those girls' names in my mind, like a pretty song—*Sissy, Michelle, Monica, Angela.*

One of the girls in the house gave me some needles and yarn. I kept busy making little things for Buster, caps, socks, and sweaters. Then I made baby things for that girl to sell out on the street. I didn't really know how much she got for my wares, but I took whatever she gave me and handed it over to Ben to contribute to the food in the house. He spent his days helping the guys in the house repair the plaster and plumbing, all the things gone to wreck and ruin. One of the guys grew marijuana up in Mendocino, and Ben began selling joints for him in Golden Gate Park, getting a cut of the profits.

I never went more than a block either way outside the house, always with Ben. I couldn't imagine going out into that big city alone with Buster, with so many weird people running about. It was funny but with Ben I felt safe.

Then one day Buster got really sick, coughing and wheezing like to scare me to death. His little face puffed up and he'd try to cry, but all he could do was honk. "We have to take him to the doctor," I told Ben. "He's got to have some medicine." I could tell Ben was thinking it over, calculating the odds that someone would recognize us. He peered at Buster where I was holding him in a blanket in my arms. His little face was all red and feverish. "Let's go," Ben said. We rushed out with Buster to catch the bus to the Free Clinic, only it wasn't free. I had to pull that fifty-dollar bill out of my sock and use most of it for the medicine. After that I only had $21.67 left, and Walter's little paring knife was gone, left back in the motel where Buster was born. What must the cleaning lady have thought when she came in after we left! The medicine did the trick, and in a day or two Buster came back to his normal, happy self. When I thanked Ben for taking us, he mumbled something about it being the only thing to do.

One night not too long after that when we had gone to bed and were lying there on our mattress on the floor in the dark, Ben whispered, "Jean. Hey, Jean. Are you awake?" He didn't want to wake Buster, who was sleeping in one of the chest drawers we used as a crib on the floor next to us.

I said softly that I was.

"I've been thinking." He spoke quietly, not turned toward me but lying on his back, as if talking to the ceiling. "You know … maybe things could be different … between us. I mean, we're both so alone. And Buster is going to need a father."

His voice was so wistful and sad it almost made me cry. How hopeless it all was. What a waste!

I was silent, my throat aching.

"I'm not what you think," he said. "Not as … bad … as you believe. We can make a fresh start. I know we can."

We both lay stock still, hardly breathing.

"Life's not like that," I finally said, speaking to the ceiling myself. "It's not bits and pieces you can pick and choose. It's whole cloth. Everything counts."

He was silent.

Sissy, Michelle, Monica …

"But maybe we could just give it a try. I like you, Jean. I've grown to like you a lot."

That wasn't something I wanted to hear. It didn't help things at all. I didn't know what to say. Finally I said, "We're going to have to part ways eventually. You know that as well as I do."

He was silent for a long time. "Listen," he said, and now he turned on his side toward me on the mattress. "There's just something about you, Jean. Something good and honest and clear. I want to stay with you and Buster. I want us to be a family." He began stroking my arm gently. I started to pull away, but honestly, it felt so good, I let him do it.

"We'll talk about that tomorrow."

"Can I say one more thing?"

I didn't answer.

"I've never met anyone like you."

"Why would you have?"

He gave a soft snort. He was still stroking my arm. Up and down, over and over.

He propped himself up on one elbow next to me and played with a bit of my hair, twirling it around his finger. "We're good together, Jean. We've been through a lot. I admire you. And I really like you. Maybe more."

Now he reached over and stroked my cheek very lightly, with just his knuckles. "You know, you're so damn pretty. You don't even know how pretty you are."

A wave of loneliness passed through me, making me yearn inside. Maybe he sensed it, because he took me in his arms and kissed me on the lips, and I let him. Something was pulsing in me, something that cried out for him or maybe just a man.

He slipped off his boxers and began touching me down there. I wanted him to, it felt so good. But when I reached down to touch him, the way I used to do with Jimmy, I couldn't help drawing back my hand. That had never happened with Jimmy! I didn't know what to make of it.

"Just help me out a little here," Ben whispered in my ear, kissing my neck, making me shiver.

I reached down again, and it had gotten littler! I pulled my hand back. I was coming back to my senses. My brain had turned back on.

He turned away from me onto his back. By the light of the streetlight outside I could see his profile, his eyes open, staring at the ceiling.

"We need to sleep now," I said. "Goodnight, Ben."

For once, he had no words.

Finally the day came. It just took one quick little move on my part to grab the gun off the chest of drawers and point it at him. The tables had turned, as tables so often do. The wheel of fortune goes round and round.

"You wouldn't shoot me, Jean," he said and before he got my name clear of his mouth, I fired one true shot right between his ear and his shoulder, missing him by no more than a whisker, which was my exact intent. I'd been around guns all my life and was a pretty good shot, if I did say so myself. That shut his mouth. The bullet hit the hanger my blue jacket was on in the closet, and it dropped like I had kilt it. People came running from all over the house up to our room to see what had happened.

"We're leaving," I said to the gaping longhairs, who were staring at the gun, looking back and forth between Ben and me. Buster had set to bawling at the loud noise. I tucked the pistol into the waistband of my blue jean skirt one of the girls in the house had made for me and picked him up off the mattress, soothing him with my hand and voice. "Let's go," I said to Ben.

"We're going, we're going," Ben said to the others, "no trouble, no trouble. We're outta here." He gathered up our stuff in a hurry, crammed it into my duffel and his backpack, and that quickly, in five minutes, we were walking out of the house we had lived in for almost four months. There was no one I cared enough about to even say good-bye to, though Ben had snake-charmed several of the girls.

"Are you going to turn me in?" Ben asked on the street. "Because if you are, just kill me now. Or give me the gun, I'll do it myself. I'm not going to prison." He was wild-eyed, scared.

"Remember how you said you wanted to see those mountains I come from," I said when we reached the street. "Well, you're going to take me to see those mountains. We're going to see my Ganny. So now you got to steal us a good car, 'cause it's a long way home."

We waited in the park where all the hippies hung out until late that night. We sat in the dark but at least it wasn't cold, waiting till the city had gone to sleep. Ben didn't try to run away, just like I hadn't tried to when he had the gun. We had got so used to being together I don't think he was all that eager to part ways either, and I didn't think I could get to Ganny's without him. Once I got to Ganny's, she'd know what to do.

When it got really late that night, we walked a mile or two up and down some steep streets until I spied a Chevy Impala station wagon, almost new. I was getting to feel like we was Bonnie and Clyde. I had seen that movie back in Tacoma, the way they got tore up with bullets at the end. I was afraid that might be how we would end, in a slow motion hail of bullets, if the police got on to us. I pointed out the Impala to Ben, and he opened the hood and hot-wired it like he was expert at doing.

Thus began what Ben called our "odyssey" back across the U.S. I was getting to see more states than I knew existed. It took weeks, sticking to the back roads, shoplifting food, stealing cars. We stopped for a week somewhere for Ben to take a dish-washing job when we needed money for gas and food. In Arkansas I think it was, he hot-wired a VW camper with a pop top, which made life a lot easier. The backseat opened into a right comfortable bed. It even had a little icebox where we could keep our food. Compared to sleeping in a car, it was downright luxurious.

Chapter Twenty-Seven

Inga

Next to me on the plane, Ron is sound asleep, snoring softly. He's often exhausted from the late hours he keeps and the stress of his job. He keeps talking about retiring and I encourage him to, but I think he's addicted to police work. It's what he's good at, what he knows. What kind of danger is this trip putting him in, if we actually find Ben? I just want him to get out before he gets hurt. It scares me every day that he's a cop.

Below the clouds are incredibly white, magnificent cumulus formations. Dad taught me the names of various clouds when I was a child, most of which I've forgotten. I wish I could just shut my eyes for a moment, drop off into an oblivious, restful sleep. I don't have to hold them open to keep this plane aloft, but the constant drone of the engines, laboring to keep us aloft, keeps me listening intensely for a stutter or stall. My body and mind refuse to relax. I'm scared about flying and I'm scared about what we'll find in San Francisco.

The tip that Ben and Jean were possibly living in the Haight came in on the anonymous crime tip line. The person didn't leave a name or a number. The message was cryptic, possibly a religious crank or simply a prank: "Those who you seek dwell in the city of love. Joseph, Mary and the child." Ron got it immediately and came straight to the library to tell me.

"The Haight. Summer of love, city of love. What better place for Ben to hide out, get lost in the crowds! A hundred thousand hippies in a few square blocks—all he has to do is wear his hair in a ponytail and flash the peace sign."

"That must mean Jean is still alive!" I exclaimed. "The baby is alive!" And Ben was alive. I'd see him again.

Ron was catching a flight first thing in the morning for San Francisco.

"I have to go with you."

"No, Inga, absolutely not. It could be dangerous. If we even find them. It's a long shot, probably a wild goose chase. The local police will be involved. You'd be in the way. It might not be pretty."

"Ron, I have to go. Don't you understand? Maybe Ben will surrender peacefully if I'm there. Maybe there is something I can say or do." All I could think about was Ben shooting Ron, or Ron shooting Ben. I had to be there, I had to try to bring about a peaceful surrender.

"I can help, I know I can. I'll go crazy waiting here. I'll die if I have to be here not knowing what is going on!"

He let his chin fall to his chest. I heard a big sigh.

"What can I do with you, Inga," he said. "I love you. But you have to do exactly what I tell you. No arguing."

Now, resisting the impulse to lift my feet off the plane's floor, I think about that: Ron loves me. Right in the midst of the mess of my life, when I felt stripped and shamed and dead, Ron came along to love me. I was a tree stripped bare by a violent storm of all its leaves, and now because Ron loves me, I am coming back, one green leaf at a time. Ron! With his big hands and feet (which sweat so much the first thing he does when he comes over is wash his feet and put on a clean pair of socks), his shaggy eyebrows and balding head, his wonderfully furry chest that I harbor against, his paunch of a stomach that I love to rest my hand on when we're lying in bed, his propensity to fart, which makes me laugh in spite of myself. He's human, all right, no god, and the best thing that ever happened to me. I can trust him totally. He's struggled with his own demons, and he's accepting of others, even of someone like me.

But what right do I have to happiness? It isn't as if the sorrow goes away, the guilt, the anguish over all that has transpired. How these things can exist along with Ron, along with love, I don't understand. But love him I do, and there is real happiness in that, mature happiness. The sound of his voice on the phone, even when he's tired and crabby from long hours, seeing too much of the raw side of life, lifts my heart. The touch of his hand soothes and thrills me. He's a natural homebody, it turns out, single only by default, as if life has constantly dealt him the wrong cards, and only now has he gotten the hand he wants. He comes over no matter what hour of the night he gets off work, taking the precaution to park around the block. We figure people know, the way they do, but why broadcast it? As long as we don't make a public deal about it, his superiors will look the other way until he retires. One time at work Larry commented on how much better I was looking, how there's such color in my cheeks—then he paused, thought a moment, and said, "ahhhh ..." and when I didn't respond, caught like the proverbial deer in the headlights, he just laughed and patted me on the back.

Now Ron sleeps beside me here on the plane, while I am overly awake with assorted anxieties. Maybe that tip didn't even mean what we thought it did. How will we ever find them, even if they're there? And what if we do? Then what? I don't see any good outcomes. No happy endings. But we have to find them, we just have to.

Why would Jean still be with him? She must have had some opportunity to escape. Ron and I have pondered this time and again. He said maybe she's too afraid, or maybe it's that she's become dependent on her captor. Maybe Ben has threatened her or the baby. Or maybe he's convinced her he's innocent. He's got a golden tongue.

Maybe if I just shut my eyes for a moment. We got up so early to catch this flight ... I hardly slept, afraid the alarm wouldn't go off ... maybe I can rest a little bit now ... I've gotten used to the white noise of the plane ... so mesmerizing ... I won't actually sleep, just ... I'm so tired, tired to the bone ... something good ... something ... something good is going to happen ... we're flying somewhere ... Ron and I ... something that makes me happy ... I'm looking forward ... going to see our son and daughter-in-law ... and their new baby ... That must be it ... I haven't seen the baby yet ... I can't wait to see ..."

I jolt to consciousness, my breathing fast and shallow. Ron jerks awake, puts his hand on mine where they're clenched in my lap. My heart is racing ... oh please, not that, not now!

"Inga, honey, it's okay," Ron says. "Com'ere," and he releases our seat belts so he can put his arm around me. He holds me awkwardly, but it still feels safe and solid and real. Ron is with me, I'll be okay.

"What is it," he says, when my breathing and pulse have calmed. "Tell me."

"I dreamed ... I mean, it was only a dream! We were flying to see them."

"Who, sweetheart? Ben? Jean?"

"Yes, only it was all different. All different! They were married, there was none of ... the other. We were going to see our grandbaby ..." I shook my head, shocked that it was only a dream.

"It's okay, Inga. It's okay." He strokes my hair, cradling the back of my head with his big hand.

"Why can't it be like that, Ron!" I cry. "Why does it have to be the way it is! It's so ... ugly! So ... wrong!"

"I'd change it if I could."

The stewardess stops by our row, a concerned look on her face. "Is there anything I can do? Is she all right?"

I pull myself together. "No, no," I insist. "I'm okay. I'll be all right. Can I borrow ... ?" but Ron already has his handkerchief out to give me.

We stand on the corner of Ashbury and Haight, surrounded by dilapidated old Victorian houses and brownstones. The street is alive with hippies, the way I've seen them on TV. The air is filled with bongo drums and a screeching electric guitar from a head shop behind us. What I first assume is the smell of incense Ron informs me is marijuana. The kids all have long hair, some, like the Blacks are wearing, in big Afros, and the girls have long loose hair and tie-dyed T-shirts, overalls, or dresses down to their ankles. I wonder where all these young people live, maybe in Golden Gate Park. Where are they from, who are their parents, and do they know their children are here, in the Haight? Are these kids okay? We have to step around one young man who is sitting in the middle of the sidewalk with a glazed look to his eyes. I catch Ron by the arm, "Are you sure he's all right? Should we do something?" "He's tripping on LSD," Ron says. "We're seeing a lot of that in Tacoma."

So this is where the famous Summer of Love took place. I'm curious to see it, and a little frightened of it. It's like all these young people have their own world here, a world that we're outsiders to, a world we can't really understand or participate in. We stick out like sore thumbs, even though we have "dressed down," worn jeans and T-shirts ourselves. Ron is wearing an old khaki sport coat to conceal his gun. But we are old, grown-ups, and these kids are like Peter Pan and the Lost Boys. They look excited to be alive, jazzed up, making it up as they go along. There's something of a carnival atmosphere but with an undercurrent of what? Like they've stayed too long at the party or maybe showed up when the party was already over.

Ron begins showing the picture of Ben to anyone and everyone we encounter. "Are you pigs, man?" one young man asks suspiciously. "Are you narcs?" "Parents, bro," Ron answers, sending the boy into gales of laughter. "High," Ron says, taking my arm as we step through the crowd. "Let me ask," I say. "Maybe someone will respond to me, rather than a 'pig.'"

"Oink," Ron sighs.

After several hours of no luck, exhausted, we finally go into a small storefront café for a cup of coffee. I realize we haven't even stopped for lunch. Ron is used to missing meals, but I'm three squares a day. We order the day's special chalked on a blackboard, red beans and brown rice. There's no meat on the menu, only hippie food, as Ron calls it. "What I wouldn't give for a medium-rare hamburger," he says plaintively. Sitar music twangs in the background.

"We're never going to find them," I say. "I'm not even sure anyone can recognize him from the photograph. He's probably changed his looks. Talk about a needle in a haystack."

A girl comes over to refill our coffee cups. She picks up the photograph of Ben on the table. "Recognize him?" Ron asks reflexively.

"Yeah," she drawls, "Willie. He's got that mole by his eye."

We both stare at her. She's a beautiful young woman, her ash blonde hair gathered into two long braids. She wears one of the Indian-style dresses we've been seeing, with tiny mirrors sewn into the bodice. She's barefoot, which I've never seen in a waitress before.

"Do you … know Willie," I stutter.

"Are you his folks or something?"

"I'm his mother."

"Cool. They're crashing over on Pine Street."

"They?"

"Willie, Dawn, and Buster. Cute kid."

"What address?"

"It's that big purple place on the corner. At least they were there last time I was over. People come and go there. Want more coffee? We have some super granola bars."

Ron whips out a twenty. "Keep the change," he says as we head out the door. I glance back and see the girl staring open mouthed after us. "Cool!" she calls.

"Willie, Dawn, and Buster," I say as we half run down the street. "Can it be? What if it's them?"

We stand in front of a large Victorian, terribly shabby, that has been painted in pinks, purples, and blues, someone's psychedelic dream. The steps are half rotted, the railing missing, and an old couch and some broken wooden chairs are scattered on the big porch across the front of the house. I look up toward the windows. The house is three stories, with a turret on top. A flimsy white curtain blows out an open window like a white surrender flag, but no faces appear.

I think about Ron's gun and my heart races with fear. "Let me go in first," I beg. "Let me talk to him first, Ron! Please!"

"Come with me," he says. We walk in the open door and stand for a moment in the entry hall, where a wide wooden staircase, grand in its day but badly neglected now, leads up to the second floor. Voices come from the back of the first floor. Ron and I look at one another, but he takes the lead, going down the hall past the dining room with a big oval table and a rickety collection of wooden chairs to the kitchen.

Three kids, a boy and two girls, none older than twenty, are sitting at a kitchen table passing a joint around. They glance up when we enter. They continue their conversation, something about cosmic love, as if strangers walk in all the time, and maybe they do. After we stand there a moment, the girl with long bangs that almost obscure her eyes offers the joint to us. "Wanna hit?"

"No thanks," I say. "We're looking for my son."

"Groovy," the young man says without much interest.

"What's his name," the other girl says.

"Wait," I say, "we have a picture." Ron shows it to them. "Do you know him?"

"That's Willie, ain't it?" the fellow says to the girls. "Is that Ol' Willie?"

"I … I don't know," I say. "I mean, he might go by Willie … here."

"I just love Willie," the girl with bangs says. "Though he's weird. But that's cool." It occurs to me that they are very high. "I love Dawn too. It's not like I have a thing for Willie. I never slept with him. 'Cause I love Dawn and Buster. I love everybody, don't I?" She asks this question to the air.

"Is there a baby? Is Buster the baby?" I ask.

"They split," the guy says. "Bang! Didn't say good-bye. Took all their stuff and split. That's their trip. Split and didn't say a word."

"When?" Ron, forcefully.

"Man, I don't know. Sometime."

"Try to remember."

"I dunno, last week? The week before … or … ?"

"They left, man, just took off. Didn't say good-bye. Took all their stuff. Bang! What a trip! Split."

"Do you know where they went?"

They all shake their heads, no. No big deal.

"Can we see the room they were in?"

"Second floor, rainbow room. You can crash there. We don't have any hang-ups about who crashes here. Even old dudes. All are welcome, ain't that right?"

"Right on."

We leave them nodding and agreeing that they don't have any hang-ups, not only about who stays there but about what people look like, if they're black or white, straight or gay …

We run up the stairs. Could we have just missed them! They had been here, in this very house. I want to see the room, I want to touch something they've touched, I want to get as close to them as I can.

We look around when we reach the landing. What a beautiful place this must have been at one time, but now the wallpaper is peeling, the wooden floors are scuffed and scarred, and there's a musty, offensive odor, like wet rotting insulation and cat piss. There are six doors, all open. We go door by door, looking into each room, until we come to one that is empty except for a tattered, stained mattress on the floor. It's a small room with a big radiator, painted a glaring yellow, with a big rainbow across one wall. It's so shabby and crummy that it almost breaks my heart. How long did they live here? What did they do? What made them leave suddenly? We can't ask the three nodding heads downstairs.

Ron is opening the small closet. "Do you recognize this?" He holds up my blue down jacket, which was crumpled on the floor of the closet.

"It's Jean's! I gave it to her when we were at Dad's. Why would she leave it? As a sign?"

"There's a bullet hole here in the closet wall."

"A bullet hole … ."

"Phew," Ron says, "what's this?"

He holds up a garbage bag tied with a knot. He undoes it—it has a couple of dirty diapers in it. "Buster," he says, "obviously has a healthy digestive tract."

While Ron goes to call the local police to bring over a forensics team, I look out the window at the view they had. What did they feel in this room? Was Jean frightened? Tortured? Had he threatened to harm the baby if she didn't do what he said. Or … and this was a startling, disturbing thought, had she fallen in love with Ben? Had he manipulated her and made her think *he* was the victim? The innocent party, wrongly accused. Where were they now?

It is late when Ron gets back to our hotel room. He stayed while the police interviewed the house occupants and ran forensics tests in the room and bath. Unfortunately the three nodding heads got busted. Some parents somewhere are going to get a phone call in the middle of the night. At least their kids are alive.

I prop up in bed while Ron takes a shower. I had fallen asleep the moment I hit the bed, but now at three a.m. I'm wide awake. How does Ron do it? He must have the constitution of a pack animal. I figure he's exhausted and probably hungry.

"Not hungry," he says when I ask him. He gets in bed beside me and props his arms behind his head. I lay my head against his chest, listening to the steady, slow beat of his heart. That's all it takes. In a few moments, we're making love.

When we've finished, we lie in the dark, wrapped in each other's arms.

Then, out of the blue, Ron says, "Let's get married, Inga."

I feel lightheaded, and a thrill runs through me. "What?"

He turns over just enough to switch on the bedside light, then gathers me back in his arms. I look in his eyes. He is looking back in that direct, serious way he has. "We never know how much time we're going to have. I love you and I want to marry you. ASAP."

"I love you, too."

"So it's a deal. What are you doing tomorrow?"

I push away from him. "Don't. We have to find them."

"It's possible we'll never find them, Inga. We probably will but it could be months, years. Ben is very adept at evading the law."

"I keep thinking about something, Ron. I don't know why. When Ben stayed on Jean's balcony those two nights, she called him a snake."

"Why a snake? Why didn't you tell me about this before?"

"I didn't think it was important. But it's been coming back to me lately. Her grandmother lives somewhere way up in the North Carolina mountains. Jean told me a story about how when she was little, she and Ganny came upon a big rattlesnake wrapped around a tree. Jean collapsed from fear but Ganny killed the snake."

Ron turns toward me, squeezing my shoulders.

"What, what is it?"

"Don't you see! That's where they'll head next."

Chapter Twenty-Eight

Jean

"You hold him for awhile," I say. "I'll fix us some lunch."

We've just pulled into a picnic area on the Blue Ridge Parkway. Ben—I never got used to calling him Willie, though that was his name when we lived in that ugly hippie house in California—has never seen this part of the country, my part, and I join him at the guardrail, where he's gazing out at the view like he's in a trance. At five months old, I reckon my little red head weighs nigh to sixteen pounds, and my arms are about to give out. I hand him over, and Buster smiles up at Ben with that goofy grin of his. "How's Mr. Buster," Ben coos at him. "Are you Mr. Buster? Mr. Buster Brown?" He lifts Buster high in the air, like he's flying, and Buster crows with delight.

We've been on the road over a month. It's the first of October now, and while the leaves are not yet at their peak, the parking lot still has plenty of leaf gawkers. Summer has come and gone, men have walked on the moon, and here Ben and I are, still together, though that is coming to an end soon. One way or another, we are about to part ways. It's been a year since he showed up on my balcony back in Tacoma. It's been nine months since I last saw or heard from Mrs. D, or anyone else for that matter. I wonder how she is, how her heart is doing, and if she has found a way to mend it.

We have some sandwich makings in the icebox in the VW camper, baloney and pimento cheese we got at a Winn-Dixie outside Knoxville. I glance over to see Ben sitting on one of the big rocks that line the parking area, bouncing copper-top Buster on his knee. Ben has let his curls grow back in brown, and he's shaved off his big beard. My own hair has grown so long I wear it in a braid down my back, light brown near my scalp but still red on the ends. Ben doesn't seem to care if anyone recognizes us or not, or maybe he figures people have forgot about us. Maybe he has forgot. I don't know, 'cause I never ask Ben any questions. One time he said that was what he liked about me. "Like people think *I* know," Ben said.

I suppose to any of the folks at the picnic area, we look like any other young couple with a baby. It's hard sometimes to keep straight what's real and what isn't. But even if we look like anybody else, we are hardly that. I do keep that little pistol tucked in my skirt waistband, hidden under my baggy sweater. No one need know it's there except Ben, and since I took it from him, I don't think he is like to forget. When we first left California, I thought Ben might light out at the first opportunity. But he's stuck with us, and I don't think it's because of the gun. Maybe he doesn't know what else to do, where else to go. Or maybe it's because of Buster, the way he reaches for Ben, the way he falls asleep in his arms, the way he looks at Ben with innocent adoration.

Calling Ben to come eat, I put the sandwiches on paper plates and carry them over to a weathered picnic table. It looks like it's been through many a winter up here on the mountain. The air now is crisp, sweater weather, and for a moment I let my eyes rest on the mountains beyond, which are taking on the colors of fall. Suddenly I feel how weary I am of my load. I plan to lay it down at Ganny's. I look at Ben, who grins at me, holding up his baloney sandwich to show he approves, and my heart kinda heaves. What I feel for Ben Daudelin I can't really say, but it isn't what I would have thought. But we are coming to the end. I feel it just like I feel the turn in the weather up here in the mountains, summer turning to fall, with winter not far behind. I know Ben is bound for the grave or jail. We will just have to play it out, one way or another.

As for me, I want to see my Ganny, to lay my head on one of her feather pillows, the feathers of which she plucked from her own geese. I want to eat someone's home cookin' for a change, not the fast food we've eaten on the road for weeks, nor the rice and beans and alfalfa sprouts we had back in California. I want a real fried chicken, its neck wrung with Ganny's own strong hands, with mashed potatoes and cream gravy, and the thin little biscuits Ganny could whip up in her sleep. Maybe there'll be some applesauce from the tart apples that will be falling from her tree about now. I've traveled many a mile to reach home.

Getting to Ganny's is no easy feat. Unless you know the way, you won't never find it. It's way up in the mountains, with the road turning to dirt and getting smaller and smaller until it's just a one track, sometimes too muddy or washed out to pass. In the winter it's shut down with snow and ice. You have to keep your nerve driving on that road, coming so close as you do to dropping off the side of the mountain, blind curves and all. But luckily there is still light when we draw near to her place.

At sunset I pull off on Laurel Ridge Road. We walk a path through the woods to the end of that ridge, as I have done many a time. The sun is a fiery ball going down behind the farthest range of smoky blue mountains. It's a beautiful sight, the near mountains turning gold and red. We watch the sun sink down like it's being swallowed, then gone. After that, the whole big sky lights up pink and orange. We linger there, the three of us, about at the end of our journey, to watch the evening come. We stand in silence, Ben and me thinking our own thoughts, and Buster not thinking at all, I suppose. I wonder then if Ben ever thinks of those girls, how he snuffed out their lives. When we turn to leave, there are tears in both our eyes, but what his are for, I can't say.

Ganny's house is down a winding dirt road on the other side of Laurel Ridge. As we start down, I can see one light on at her place, with just the faintest trace of chimney smoke in the navy blue sky. Her place is set in Morgan's Hollow, nestled by the ridges around it, like you might cup something in your hand. There's her rusted old tractor, the Airstream trailer someone abandoned long ago, the pickup she no longer drives, and the falling-down barn, which has sunk even more since the last time I was here. At least there's no sheriff car around. All looks peaceful. Now that we are bouncing down the dirt driveway that leads in, I feel both excited and calm. I'll show Buster to Ganny, and she'll know what to do about Ben.

In the yard I turn off the engine and we sit there a moment, letting the bouncing leave our heads.

"Well," Ben says, "You're finally home, Jean."

"This is it," I say.

"Maybe I shouldn't come in." His voice is choked, the first time ever.

"What else you going to do?"

"Maybe it's time for me to push on."

I turn that over in my mind. I turn and look at him, his downcast eyes, his mouth taut with tension. There's beauty in that face, and horror. The best and worst of man.

"You might as well spend the night," I say. "Meet Ganny. Then we'll see."

Just then the door to the house opens. I see lit from the porch light the little figure of Ganny peering out, her hand over her eyes as if it is us rather than her in the light. I bound out of the car, across the dirt yard, and up the three rickety steps to the porch, calling, "Ganny, Ganny, it's me! I'm home. It's Jeannie!"

"Why, lawdy me!" Ganny says, clutching me to her with what feels like chicken claws. "Lawd, child, is it really you come home?"

I'm laughing and crying, then suddenly I remember Buster, who Ben had been holding as I drove in. Ben brings him up to me and I take him under the arms and hold him out for Ganny to see.

"Ganny, this is my baby. Buster. The one I gave life to."

Ganny sweeps her gnarled hand over his head. She holds out her arms and I hand him over, all wide-eyed and blinking in the light. "And Ganny," I say, nodding to Ben behind me. "This is Ben."

"I know Ben," she says, and beckons us to enter with a tilt of her head.

I step into the kitchen, onto the worn linoleum floor. It's all just the way I remember it, though it seems I've been gone forever. Ganny's shotgun where she keeps it by the door, the cast-iron woodstove she cooks on, the long table covered with oil cloth, pushed up against the window, laden with ancient almanacs, empty mason jars, a ball of twine, cracked butter molds, dried milkweed pods, a big wash basin speckled black and white. A delicious smell steams the windows: chicken and dumplings! Like she knew I was coming. Like she was ready. There's a pone of corn bread on the back burner, and on the table a cut-glass dish with butter Ganny churned and molded with a flower impression on top. "Y'all take off your jackets," Ganny is saying, "hang 'em up there." She points to the pegs by the door. "Toilet's out back," she indicates to Ben with a wave of her hand. "There's buttermilk or coke, or maybe the gentleman wants something a little stronger."

Ben smiles and sits down at the table. "Coke'll be fine." What did Ganny mean, she knows him? Does she know about Ben? Or is that just an expression, like *glad to know you*? Ganny has her own way of expressing herself, and she doesn't seem upset a'tall about Ben.

She sits in her rocking chair, the one with the carved back she always sits in, and I put Buster in her lap. He looks up at her grizzled face in wonder, torn between crying or laughing. When she makes a face at him, laughing wins out. Ganny is missing right many of her teeth, her skin brown as an Indian's, and she isn't much taller than a child. I notice that she grabs on to things when she walks, like she can't totally count on her legs to hold her up. How much longer can she keep on up here on her own? She comes from hardy Scots-Irish stock, but there is a limit even to that.

I dish up bowls of the chicken and dumplings and get the mismatched silverware from the drawer. All the time something in me is singing, "Home, home," and a lightness has come into my heart. I have been a wayfaring stranger, but now I am home. Ganny will take care of me, she'll know what to do.

I eat enough for three men, but I notice Ben doesn't have much appetite. Ganny and I make small talk, about her cow, chickens, and geese, and what the weather has been like. The farmer's almanac predicts a hard winter. Lots of cold and snow.

"I can't chop wood like I used to," Ganny says.

"Maybe I could help you out tomorrow," Ben says.

"May be," Ganny says.

After dinner we drowse in the warmth of the room. Every now and then Ganny stokes the woodstove. She opens the door to the back bedroom, so it will get some heat. Normally, it being just her, she doesn't heat it, but that's where Ben will sleep tonight. There's a double bed in the far corner of this room, where Ganny always sleeps. Buster has fallen asleep in my lap, so I lay him on the bed, covering him with Ganny's hand-stitched quilt. I feel heavy and warm myself, and could curl up in bed right next to Buster.

"What's this, Ganny," Ben is saying. He has spied her autoharp and is holding it up to examine. She used to play it for me when we'd visit, and sing old ballads and hymns. She wanted me to learn but I never did.

"I bet you never seen one of 'em harps," Ganny says, rocking away.

"Do you play?" Ben asks. "Would you play us a tune?"

Ganny is silent for a long time. I wonder if she has heard Ben, but finally she says, "Might as well."

He hands her the autoharp, which she puts across her lap. "This is an old favorite of some," she says, and begins strumming. The autoharp has a strange keening quality. It about puts me in a trance.

Then Ganny begins singing, her own voice a mountain voice, with that peculiar twang that seems a perfect accompaniment to the harp.

"Who's that knocking at my door, have I heard that knock before?
Is it evil trying to get into my room
Who's that's tapping at my window, who's calling me to go
To a place that's filled with dark and gloom.
Oh this life that I'm living, it seems so unforgiving
I find trouble everywhere I go
I always seek it first, just to quench my burning thirst
In waters that are cool as fallen snow
But the waters are so deep, what you sow you must reap
Now I hear a knocking at my door
It's evil standing outside, there's no place to run and hide
It plucks my soul and presses me to the floor
Oh I've been down that pathway, it always leads the wrong way
But this time I don't think I'll be back
Feels like a freight train pulling me, there's a dark tunnel ahead I see
This train's going down a one-way track

I feel the hair on the back of my neck stand up. For a long time none of us speaks, bewitched maybe, with just the crackling of the fire in the stove the only sound. When I finally dare look over at Ben, he has the strangest expression on his face, one I've never seen before, like he's seeing that dark tunnel ahead.

"Time for bed," Ganny says, laying the autoharp aside, breaking the spell she's cast. "Ben, son, you won't be too cold I hope. There's lots of them quilts in that cedar chest. And Jeannie, you can snuggle up with me."

With that Ganny goes into the kitchen and gets her shotgun. She brings it back to the bed, where she leans it carefully against the wall.

"Up here in the mountains," she says, "we got big cats and bears and rattlers and no telling what all in them woods. Always sleep with my gun."

Chapter Twenty-Nine

Inga

As soon as he learns about Ganny, Ron calls the North Carolina authorities and tells them to get directions to Ganny's house from Jean's mother and follow up on his hunch that that's where Ben and Jean might be. Now he's come back to lie beside me on the bed in our hotel room in San Francisco. We stay that way in silence for a long time. What is there to say? If I had recognized early on that something was wrong in Ben, those four Alpine Lake girls might still be alive. If I had called the police when Ben showed up on Jean's balcony last fall, the girls in Modesto might never have been harmed. If I had done the right thing when Ben showed up at Dad's, at least Jean might have been spared. I didn't intend to withhold information from Ron about Ganny, but he must think I did. I watch the ceiling panels go from black to gray as night turns to dawn. I listen to Ron's quiet breathing. I can tell he isn't asleep either. Finally, when the sun shines in the window, he stirs, gets up, takes a shower, calls room service for breakfast. He orders what he knows I like, a large orange juice, a poached egg on toast, and a side order of corned beef hash. For him toast and coffee.

"Get ready, Inga," he says. "We have a plane to catch." I rouse myself, stand in the shower, and then, in spite of everything, I realize I'm starving. How this can be I don't know, but my stomach burns with acid and demands something be put in it.

While we sit at the little table in the room, Ron occupies himself reading the newspaper that came with room service. We haven't heard anything back from the local sheriff in Franklin, North Carolina, who has gotten the task of going out to Ganny's. We don't know if they've found Ben there and taken him into custody, shot him dead, or just frightened an old lady. Maybe they haven't even gone out to Ganny's, for all we know. Maybe Ron's wrong about where Ben and Jean would head. We're totally in the dark.

After we finish breakfast and Ron has set the trays outside the room, he sits back down at the table and clears his throat, as if about to make a speech. He looks at me for a long moment. Then he reaches over and takes my hand. He rubs the top of my thumb with his thumb. In a movie or over dinner, he'll often take my hand that way, rub my thumb like that. "Let's just get back to Tacoma. I have a lot going on in my head right now."

I nod and set about packing. We're courteous and careful with each other on the trip home, both preoccupied with what the authorities will find at Ganny's and what lies ahead for us.

Ron comes over that night after we get back. I didn't expect to see him so soon. I have purposefully kept the news off all afternoon and evening, afraid of what I might hear. So I know he has something to tell me, I just don't know what.

"Tell me."

"It's not what you think, Inga," Ron says. "Come sit down."

He takes me by the elbow, the way he did that first time he came to the house. Gentle, polite. He deposits me on the sofa but takes the wing chair himself, as if we're strangers.

I search his face. It's only in lovemaking that it softens, relaxes. He's shaking his head, as if bemused.

"All they found at Ganny's was a cantankerous old woman. They're not there, Inga, and never have been. I was wrong about that." He tells me how Ganny met the sheriff at the door with her shotgun cocked. Once they convinced her they were the law, she let them in and showed them around the property. No sign of Ben or Jean. The only tire tracks in the dirt yard matched the neighbor's truck across the ridge. "The sheriff said he'd keep an eye on the place," Ron sighs.

"But you were so sure they'd head to Ganny's."

"Okay, whatever. I guess that isn't where they headed." He rubs his face hard. "They could be anywhere."

"I see," I say, hardly knowing what I feel.

"There's more," Ron say. "A man has confessed to the Modesto killings."

Ron tells me how a young woman whom the guy met at a bar escaped from his car as they were supposedly driving to her apartment for a drink. When he made a turn different from the directions she had given him, her instincts told her something wasn't right. She leapt from his car even though they were going about forty miles an hour, fracturing her arm but saving her life. When he tried to grab her, he swerved the car, crashing into a telephone pole. It was just one of those lucky breaks, for her and the police, which so easily could have gone the other way. The police found duct tape, clothesline, and a knife in his trunk. When they took him in for questioning, he confessed to the Modesto killings, giving a chilling, precisely detailed account.

"But he didn't admit to any of the murders Ben was arrested for," Ron says wearily. "All us law enforcement people were convinced Ben did the Modesto killings, as well as the four Alpine Lake girls. The Modesto guy's lawyered up, and his lawyer is trying to work out a plea bargain, but apparently nothing can shake a confession for any of the other murders out of him. Kind of makes you reconsider the merits of torture."

So Ben didn't kill those girls in Modesto. He said when he showed up at Dad's that he hadn't had anything to do with them. Now it turns out that that, at least, is the truth. Could he possibly not be guilty of the others? He said he was innocent at the jail. I try to remember exactly what he said at Dad's. Had he denied the four girls the same way he did the Modesto crimes? But all that speculation. He couldn't have just been theorizing.

"I'm going to retire," Ron says. "I just decided driving over here. I'm going to put in for two weeks vacation right away and then retire by Christmas."

Alarm runs through me. I see how his eyes have bags under them, how his color is off. All this stress is surely taking a toll on his health. I want to put my arms around him, ease him, but I don't move. I'm not sure I have that right. "When was the last time you took time off?"

"I don't really take time off. But right now I can't believe how sick I am of all this. There're other things I want to do with my life—like hike those blue mountains I was telling you about."

"That's good, Ron. A good idea."

He leans back in the wing chair, tipping it up on the back legs, something that old chair isn't used to. "Oops," he says, when it groans, threatening to crack. He tips back and comes over to the sofa and lies down across it, putting his head in my lap. I shift to make us both more comfortable, hardly daring to breathe. His legs and feet extend over the end of the hard little sofa. I can't help smoothing his bald head, just to touch him.

"When did I get so dog-tired, Inga? The funny thing is, this fellow they arrested in Davis? The one who confessed to killing those girls in Modesto? I was just so sure it was Ben. So damn sure! I didn't really talk about it much to you, but in my own mind, I was convinced Ben had killed those girls, too. Now, it turns out, he didn't."

What if we were wrong, I'm thinking. *What if we were wrong about Ben all along?*

He's silent for a long time. "But it doesn't matter what I think," he says. "What any of us *think*. He has to be apprehended, brought to trial. Maybe I should leave that to others. Considering everything."

Ron sits up and looks at me. He takes my cold hands in his. "Let's get married. I want us to get married now. I know it's sudden and I know you're unprepared for this, but it's the right thing. Nothing has ever felt so right to me in my life."

I'm thinking of all the reasons we shouldn't. It's so sudden, we have a rocky past, he doesn't really trust me, he's in an altered state, he'll change his mind, he'll regret it. And what about me? I'm not really marriage material. And Ben. He'll always be there, between us.

I take a deep breath. I'm going to tell him all this, all the reasons it's a bad idea. I'm going to tell him how we need to go slow, take our time, not make a mistake. But I don't speak.

"Look at us, Inga," Ron says. "How are you going to go on without me? How am I going to go on without you? We have a chance at some kind of happiness, together. The nearest we can come now to happiness."

I'm listening.

"We have to move forward. That's all there is to it. Ben … I don't know. Whatever happens there, we'll face it together. I'm here for you—and I want you here for me."

All I can do is nod.

"Is that funny face you're making a yes, then?"

I bury my face in his shoulder. He rubs my back, letting me cry it out. When I've calmed, I say into his neck, "Yes."

We get married in the courthouse in Tacoma a week later. Lorraine and Larry are my witnesses, and Ron's sister comes over from Puyallup for him. "Maybe the fourth time'll be the charm," she says wryly to Ron. I like her, a squat woman with thinning hair and an obvious affection for her kid brother. I have no family myself. In another life, Ben would be here, wishing me well, and Jean would be here too, where she belongs. I'd toss her the calla lilies Ron brought over to the house this morning, and I'd put my arms around her, giving her a long hug. The municipal judge who marries us wears the most god-awful plaid sport coat I've ever seen, and has an obvious toupee. We tie the knot over the lunch hour, so that Lorraine and Larry can make it on such short notice. We go back to my house and have a quick glass of champagne with a cake from the grocery store before Lorraine and Larry go back to work. Ron and I go to bed, loving each other.

Afterwards, lying in bed, Ron says something unexpected. He's full of surprises.

"I've been thinking. Maybe we should move. Leave this town. Get a fresh start. I have a good pension, we can both sell our houses. We could get different jobs somewhere. Whadda ya think?"

"Leave Tacoma?"

"What's keeping you here, Inga?"

"I … I … don't know, really. I like it, I guess. Or do I? Maybe not, not anymore."

"It's got a lot of history for us both. Too much. We could go somewhere where people don't know you as Ben's mother, where they don't know me as a cop."

"They'll find out about Ben. It won't go away."

"I know. But it wouldn't be the same. Not so … what's the word—intense. Maybe people would leave us alone."

"Where, Ron?"

"I was thinking about those blue mountains. You gotta see them. There's just a feeling there, I can't explain it. It's peaceful and beautiful, with lots of room. Lots of woods. And you don't feel like you're so important there, that you matter so much. Not as much as the trees and mountains, at least."

"Jean loved—loves—those mountains. I *would* like to see them, but I don't know. I've never thought of living in the South!"

"We don't have to decide right away. I've got those two weeks starting next week. Let's just take a trip. A honeymoon, call it. Exploratory."

"Can we go see Ganny?"

"They're not there, Inga honey."

"It's not that. I'd just like to meet her. Jean talked so much about her. I'd like to pay my respects. Tell her I'm sorry."

"I guess it couldn't hurt," he says. "But enough talk about old grannies." He's reaching down between my legs, starting again.

I'm as hungry for him as ever. But at the same time I'm thinking about Ganny, about going there, seeing her. In some way I feel I owe it to Jean.

We fly to Charlotte the next week and rent a car to drive to Asheville. It's the first of October, not yet the height of the leaf season, but the Blue Ridge Parkway already has a lot of traffic. Ron wants to see the Biltmore Estate, so we spend a day touring the house, which is so grand it's amazing. "This is the closest I'll ever get to Europe," Ron says, for indeed, the house and grounds don't seem American but more fit for royalty. We walk the formal gardens holding hands. The weather is perfect, crisp and sunny, with not a cloud in the sky. That first night we stay at the Mountain Laurel Motel on the edge of Asheville and walk around the town the next day, up and down its steep hills. I like how it's surrounded by mountains. The mountains aren't like the Olympics. These are gentler, not so big and rugged. Ron's right, they are peaceful, spiritual in the way of mountains, as if they'll go on long after all of us and our human problems are gone. Asheville has obviously seen better days, back around the turn of the century when it was a resort town. Ron says the town must not have had the money since to tear down the Art Deco buildings and put up new ones, so at least they've been preserved. They'll be here when the town has a revival. Maybe it would be a good place to live, a place to get a new start together.

We decide to drive over toward Brevard and stop at Ganny's on the way. Ron's gotten the directions from the Franklin sheriff, who has been driving up to Ganny's every few days, though Ron said his interest is waning. I read the directions to Ron as we turn off Highway 16 near Glenville and then make several more turns onto progressively smaller roads. Finally, we're bouncing down a one-lane track; if another car comes, we'll have to back up to a wide enough spot to pass, and there aren't many of those.

"How can an old woman live up here all alone," I muse.

"Probably a tough old bird," Ron says. "Still sure you want to do this?"

"If you don't mind too much. It'll mean a lot to me."

He smiles over at me, and a swell of love fills my chest. I was moved by the vows at the courthouse: through sickness and health, till death do us part. I'm getting another chance, when I had about given up on just about everything. I look out the window at the near woods. The leaves are falling, some of the trees already bare up this high. You can tell winter's on the way and that it will be a long, hard one up here in the mountains. It puts me in a pensive mood.

At the bottom of the dirt road is an old wooden farmhouse, an Airstream trailer off to the side, old farm equipment. The place looks gone to ruin—almost deserted—but there's a little wisp of smoke coming out of the chimney. I notice a VW camper off to the side, as well as an old trailer and pickup truck. Ron is silent behind the wheel, studying the scene. We pull to a stop in the dirt yard.

Just as I start to get out, the front door of the farmhouse swings open. Jean comes flying down the steps, her long hair loose and swirling about her like a vision, her face full of ecstasy and terror. "Mrs. D, Mrs. D!" she is calling. "I knew you'd find me! Thank God you're here at last!"

Coda

Jean

I don't know why it should be so fascinatin' to watch pure water pour over bare rocks, but it just plain is. I sit out here on these big boulders whenever I can, especially on these fine August mornings. Today is Sunday, and when the folks start leaving the cabins around eleven, I can start cleaning. Cleaning's my job and I enjoy it. The cabins are easy to keep, being so simple and all. Folks who stay here have been coming for years, not like strangers just passing through who don't care. The guests don't even have to stop at the office and reserve their week for next year. It's just automatic, unless they say otherwise.

The water is so clear you can see down to the bottom of the lake, three or four feet deep. It washes over these rocks, which must be old as Moses, like it's trying to cleanse the world, over and over, again and again, world without end. When I'm cleaning the cabins, I get down on my hands and knees to scrub the linoleum floors. I use the same motion as the lake, back and forth, over and over, though the floors never look as clean—sanctified, you might say—as these rocks.

Still, sometimes when I least expect it, though not as often now, the clear water will turn blood red. Like someone has poured a bucket of blood in the lake, and it's washing up on these rocks. I know that's just in my mind. I mean, there isn't any blood in the lake, but when I see the water turn red like that, my breathing gets tight. I calm myself by concentrating on the way the water just keeps coming, lapping over the rocks. It eventually washes the blood away, until it's clear as glass again.

When we first returned here, I couldn't stop thinking about that last day in the mountains, when there was so much blood. I didn't think I'd never get better, that it would ever go away, and it hasn't—gone away—but I can say it has dimmed over time. It's been almost a year now. That's a long time in some ways, and no time at all in others.

That last morning started out peaceful enough. We had gotten to Ganny's the night before, and were dog-tired, having traveled hither and yon across the country. We slept 'till nearly ten that last morning, having been up so late the night before, what with Ganny playing her autoharp and all. She fixed us eggs fresh from her chickens, scrambled with chives that had grown in a big clump out her back door for as long as I could remember. She had some boiled custard I fed Buster, and her homemade bread. She heated water on the stove for Ben to take a sponge bath in the back.

It was in the afternoon that we heard a car coming down the road. There weren't many cars that ever came by Ganny's, so it was an occasion. The three of us went to the window to see who it could be. I know Ben for one and me for another were nervous. Buster was propped up on Ganny's bed with feather pillows, his little face alert, not wanting to miss a thing. I reckoned it might be the police, and I imagine that was on Ben's mind too. But it weren't any police or sheriff's car, just a shiny gray sedan with two people in the front seat.

It was only when they pulled right up into the yard that I recognized Mrs. D. As soon as I saw her I went flying out the door, barefoot, my hair loose like a wild thing's. I threw myself into her arms as soon as she stepped from the car and she grabbed me so hard it about cut off my breath. I kept saying her name over and over, beside myself, hugging her to make sure she was real.

The man who was driving must of got out of the car right about then too, but I can't say I noticed, the way my eyes were spilling over with tears. Suddenly a loud shot rang out and echoed off the mountain ridge above us. Mrs. D and I dropped to the ground, covering our ears with our hands, and I for one had my eyes squeezed shut. I knew immediately it was a shotgun blast and that it had come from the house. I figured the next instant I'd be dead, but before I could catch my breath, Mrs. D had sprung up and sprinted around to the other side of the car. I stood up then enough to see that the man she was with—that police fellow from

Tacoma—was down on the ground, a bright red fountain percolatin' out of his chest. Mrs. D dropped down beside him, cradling his head, calling his name, making such pitiful sounds that I began whimpering and crying, too. He was dying, he was dead, right there in her arms. Then I remembered Buster propped up on those pillows in the house. Even a bullet couldn't have stopped me from getting to him. I ran screaming and stumbling back to the house, yelling "Buster! My baby!" like something possessed.

As I ran, I pulled the pistol from my waistband. I mounted the steps to the porch in one big leap, holding the pistol out in front of me with both hands to steady it. The front door was wide open, and right there was Ben pointing the shotgun at me, level with my chest. We both froze, as if someone had taken our photo and locked us that way forever.

"I'll shoot you dead if I have to, Ben," I said. "I want my baby."

"That won't be necessary, Jean," Ben said. He slowly stooped down and laid the shotgun on the wood floor. He stood back up, his hands raised in surrender. "Because I could never kill you," he said.

The next thing I knew I found myself flung over to the side of the porch, down hard onto my knees, firing a wild shot into the porch roof. Mrs. D had come up behind me and shoved me out of the way with all her might. That's when I heard the shot. *Nooooo!* I screamed, covering my ears again. When I turned I saw Mrs. D standing there on the porch, staring in to the open doorway, holding a revolver straight out in front of her with both hands. I got shakily to my feet and went over to her, afraid of what I'd find. All the color had drained from her face. I wondered if she had been shot, for there was blood on her face and in her hair and all down her front. Slowly she lowered the gun to her side. That's when I looked inside the house. She had shot Ben right in the forehead, making a neat third eye. He had slumped down to the floor, his eyes already glossing over with death. I rushed over to Buster, who was howling his head off on the bed, and picked him up. That's when I saw Ganny. My breath caught in my throat. The side of her face was bashed in, her poor little neck broke where she had fallen against the stove and hit her head. They must of struggled for the shotgun, he must of hit her with the butt of it when he wrested it from her. I put my hand over Buster's eyes. He had already seen enough for a lifetime.

That's when I noticed Mrs. D wasn't making a sound, just looking like a bloody ghost. Slowly she raised the revolver and pointed it right at her own temple.

I got to her in two shakes and fell down in front of her on my knees, clutching the baby to me with one arm and grabbing her around the legs with the other, almost knocking her over. "Don't do it!" I cried. "You're all we got. Don't leave us now!"

I could see she was tore. I could see it all pass over her mind like a cloud over a mountain: how she had kilt her son, how that policeman lay dead in the yard. I don't even know if she had seen Ganny yet. And me sobbing there at her feet, Buster crying too. All the blood and tears.

I don't know how long we stayed like that—me on the floor, her like a statue. But finally my sobbing turned to hiccups and I struggled to my feet. "This here is Buster," I said to her. She still had that gun to her head. "This here's my son." I cradled him in the crook of my arm, and he looked at Mrs. D in surprise and stopped crying.

She took a deep, long look at him, like a long drink. I don't know what she was seeing, my Buster or another baby from long ago. She didn't look over at Ben. Slowly she lowered the gun. "We're going to need some help, Jean," she said. "Though I don't really know for what now."

"Yes ma'am," I said. "I'm on my way." Though where I was going, I couldn't say.

Mrs. D turned and stepped off the porch into the yard. She sat down on the ground by that policeman, picked up his hand, held it to her face. She gathered his head up into her lap, and that's where I left her, rocking and rocking.

Ben had left the car keys in the VW. I held Buster in my lap and drove like a hellion down the mountain to the main road. I kept saying to myself, *Three dead and three left standing, three dead and three left standing.* I drove in the middle of the road and forced the first truck coming at me to stop. That's what I said to the driver who came up to my window to cuss me out, "Three dead and three left standing!" He turned white as a sheet. I told him whereabouts—he knew my Ganny—and he said he'd drive to the bar down the way and call for the sheriff. "It's all over now," I said to him, but really I was talking to myself. "It's all over now," though it's taken me a long time to really believe it.

• • •

Mrs. D's hair turned snow-white after that. After they came and took away the three dead, and she and I went back to Tacoma to get our things. After that we moved up here, to Walter's, by the big lake. That first winter we just made do, licking our wounds. We'd cry when we felt like it, or be silent for days at a time. Sometimes we'd play cards or watch TV. We even laughed once in a while, though that was rare. The neighbor people were nice, bringing in food, helping out, keeping the woodpile high. It snowed eighty-four inches that winter, like to have buried us, but that was okay by us. Buster kept us entertained, learning new things. Mrs. D took a shine to him, and by spring he was walking and trying to talk.

One day this summer a colored fellow showed up, something we don't see much of way up here. It was Denny, Jimmy's buddy from Nam, the "Soul Man" Jimmy wrote me about. He had hunted me up from home; Mama gave him where to find me. "So you're Jean," he said when we understood who he was and invited him in. Tears began streaming from his eyes. "Jimmy told me all about you and that you were going to have a baby. It made him so happy," he said when he was able. "This here is Buster," I said, pointing to where Buster was sitting on the floor with his wooden blocks. "Hi, Little Man," Denny knelt down and started crying again, like he was the baby. Mrs. D and I waited until he was through. We was well acquainted with tears.

We invited him to stay for dinner, to spend the night if he wanted, but he said he had to be getting back to the Cities. He told me he was with Jimmy when he got shot, and that he hadn't suffered. "I took these things for you," he said, getting out a white envelope from his coat pocket. "I knew he'd want you to have them." He handed the envelope over.

It was the wedding band I had given Jimmy, and a picture of us, back home, taken right before we was married. I looked at the girl in that picture, and if I had ever known her, it was too long ago to remember.

I thanked Denny for coming, and we hugged in a big bear hug. He hadn't told me any other details, just that Jimmy hadn't suffered. That was enough.

Mrs. D and I never talk about those other days. For us there is only now, there is only here. And what is there to say? Can you say love triumphed? Not really, though love is here. Can you say good won out over evil, the way it's supposed to? All I know for sure is that there have always been snakes and always will be, ever since Adam and Eve ate of the fruit of the Tree of Knowledge of Good and Evil and God pushed them out into the world to fend for themselves.

Sometimes I look at Buster, and I can't help but wonder, given all he has seen in his short life. It was sad how he missed Ben at first, even though he had no way of saying so. But I could tell by how he was always looking around, searching for him. I suppose by now he's forgotten, though I do notice how often his little face is clouded up, contemplating the mystery of it all.

The End

Acknowledgments

So many people helped me in various ways survive the long journey that writing a novel is. I'm extremely grateful to those who read the manuscript at various stages and offered helpful feedback: my sister Betty Bates, Marisha Chamberlain, Miles Frieden, Richard Gilbert, Alan Kelly-Hamm, Vicky Lettmann, Katherine Schaefer, Cheryl Strayed, and Susan Welch. I hope I haven't left anyone out.

Emily Meier was invaluable as writer and friend at every stage, providing a comprehensive early critique, cheering me on through the years of the novel, and educating me every step of the way about the publishing process. Kipp Wessell's support, understanding, and humor made the trip a lot more fun. Several people provided valuable professional expertise (and when I get things wrong, it's on me, not them): Pamela Holt on librarians and libraries; John Stuart, Minnesota State Public Defender, on legal questions; psychologists Chad Breckenridge and Nicole Shackelford on deviancy; and Christine Morris on police work. Thanks to Judy Liautaud, Arlo Haskell, and Susan Wilson for input on the cover; to Rebecca Swift for my imprint logo, which I love; to David Janik for hanging in there with me over many drafts of covers until we came up with a great one; to Mary Keirstead, who copyedited the manuscript; to my mother-in-law, Meredith Alden, for time at her cabin where I could write; to the good folks at www.52novels.com for formatting the manuscript for ebook and POD versions; special, heartfelt thanks to proofreader extraordinaire James Ashley Shea in Thailand who made a number of excellent "saves" in the final manuscript; and huge gratitude and good wishes to my agent, Joy Azmitia, who loved the book and believed in it, which boosted me immensely.

And finally, love and gratitude to my husband, Jeff Alden, who edited the manuscript again and again, making me take out extra words and as many weepy parts as he could pry loose, and whose constant, unwavering support and love amaze and sustain me.

About the Author

Paulette Alden is the author of *Feeding the Eagles*, a collection of short stories (Graywolf Press) and *Crossing the Moon*, a memoir (Penguin). Her work has appeared in *The New York Times Magazine*, *Ploughshares*, *Stanford Magazine*, *Antioch Review*, and *Mississippi Review*, among others. A former Stegner Fellow and Jones Lecturer in Creative Writing at Stanford, she has taught memoir and fiction writing extensively, at the University of Minnesota, Carleton College, St. Olaf College, the Key West Literary Seminar and the Madeline Island School of the Arts. Originally from South Carolina, Alden lives in Minneapolis, where she critiques literary manuscripts and blogs on books and writing on her website, www.paulettealden.com

Paulette Alden is available for readings and book groups. Please contact her via her website, www.paulettealden.com

If you enjoyed this novel, please post a review on Amazon and Goodreads. Thanks!